# THE FAIRFAX LEGACY

# THE FAIRFAX LEGACY

Pamela Oldfield

This first world edition published 2008
in Great Britain and in 2009 in the USA by
SEVERN HOUSE PUBLISHERS LTD of
9–15 High Street, Sutton, Surrey, England, SM1 1DF.
Trade paperback edition published
in Great Britain and the USA 2009 by
SEVERN HOUSE PUBLISHERS LTD

British Library Cataloguing in Publication Data

Oldfield, Pamela
  The Fairfax legacy
  1. Family secrets - Fiction 2. Inheritance and succession -
  Fiction 3. Domestic fiction
  I. Title
  823.9'14[F]


ISBN-13: 978-0-7278-6710-0   (cased)
ISBN-13: 978-1-84751-092-1   (trade paper)

*All Severn House titles are printed on acid-free paper.*

Typeset by Palimpsest Book Production Ltd.,
Grangemouth, Stirlingshire, Scotland.
Printed and bound in Great Britain by
MPG Books Ltd., Bodmin, Cornwall.

# One

Elena clutched the banister rails and peered through at the scene below. It was long past her bedtime but loud voices had woken her and, ever curious, she had tiptoed out on to the landing to investigate. Her beloved father was urging her mother to keep her voice down, but she obviously had other ideas.

'I shall tell her. Why should I keep my voice down? I have things to say and I shall!' Hermione Fairfax sucked in a furious breath. 'She'll have to know some time, Oscar, so why not now? Why let her cling to the idea that her wonderful papa is—?'

Elena's father turned away, but her mother clutched at his sleeve. 'Don't you dare turn your back on me, you hypocrite! At least be man enough to stay and talk.'

Roughly he removed her hand from his sleeve. 'Let me go, Hermione. You are overwrought. And please keep your voice down or the girl will hear you and—'

'What does it matter if she hears us? You should be ashamed of yourself. When the truth comes out it will ruin her life – have you thought of that?'

Despite the warm nightdress she wore, Elena shivered. It was long past her bedtime and the house was cooling down. Her bedroom was cosy enough with its coal fire that her nanny kept lit all night, but the top of the stairs was draughty and eight-year-old Elena had been sitting there for a long time.

Her father regarded his wife steadily and when he spoke again he had moderated his tone. 'Look, Hermione, let's please talk reasonably about this. You said a few weeks ago that you wanted to make a fresh start. D'you remember? After all these years I was surprised but delighted. I still don't understand what has gone wrong. You said you forgave me and that you wanted us to have another child. You wanted a boy.'

There was a silence. Elena frowned.

Then her mother said, 'I wanted to try again – for all our sakes. I wanted to give you a son.'

'But the doctor has always said that . . . that physical relations between us were unwise from a health point of view.'

'He didn't say it was impossible to have a baby. Just unwise.'

*They were talking about a son!*

Elena's eyes widened. That meant she would have a baby brother!

Her father went on. 'You seemed to be determined to make a fresh start, but now, a few weeks later, you suddenly say you've changed your mind again. What's happened, Hermione?'

'I thought I could forgive and forget, but I was wrong. That's what happened.' Sighing, she walked to the sideboard and poured herself a drink.

Elena waited, hypnotized by the drama, but understanding very little. Mama was going to forgive Papa, but for what? Had Papa done something bad? Elena couldn't, wouldn't believe it. Not her darling papa.

Suddenly Nanny was beside her, tugging her to her feet, whispering urgently in her ear. 'Come to bed, you naughty girl. You'll catch your death of cold.'

Her words were sharp but her tone was gentle. Elena rose obediently and, clasping her nanny's hand, hurried away from the angry scene below, along the landing and into the large room, which was still referred to as 'the nursery' to Elena's mortification.

Elena's bed was situated to the right of the fireplace and Nanny's was to the left, hidden behind curtains that acted as a room-divider and gave her a little privacy. Small rugs were placed strategically on the polished wooden floor and at Elena's end of the room there was a toy cupboard and a few shelves which contained books and a variety of small toys from board games to knitted animals. Pride of place went to an ancient rocking horse. There was a large metal fireguard around the fire and a few garments were airing on a wooden clothes horse.

'Mama said Papa was wonderful.'

'And so he is.' Her nanny stirred the fire with the poker and topped it up with two more lumps of coal then seized the bellows and gave the coals a few puffs of air to get them going.

Elena watched her thoughtfully. 'She never says—'

'Who's "she"? The cat's mother?'

'Mama never says I'm wonderful.'

'Of course she does.'

'She doesn't. She doesn't say anything nice to me. She – I mean Mama – hates me!'

'Hates you?' Nanny glanced up from the fire. 'Now where did you get that silly idea? Of course she doesn't hate you. Nobody hates you.' Satisfied with the fire, she returned the bellows to their place behind the coal scuttle and straightened up.

Elena wondered, not for the first time, how old her nanny was. She knew it was bad manners to ask, but she did worry in case Nanny was old and might die. She had learned a lot about Nanny by keeping her eyes and ears open and had perfected the art of appearing to be disinterested in all adult conversations.

Now Elena said, 'I wish I had curly hair like yours. Mine's straight and I hate it.'

'You have lovely hair, like your father. A dark chestnut brown.' Nanny smiled and put out a hand to stroke Elena's hair. 'A chestnut mane. Like a little chestnut pony.'

Enchanted by the idea, Elena began to prance round the room, neighing, but Nanny said hastily, 'Now, don't start that. You should be fast asleep.' She straightened the bedclothes and patted the bed. 'Get back into bed and forget all about that silly scene.'

'But why is Mama so cross?'

'She's just upset. I expect she has a bad headache. You know how she is when she's unhappy.'

'She's always cross with Papa and me. Sometimes she cries.'

'Nonsense!'

'And she gets cross with you.'

'What are you saying? She hardly says a word to me.'

'That's what I mean. That's because she's cross.'

Nanny rolled her eyes despairingly. 'Your mother gets upset easily. She's . . . she's very sensitive.'

Elena gave her a very steady stare until her nanny turned away.

'Nanny, what's a hippercrit?'

'It's nothing for little girls to worry about. I've told you before not to listen to private conversations. It's not nice. In fact it's horrid.' She retied the belt of her plaid dressing gown.

She looked familiar and comfortable to Elena. Nanny had been around as long as she could remember – first as a nursemaid to the young Elena and later as her nanny. Elena had found out that Nanny's real name was Winifred because she had found a letter in an envelope in Nanny's drawer where she kept her silk bloomers and handkerchiefs and the two lavender bags. It was addressed in capital letters to Miss Winfred Franks, but inside the envelope the letter itself was written in joined-up writing which was impossible for Elena to read.

'Is it like a hippopotamus?' Elena yawned as she snuggled down into the bedclothes and reached for her teddy bear.

'I have no idea. I told you to forget all about it.' Nanny stared at herself in the mirror above the fireplace, sighed and tidied a few stray wisps of hair.

Elena said sleepily, 'I might be having a baby brother. Will the same stork bring him? A stork brought me. A nice friendly stork. He had a long beak, but he didn't peck people. Papa told me.'

Nanny turned abruptly to stare at her, obviously startled by the snippet, and Elena felt a small flash of triumph.

'A baby brother? Don't be silly . . . Are you sure?'

'Papa said she'd changed her mind . . .'

Suddenly Nanny looked annoyed. 'Spying again! How many times have I told you about that? How long were you sitting on the stairs for heaven's sake? I didn't hear you get out of bed.'

'I don't know how long it was,' Elena replied carefully. 'Not long, I promise.'

Nanny was hovering now at the end of the bed. 'So what else did they say – about the baby brother?'

'Don't know.' Regretting that she had mentioned the baby brother, Elena closed her eyes, produced an exaggerated yawn and slid down further into the bed, hoping to avoid any more questions.

'They must have said something else, Elena.'

'They said it wasn't impossible.'

'Did they? Ah!'

Peeping above the bedclothes, Elena thought she looked worried. 'Then you'd have to look after us both! Would you mind? I could help you. I like baby brothers. We could call him Oscar, like Daddy. Daddy's name is Mr Oscar John Fairfax . . . or we could think of a different name.' She frowned. 'It's not fair, is it, because you might not like your name? I don't like mine. I'd like to be called Arabella . . . Nanny! You're not listening!'

'Arabella? That's nice.'

Elena regarded her through narrowed eyes. Had she been listening? You could never tell with grown-ups. 'You could call me Arabella,' she suggested hopefully. 'It could be our secret.'

'We have quite enough secrets in this house already!' Sighing heavily, Nanny leaned over and kissed her lightly. 'Go to sleep, little one.'

'But it could.'

'We'll think about it tomorrow.'

She tucked the blanket around Elena's neck and made her way to her own bed.

Elena said, 'Can we play the gramophone tomorrow?'

'You know you can't. Your mama doesn't allow it.'

'But why? It belongs to Papa.'

'It's all very delicate and new and you might break it. Only grown-ups can use it.'

'You could do it. When Papa opened the box he was so excited. He said it was a very special Christmas present. He gave Mama a thank-you kiss.'

'Did he?' There was a long silence. 'He never plays it though.'

'He does sometimes. He plays his opera records. I've heard him. He would let you play it.'

'I wouldn't touch it with a bargepole!'

'What is a bargepole?'

'For heaven's sake, Elena! Just go to sleep.' Nanny climbed into bed.

When the springs of Nanny's bed stopped creaking, Elena said demurely, 'Goodnight, Nanny.'

'Go to sleep, minx!'

Elena smiled. Minx was what her father sometimes called her and she assumed it was a compliment. She poked her head out and squinted up into the darkness, trying to remember if she had heard anything more about the baby brother, but nothing came to mind and within minutes she was fast asleep.

Next morning early, once Nanny had gone downstairs, Elena crept from her bed and hurried over to Nanny's part of the room. She went straight to the small chest of drawers where Nanny kept her 'treasures'. One of these was a photograph of Nanny looking much younger and holding a small baby. Nanny was smiling broadly, the baby held close to her chest. On the back someone had written 'My Darling Girl' in the left-hand corner and the date 1913. Elena had never been able to ask about this child for fear of revealing that she had searched through the chest of drawers, but since Nanny had no children Elena imagined that this 'darling child' must have died. She found it tragic and yet romantic and often returned to look at it. Aware of the special nature of the photograph, Elena hugged the secret to her heart.

Months passed and summer and autumn with it. One morning in late November, an early snow was falling as daybreak revealed the Kentish countryside. Large feathery flakes had managed to cover everything with a heavy white dusting. Green fields, leafless trees and the rooftops of Hawkhurst had all been decorated with a bright layer of pristine snow.

As Nanny shook her small charge awake she said, 'I've

got a big surprise for you, Elena. Come to the window and see!'

Elena sat up, wide-eyed. 'Is it my baby brother? Has the stork come? Can I see the stork before he flies away?' She was scrambling out of bed as she spoke, her face pink with anticipation.

'It's not that,' Nanny said, shaking her head. 'You have to wait a few more weeks for your brother or sister. Come and see for yourself!' She held out her hand, smiling. 'Shut your eyes!' She led Elena towards the window. 'Now open them.'

'Snow! Oh!' Elena clasped her hands excitedly, staring entranced at the change in the garden that the snowfall had wrought. There was a thin white cushion on the seat of the swing, a white carpet on the pathways and the summer house was wearing a little white hat.

At that moment the telephone trilled in the hall below them and almost immediately they heard the maid's footsteps on the stairs followed by a knock on the nursery door.

Nanny called, 'Come in, Millie.'

Elena said, 'Shall I tell Mama the telephone's—?'

'No, dear. We mustn't disturb your mama. She needs her sleep.'

The maid came in. 'It's Mr Hatton. He wants to speak to the mistress.' Millie was an awkward, moon-faced girl, who was nearing fifteen and had an apparent grudge against the whole world.

'Mrs Fairfax is still asleep, Millie. Ask him to ring back later.'

'He's asking about the new arrival.' Millie cast a quick look in Elena's direction.

Elena glanced at her nanny. 'He means my baby brother. That's what "new arrival" means.' She turned to Millie. 'Or it might be a baby sister, but Papa wants a boy.'

Millie said, 'I'm talking to Nanny, not you! Children should be seen and not heard!'

'There's no need to speak to her like that, Millie. Remember your place. As for Mr Hatton . . .'

Millie tossed her head. 'He rang three times yesterday and had me running up and down the stairs and all over. Wearing

me out, it was. I said to Cook, "What's the bloomin' hurry?"
and Cook said, "What's it got to do with him? He's only
the solicitor."'

Elena said, 'It's about the will.' They both stared at her. 'I
don't know what that means,' she went on, 'but I heard
Mama talking to him on the telephone.'

Millie rolled her eyes. 'Well, aren't you the sneaky little
thing? That's eavesdropping, that is. Anyway a will's about
when you're dead and nobody's dead.'

Millie had a morbid fascination with death.

Nanny said, 'Don't keep the poor man hanging on the
telephone, Millie. Go down and give him the message and
do it politely!' As the maid made no move to obey she gave
her a token push. 'Don't argue, Millie. Just go!'

Millie retreated to the door. As she fled along the landing
she muttered, 'Talk about bossyboots!' before clattering loudly
down the stairs.

Nanny tutted. 'I don't know why they keep that girl on.
She has no manners and no idea how to behave.' She asked
casually, 'What did your mama say about the will, Elena?'

'She said, "I'll talk to him. I'll insist." What is a will, Nanny?'

'What is a will? I wouldn't worry yourself about that.
And you shouldn't have been listening. Were you under the
big table again?'

One of Elena's favourite hiding places was beneath the
small circular table in the bay window of the sitting room.
It was covered with a large chenille cloth that hung down
all round and aided concealment. Elena had long since been
forbidden to sit there, but people invariably forgot to check
and the child continued to accumulate snippets of confused
information. These meant nothing to her, but were sometimes of interest to her nanny.

Without answering Elena turned, her eyes gleaming. 'I
shall make a snowman to show to Mama! All by myself, and
Toby can watch me if he's good and doesn't bark and get
too excited. Last year he jumped up at it and made his arm
fall off! Shall I wake Mama? She loves the snow. She might
want to help me with the snowman.'

'I shouldn't, Elena. She likes to lie in.'

'I'll give him a scarf and make his eyes out of two pieces of coal.' She paused. 'Is it the weekend? Is Papa home from work? Are we going to church?'

'Yes, it's the weekend. Sunday. Yes, your papa is at home, but he has gone for an early walk with the dog, and yes, you are going to church while I stay here in case your mother . . . Well, just in case the stork arrives. Your mama has now decided that he might come early.'

'But I will have time to make the snowman, won't I?'

'You will if you hurry and wash your face and hands and then dress. You can make a start and I'll call you in when breakfast is ready.'

'Will it be porridge?'

'I expect so. To warm your tummy.'

'With honey?'

'I'll ask Cook.'

Half an hour later, while the child was busy in the garden scooping up handfuls of snow, Winifred busied herself preparing for breakfast in the nursery at the table which she and Elena shared – porridge with honey and thin bread and butter which had been sent up from the kitchen. The only time Elena shared a meal with her parents was on Sunday when the family sat round the big table in the dining room for Sunday lunch and enjoyed a roast dinner while Winifred joined the staff in the kitchen for a similar meal.

Now, as she set the table, she wondered about Hermione Fairfax and the frequent calls she received from Douglas Hatton. Over the last three weeks his calls had become more frequent – or was that just paranoia on her part? The reference to the will was rather worrying, she thought. Was Mrs Fairfax planning to change it? How could she? The will had been made by her husband. Maybe she was going to put pressure on him for some reason. But why?

Sighing, she wished she could talk to Mr Fairfax, but there had been a distinct coolness between them lately that had started with Winifred's discovery that he and Mrs Fairfax were trying for another child. That had been entirely un-expected because over the past years Mrs Fairfax had made much of the fact that her health was too unstable for the rigours of further childbirth. The husband and wife had slept in separate bedrooms for years.

Winifred would prefer to think of Mr Fairfax as Oscar, but that would clearly be foolhardy and she recognized that. The relationship they had once had, many years ago, had ended and Winifred was now no more than a nanny to his daughter. She dared not risk calling him by his Christian name within Mrs Fairfax's hearing.

'Something has happened,' she murmured, 'but what?' She sensed change and it unsettled her.

The baby was not due for several weeks, but Hermione Fairfax was becoming anxious and it made her irritable. The exasperated midwife had been told to expect a call and the family doctor had been made aware of the situation and could be summoned if there were an emergency.

Winifred wondered how Elena would feel towards the new baby. At the moment the child was thrilled by the idea, but often, as time went on, a new baby could diminish the older child in importance and cause jealousy to rear its ugly head. They would have to make a big fuss of Elena to avoid this and for Hermione Fairfax that would not be easy.

Downstairs in the kitchen, Cook sipped her tea as she watched Millie butter a slice of toast. The room, though not large, was in keeping with Downsview – the house inhabited by the Fairfax family which had been passed down to Oscar on the death of his father fifteen years earlier. It was a substantial white weatherboard property on the outskirts of the village and boasted a sizeable garden. Most of the fittings and furniture had also been passed down, but there had been a few improvements. In the kitchen a new gas cooker now stood beside the old range, shelves had been added to accommodate the many pots and pans, and the old chipped sink had been replaced.

'Can't you get any more butter on that toast?' Cook demanded. 'I don't know what Mrs Fairfax would say if she saw the way you eat. The word pig comes to mind.'

Millie flashed her a sullen glance. 'I'm a growing girl – not

like some people. At least . . .' She thought of a barbed reference to the elderly cook's own increasing bulk but wisely
decided against it. 'I'm young. I need—'

'Don't eat with your mouth full, girl!' Tutting, Cook leaned
forward and rested her meaty arms on the table. 'You have
to smarten yourself up, Millie,' she said earnestly. 'You won't
find a nice young man the way you carry on. You'll never
be a beauty, but you could try a bit harder. Smile more –
you've got nice teeth. And you need to learn a few manners.
You have to soften the rough edges – unless you plan on
becoming an old maid!'

Cook had never had any children of her own and the
maids that came and went were the nearest she came to
having daughters. She liked Millie in spite of her uncouth
ways and genuinely wanted to help her improve her chances.
'You could do something about your hair, too. Straight as
a poker, like mine, but I make a bit of effort. All you need
is a few curling rags last thing at night. You'd look quite
pretty with a few curls. It softens the face, you see?'

'I like it straight!' Millie reached for the bread knife, but
Cook slapped her hand.

'You've had enough for one breakfast,' she told her. 'Go
up to Mrs Fairfax and—'

At that moment the bell from Mrs Fairfax's bedroom
jangled furiously and went on jangling. They both leaped
to their feet, startled by the bell's intensity.

Cook said, 'Crikey Moses! That'll be it! That'll be the
baby.'

'What – already? I thought—'

'Go and find Winifred and tell her to go up there. That
is, ask her to do it. Don't tell her.' She clapped a hand to
her generous bosoms and took a deep breath. 'Lordy! I'm
all of a flutter and nothing's happened yet. This will be the
first pains – or the waters breaking or whatever they do.'

Millie moved as slowly as she could and Cook said, 'Just
get up to the nursery and find Winifred.'

Upstairs the nanny was already on her feet and was halfway
along the landing as Millie rushed up the stairs.

'I'll answer the bell,' she said to the maid. 'Remind Cook

to get plenty of hot water on the go. Though it might be
hours yet. And it might be a false alarm.'

Hermione Fairfax was sitting up in bed, clutching her
swollen body, and the remains of her breakfast tray were scattered over the floor. Obviously the pain had come suddenly.
Hermione's face was white with shock.

'Telephone the midwife and tell her to come at once.
And where's my husband?' she demanded.

'He's out with the dog. He should be back shortly.'

Winifred turned to go downstairs to the telephone, but
Mrs Fairfax reached out for her.

'Wait a moment. I don't want to be here alone.' She looked
frightened, thought Winifred with a jolt of compassion.

For a moment she clasped the outstretched hand, but then
she said, 'I have to telephone the—'

'Oh, yes! Of course. But you will come back?'

'If you wish but there is Elena to consider.'

'If he's back in time, Oscar can stay with her until she
goes to church with Millie – and tell Millie to take the long
way home from church. I don't want Elena home too soon.
She'll only get in the way.'

She released the nanny's hand and the latter made her
way downstairs and along the hall. She rang for the midwife
– a Mrs Benby – and was reassured she would arrive within
fifteen minutes.

The snowman was almost finished by the time Millie
appeared to take care of Elena.

'Look, Millie! My snowman!' Elena's face glowed with a
combination of excitement and exertion.

'It's a bit small,' Millie began, but suddenly remembering
Cook's recent homily she added hastily, 'but it's nice enough.
I've come to take you up for your breakfast and then get
you ready for church.' She scooped up some snow and added
it to the top of the snowman's head. 'There! I've made him
a bit taller. He's got no arms, poor thing.'

'He's not quite finished. I'm going to give him some arms
and a face and some buttons down his front. You can help
me if you like.'

'Can't. There won't be time. We have to come back from

church the long way round because of the baby coming and everyone's fussing and rushing about like headless chickens.'

'I don't want to walk the long way home. It's miles and miles and it makes my legs ache.'

Millie disliked the idea too, and saw her opportunity. 'I know what we'll do then. Instead of going all that way we'll walk slowly round the churchyard and look at the graves. You'd like that and it will take ages and no one will know.' She took hold of Elena's hand and led her firmly away from the snowman.

'Will I?'

'Will you what?'

'Will I like the graves?'

'Of course you will. Everybody loves them. All those graves with pretty flowers on them – and mouldering bones and things underneath. It's fun.'

'What are mouldering bones?'

'Skeletons. Come on. You can have some breakfast and then we'll go. If we're late for church we'll be in trouble.'

She walked back into the house with Elena trailing after her.

In fact Elena liked going to church because she could be seen by all and sundry in her best Sunday clothes. She was secretly delighted to realize that she looked smarter than Millie. The snow was still falling and a cold breeze was blowing the snow into shallow drifts. Halfway to the church they met Elena's papa returning from his 'Sunday constitutional'. He looked fit and had obviously enjoyed his walk, but the golden retriever was picking his way unhappily through the snow and gave Elena a reproachful look.

She cried, 'Oh, poor Toby! He doesn't like walking in the snow. It makes his paws cold.' She was going to ask her father to carry the dog, but Millie spoke up importantly before she could.

'The baby's started, sir. They've sent for Maggie Benby.'

'Already?' He looked startled. 'Good heavens!' For a moment he frowned but then forced a smile. 'Well, that is good news. The sooner the better. I must get back at once.

D'you hear that, Toby? No more dawdling. We have to get back! Exciting, isn't it, minx?'

'A baby brother!' She beamed.

'Or a sister – but a brother would be best.'

She wanted him to pick her up and whirl her round as he'd often done when she was younger, but instead he hurried away and briefly she felt herself overlooked.

Once in church, however, she forgot her disappointment and concentrated on the service. She watched their fellow worshippers with interest and enjoyed the music. When it was time for the vicar's sermon she allowed her mind to wander to the baby brother she was expecting. It would be fun to help Nanny bath him and to feed him spoonfuls of food when he was older. She would walk beside his pram, and if he threw out his toys she would pick them up again and shake off the dust before handing them back to him. She wondered what they would call him and hoped it wouldn't be Bertie like the butcher's boy or Stan like the postman's son. But no. Surely Mama would insist on Oscar . . .

Millie nudged her. 'Kneel down!' she hissed.

Elena realized that the hymn had ended and settled herself comfortably on the velvet hassock. And what, she wondered, would Toby think of her baby brother? She would have to share the dog with her brother but she wouldn't mind that. They could take turns to brush him . . .

They sang one more hymn and then it was all over and all the people made their way slowly out of the church. The vicar shook Elena's hand which always made her feel very grown up and then asked Millie about Mrs Fairfax.

'They've sent for Maggie Benby,' she told him shortly, and tugged Elena past before the conversation could continue. 'Nosy old devil!' whispered Millie.

Elena, who was hoping the vicar had noticed her new astrakhan hat, collar and cuffs, nodded earnestly.

The churchyard was an area Elena had never been allowed to explore before. She followed Millie along the narrow paths admiring the flowers on the graves even though many of them had now shrivelled with the cold and hung their heads.

Millie said, 'See! Even the flowers are dying! A church-yard is a place of death. Remember that.'

She stopped by a relatively new headstone and carefully read the inscription. 'In Beloved Memory of Ellen May Wittering.'

'Mrs Wittering's not dead. Is she?'

'Course she is. Died three weeks ago.'

'But we buy our stamps from Mrs Wittering. At the post office.'

'Not any more, you don't. She died of a cough. Coughed herself to death. That's what they said. It was her lungs.'

'But where will we buy the stamps?'

'I dunno. I 'spose her husband will sell them.'

They stopped at a smaller headstone: 'Dearly Missed but Not Forgotten'. Millie frowned as she tried to work out the age of the owner of the headstone.

'Eleven years old! Patrick John Deeps. Crikey! I remember that. I'd just come to your place and there was this accident. The boys were fishing, one of them fell in and this boy tried to rescue him, but he drowned instead – and the first boy was saved.' She sighed heavily. 'You think about that, Elena. Eleven years old. I could have died at eleven. I could be buried there.'

'You could die now,' Elena said helpfully.

'Well, thanks very much!'

Elena said quickly, 'I shan't let my baby brother go fishing. Not ever.'

'How will you stop him? You can't. Boys are always off, getting into mischief.'

'How do you know they are?'

'How do I know? Because I've got three brothers, that's how. One older than me, two younger and all are always in mischief!'

Elena was impressed. Millie had three brothers. She revised her opinion of Millie.

They wandered on, time passing, and suddenly the vicar appeared beside them.

'Shouldn't you two young ladies be getting along?' he suggested. 'It looks as though it might snow again.'

'I've lost something,' Millie lied. 'My hankie. I'm just looking for it.'

Elena said, 'So am I. I've lost mine, too.'

'My! What a coincidence!'

Elena thought he hid a smile.

He said, 'Don't be too late home then. Your parents might worry.'

Millie shook her head. 'Mine won't worry because they don't know I'm here because I'm fifteen and I'm in service at her house.' She jerked a thumb in Elena's direction.

Elena hesitated. 'My nanny won't worry because she's busy helping Mama. They're all waiting for the stork to bring my baby brother.'

'Or sister,' said Millie.

The vicar raised his eyebrows. 'How exciting. A baby brother. I'll look forward to meeting him one day. Well, I'll be getting along then.' With a farewell smile he set off for the vicarage and they watched his retreating figure.

'Trust you – saying you'd lost your hankie,' Millie said crossly. 'He would've believed me.'

'He called us young ladies!'

'More likely call us liars!' She wandered on and then stopped abruptly in front of one of the headstones. 'Here, Elena! Come and look at this.'

She began to read out the inscription. 'In Loving Memory of Edward Oscar Fairfax . . .' She turned. 'Fairfax. Same name as yours! Might be your Uncle Edward or your grandfather – or no relation at all.' She shrugged.

'I haven't got an Uncle Edward.'

'Course you haven't. If he's been buried here in the church-yard, he must be dead. Could've died before you were born.'

'Is he mouldering bones then?' Elena felt a shudder run up her back.

'Course he is!'

Before Millie could read any more of the inscription, the clock on the church tower struck the half hour and Millie grabbed her hand. 'We'd better go home. And remember – we went the long way, like they told us and we didn't look at the gravestones.'

'Can't I tell them about Uncle Edward?'

'No, you can't, you silly thing! Cos if you do they'll know we didn't go the long way round.'

When they reached home, the house was still in an uproar and Millie was needed. Elena was told to go back into the garden and finish her snowman. Cook gave her a carrot for his nose and a tea towel for his scarf and when he was finished Elena decided he deserved a name and called him Uncle Edward.

# Two

A week later, first thing Monday morning, Douglas Hatton knocked on the door of his partner's office and entered, trying to hide his nervousness. John Granger glanced up from the letter he was dictating to his secretary and gave him an enquiring look.

Before Douglas could change his mind, he said, 'Sorry to interrupt, John, but could I have a minute.'

'Is it important? I'm in the middle of—'

'It is rather.' He stared pointedly at Miss Terry who rose to her feet uncertainly.

John sighed somewhat irritably but said, 'Give us a few minutes, will you, Miss Terry? I'll ring for you once we're through.'

His impatience was barely hidden and Douglas steeled himself as he sat down in the recently vacated chair, in response to his partner's nod.

'It's about my address,' Douglas began. 'My home address, that is. The fact is . . . Actually, I'm in the process of moving. I thought I should tell you and give you the new details.' He placed an index card on John's desk. 'The fact is,' he repeated, 'I needed . . . that is, I need a bigger place. I'm leaving home and renting a small house.' His bright blue eyes blinked several times, a sign which meant he was under stress. He crossed his fingers under the desk and tried to smile.

'Moving?' John Granger was obviously surprised. 'What's happened? You haven't fallen out with your family, have you?'

Obviously intrigued, John sat back in his chair, his hands behind his head. He was tall and thin with soft fair hair and grey eyes which peered at the world through a pair of steel-rimmed spectacles.

This was the moment Douglas had been dreading because

he needed to say just so much and no more, but John Granger, two years his senior, knew him better than most people did. They had studied and trained together and had set up partnership as soon as Douglas finished his studies and was able to access the money his grandfather had left him. He put money into the budding firm and became a partner. Instead of working from a small room in the house of John's parents, they had bought office space over a shop in Hawkhurst's main street and the business had flourished.

'Fallen out with them? Of course not.'

'Tell all, then.'

Douglas sat down and ran nervous fingers through his hair. It was a bright sandy colour bordering on ginger and it framed his pale complexion and generous sprinkling of freckles. He said, 'Somehow, John, you know when the time is ripe . . . I mean, you get a feeling and I felt – rather I knew – that I had outgrown my home. I wanted my own accommodation so I've rented a small house.'

'You've rented a house?' Suddenly John leaned forward with a broad grin on his face. 'Not a flat – a house!' He snapped his fingers. 'Eureka! I know what's going on! You've found yourself a young lady! Don't try and deny it!' He gave a short triumphant laugh and sat back in his chair. 'I'm right, aren't I? I can see by the look in your eyes.'

Although aware of the need for discretion, Douglas was suddenly seized by a desperate desire to share what was happening in his private life.

He said, 'Well, sort of . . . I suppose.' It was his turn to smile as the words began to tumble out. 'It is a woman but not quite the way you imagine, John. She's . . . She's not a young lady . . .'

'She's not a lady? My God, John, what is she? Not a . . .?' In a whisper he asked, 'Not a fallen woman?'

John, comfortably married for more than a year now, was put out. Douglas would be the first to admit that he was not comfortable around women and John had insisted that he would find his partner a suitable woman. Now it seemed, he, Douglas, had found one without John's assistance.

'Who is this mysterious woman?' John demanded. 'Do I know her? What's her name?'

Douglas clasped his hands and tried to think how much he could tell his friend without upsetting him. It was against his nature to lie, but if he told the whole truth, there might be serious consequences for which he was ill prepared.

'You might know her . . . or rather, you might know of her.'

'Not one of my ex lady friends!'

'No.' He was already wishing he had said nothing at all – but he had needed to pass on the new address and John would have been curious. 'What I meant was she's not that young. She's quite a bit older than me, in fact.' He glanced down, feeling vulnerable beneath John's scrutiny. The silence deepened and Douglas closed his eyes. Don't ask that particular question, he thought without much hope. John wasn't slow-witted and would almost certainly guess.

'An older woman?'

'I like older women! Lots of men do. Don't be so narrow-minded!'

'Dammit, Douglas! She's not married, is she?'

Douglas became distracted by the pencil which John twirled in his fingers.

'And she's moving in with you? My God! You're a dark horse! A married woman!' His mind made the next leap. 'Does the husband know?'

'Not yet . . . but he will.' Suddenly unable to hold back, Douglas leaned forward. 'Look, John, she was the one who . . .' He smiled at a passing memory. 'It was very flattering and I simply went along with it.' He shook his head, bemused by what had happened. 'And don't blame her, John. I knew she was married. Unhappily married, I might add. I would never have dared, but . . .' He shrugged, trying to hide his elation. 'She was obviously smitten. Don't ask me why. She says I make her happier than she's been for years. Her husband was unfaithful. He doesn't appreciate her.' He laughed shakily. 'I have to admit I was bowled over. Still am. I can't believe my luck.'

John rested his arms on the desk. By now his surprise

had given way to caution. 'You sound as if you're getting in awfully deep, Douglas. It's wonderful that you are so happy, but, if you'll forgive me, I must say this. Once she leaves her husband there'll be no turning back. And it will all be pretty ugly – a divorce and all that entails.'

Douglas nodded. 'I know you're right, John, and I do forgive you, but she's worth it. At the risk of sounding melodramatic, I've never been happier and I'll suffer any consequences with a cheerful heart.' He steepled his hands then locked his fingers. After a moment his expression changed. 'It's going to break my parents' heart when they learn what's happened, but I'll face that when it comes. Not that they won't love her . . .' He stopped, aware that he was saying too much.

As one they each stopped talking and an awkward silence fell. Douglas was trying to recall exactly how much information he had given to his partner. His tongue had run away with him and John was shrewd. He waited, hands clasped fiercely under the cover of the desk.

At last John said slowly, 'Good grief, Douglas! You and a married woman! God dammit, joking apart, you must be quite mad!'

His tone shocked Douglas who leaped to his feet as an unexpected panic swept through him. He had definitely told his friend too much. He had trusted him too far. His stomach churned. Would John put two and two together?

Seeing his expression, John stammered, 'I didn't mean that! I'm sorry, Douglas. It's none of my business.'

'No! I shouldn't have told you. It's not fair on you. Look, I'll go now and I won't mention it again. We won't talk about it.' His earlier elation had faded leaving him shaken. Trying to retrieve the situation he said, 'Anyway, you have my new address. You must come round one evening and . . . and see the house. Bring Moira.' His attempt at a casual response failed miserably.

John stood up slowly. 'Will she be there? I mean—' He broke off, embarrassed. 'That came out all wrong. Sorry Douglas.'

Stricken, Douglas was staring at him speechless. Surely

this wasn't going to spoil their friendship. As partners they had a good working relationship and if that were ever lost – it didn't bear thinking about.

John also seemed to be struggling. He thrust out his hand. 'Of course I'll come round, Douglas. Love to. And I'll look forward to meeting her.'

These words, intended to reassure Douglas, merely highlighted another inescapable fact. When John discovered who she was, there would be more trouble. Serious trouble. He said, 'Thanks John,' and they shook hands awkwardly. 'You'll tell your wife, I take it. You'll tell Moira.'

'Yes. I'll have to. She'll understand.'

'Will she?'

'Affairs of the heart and all that! Women love all of that.'

There was an awkward silence.

Douglas broke it. 'I'll send Miss Terry back to you, shall I?'

'Please.'

Douglas passed on the message, went back to his office and sat down heavily. His legs felt weak and he was trembling. Before long other people would know and the fat would be in the fire then. For the first time he was frightened by the speed and inevitability of what was happening. But he loved and adored her. Tomorrow he would see her again. She was depending on him. He decided to go and tell his parents and break the news – or should he wait. But that was cowardly, he decided.

Tell them today, face to face, he told himself. Make them understand what she means to you.

Better still he would take the bull by the horns and bring his mother to the house for her approval and then tell her about the woman he loved. If he could win her round first to his way of thinking, she would ease the way to the confrontation he dreaded with his father.

'I can do it!' he said to himself, without much conviction. Once he started working on the house, everything would seem easier. He would buy some basic furniture – a bed, a table and chairs, cutlery and crockery. Or perhaps he and Hermione should choose the smaller items together. That would be fun.

'But where?' They could hardly shop locally where they were known and would be recognized. His face cleared. London! They would go up to London for the day and choose things and have them delivered. They would need curtains and carpets – and there was the small garden to consider.

'We can do it!' he said to himself. 'We must do it!'

It wouldn't be easy, but he would be strong for both of them. Please God they could bring about the happy ending he so desired.

While John and Douglas were facing the start of a crisis in Hawkhurst, less than a mile away, Cook and Millie were discussing the new baby.

Cook whipped egg whites for the queen-of-puddings and Millie ironed napkins and pillowcases.

Cook said, 'I don't mean to be unkind, but it's a funny looking thing, if you want my opinion. Pale as a cucumber and all scrunched up.'

'Not to mention his hair. All gingery and not a bit like his pa or his ma. But can't be the milkman because he's as bald as a coot!'

Cook grinned. 'But he might have had ginger hair before it all fell out.'

Millie shrugged. 'Ma says my oldest brother was pale and scrawny, but he's grown up real handsome. A heartbreaker, that's what she calls him. So James Oscar Fairfax might get better as he gets older. Poor kid. I feel sorry for him. I mean Mrs Fairfax is hardly the motherly type.'

'Poor little Elena doesn't get much attention,' Cook said, 'but maybe that was disappointment because she wasn't a boy. Not that she can help it . . . Change that iron, Millie. Can't you see when it's too cool? Look at that last napkin! Still crumpled. Do it again with the next iron.' She watched the girl stand the iron on top of the hob and take the newly heated iron. Frowning, she tried to pick up the thread of her conversation. 'Yes, now they've got a boy she might be different.'

'A pound to a penny she isn't!' Millie laughed. 'I mean, the poor little thing has already been banished to the nursery.'

'Much to Elena's delight. I thought she might come over all jealous but she adores him. Loves him to bits!' Cook began to beat the sugar and eggs together. 'As for being banished, the poor thing's better off in her nanny's care than Mrs Fairfax's. Uh-oh!'

Her sharp ears had picked up the sound of Elena's foot-steps and they were both bent over their tasks industriously when the girl entered the kitchen.

Cook looked up and smiled. 'Let me guess, Elena, you'd like a handful of currants. Well, I'm busy, but you know where they're kept.' She nodded in the direction of the larder and Elena took the opportunity to help herself.

She seated herself on the tallest stool she could find and said, 'Toby's been naughty. Mama says he's jealous of the baby.'

'What's he done then?' Millie asked.

'Chewed up Mama's slipper. Her best velvet ones that she had as a present.'

Millie grinned. 'Sure they weren't glass slippers? You know – like Cinderella.'

'No, they were velvet. Black velvet with little black bows. It's James's birthday today.'

'How come?' Millie demanded. 'He's only just been born.'

'Because he's one week old today.'

Millie snorted. 'He has to be a year old to have a birthday.'

Elena let that pass. 'Mama says he's the image of his father. But Papa's got dark hair like mine so he can't be the image of Papa.'

Millie caught Cook's eye and winked.

'What?' Elena missed very little. 'Why are you winking?'

'I wasn't!'

Cook said, 'Stop it, Millie!'

Elena scowled. 'Mama smacked Toby and sent him outside because the slippers meant a lot to her. I don't know why.'

Undaunted, Millie said, 'Maybe someone special gave them to her. A mystery man!'

Cook said, 'Millie! I'm warning you.'

Elena leaned closer to look at the creamy meringue standing in peaks. She knew there would be custard, a thick layer of cake crumbs and at the bottom the best part of a jar of jam. She hoped it would be raspberry jam. The pudding was one of her favourites.

Cook said, 'When you're a bit bigger, Elena, I'll show you how to make this pudding. Would you like that?'

'Yes, please. I could make one for James when he's a year old – a birthday surprise!' She beamed. 'Mama said they were a present from someone special. The slippers, I mean. Poor Toby. He didn't know it was naughty.'

'Course he did,' said Cook. 'He never chews things. Never has done. I wonder what got into him.'

Millie pounced. 'And who was this someone special that gave her velvet slippers?'

'I don't know. It's a secret.' Lowering her voice, Elena added, 'I expect it was Papa.'

'Let's hope so!' Cook exchanged glances with Millie over Elena's head.

The girl studied the currants that remained in her hand, selected three with great care and popped them into her mouth.

There was a sudden scratching at the back door and Millie said, 'Poor thing! Let him in. It's chilly out there.'

'Let him be!' said Cook, but Elena had already finished her currants and had rushed to the door. Toby hurried in looking chastened and crept into his basket.

While Elena was whispering comforting things to him, Mrs Fairfax came into the kitchen and Cook and Millie looked up in surprise. Still in her nightdress and wearing a pink silk dressing gown, she looked unusually cheerful.

'Shouldn't you be in bed, madam?' Cook asked, her tone solicitous.

Hermione Fairfax nodded. 'But I've only just come down for a few moments to stretch my legs. Now, about tomorrow. Mr Hatton is coming by about eleven so I shall dress and come down and sit in the drawing room while we discuss certain matters. The new baby changes things, naturally. We shall want a tray of tea and biscuits and I shall ask Miss Franks to—'

Elena piped up. 'Can I have some tea and biscuits?'

'"May I" not "Can I"! How many times do I have to tell you, Elena? No, you cannot join us for the tea and biscuits. It's a business meeting not a social occasion. And don't interrupt again. It's very rude.' She turned back to Cook. 'I shall ask Miss Franks to bring the baby down since he will be the subject of our discussion.'

Cook said, 'So will the master be present? Will it be a pot of tea for three?'

'Unfortunately he cannot be here. He has to oversee some developments in the Rye shop – but we shall manage well enough without him.'

When she smiled, as she did then, Cook suddenly remembered how beautiful Mrs Fairfax had once been. There was a framed photograph beside her bed, of her with her husband, and Cook imagined that there was a certain glow in that photograph, as though at that time in her life she had radiated happiness. Since losing her first child she had understandably lost some of her zest for life and for many years, even after Elena's appearance, she had seemed generally anxious and sometimes downright unhappy. Today she was somehow different and Cook looked at her curiously, wondering suspiciously what had brought about such a striking change. Presumably it was the new baby.

Mrs Fairfax was still slim and her face bore very few lines. She had green eyes and soft fair hair that she wore swept up in unfashionable curls on top of her head.

Still smiling, Mrs Fairfax went on. 'As I said, Mr Hatton will be here around eleven so please bring in the refreshments when I ring for them and not before. And we are not to be disturbed. I shall keep the door firmly closed in case Toby decides to join us.'

Millie butted in. 'Why? Doesn't he like dogs?'

Mrs Fairfax's expression changed. 'He's . . . he's allergic to fur – and I was talking to Cook, Millie, not to you. You really are a silly girl and I'm seriously wondering whether you are up to the job. Now get on with whatever you are doing and mind your own business.'

Millie's mouth tightened. She replaced the iron she was holding and took up the next iron. As soon as she laid it on the pillowcase there was a pungent smell of burning and Cook let out a shriek of horror which made Millie drop the iron on the floor. As she fled into the garden Cook began to stammer an apology, Mrs Fairfax rolled her eyes despairingly and Elena, expecting a drama, waited hopefully. Mrs Fairfax, however, refused to allow anything to ruin her cheerful mood. With a casual shrug of her shoulders she turned to go.

'I shall deduct that from her wages!' she told Cook mildly as she closed the kitchen door behind her.

That evening Marion Hatton accompanied her son somewhat unwillingly to view the house he had rented. She was a sensible woman with only one child, a son whom she adored, and she and her husband Ivor had done their best by the boy. They had educated him at an expensive private school and he had rewarded them by gaining a place at Oxford and surviving the war.

Mrs Hatton, now in her early fifties, and with a semi-invalid husband, had settled into a quiet but pleasant life and had gone as far as she dared towards modernity, wearing her wavy hair in a shortish bob and covering it with a small cloche hat. Her shoes were laced and she wore her skirts and coats just above the ankles.

She failed to see why, on an apparent whim, her only child had decided to move to a rented house. She and Ivor were disturbed that he had taken such a rash step without even consulting them.

At half past six she and Douglas stepped inside a small cottage at the lower end of Highgate Hill and Marion Hatton, gathering herself, made a genuine effort to be positive. After all, she argued, it was a fait accompli and there was no way she could undo her son's commitment. With a tight smile on her face, she looked along the narrow hallway and up the bare steps of the staircase. There was a musty smell in the air and the whitewashed walls were slightly stained.

'Very nice, dear,' she murmured unconvincingly, and peered into the small front room as he threw open the door. 'How are you going to furnish it?'

'Partly second-hand furniture, partly on the never-never!' He laughed.

'Oh, Douglas!' The two words conveyed her concern. Married to a reasonably wealthy man, Marion Hatton had a natural horror of the never-never system of borrowing and paying back the money with interest, over a longish period. Wisely she said no more on the subject and reminded herself that she had decided that, whatever the provocation, she would resist the urge to quiz her son. Her husband, Ivor, had asked her to find out what was behind their son's decision, but Marion was reluctant to be inquisitive. 'If he wants us to know he'll tell us, dear,' she had told Ivor, but now she was already wavering although she had only been in the house a matter of minutes.

The kitchen was the usual combination of kitchen and scullery, and with a stretch of her imagination she could almost see her son standing at the fairly new gas stove making some porridge. She asked, 'Can you cook now, then, Douglas?'

He paused. 'I shall learn, Mother. It won't be beyond me to boil an egg or make a slice of toast – and I can always pop into the Dog and Ferret for a pie at lunchtime. Don't worry. I shan't go hungry.'

The garden was a small area partly paved with brick and partly covered in a sickly looking lawn.

'Come upstairs,' he urged.

The front bedroom boasted a small fireplace. 'I shall keep nice and warm,' he told her.

'Do buy a brand new mattress,' she advised, 'whatever else you do. You never know who has slept on a second-hand mattress. You don't want to be woken by bedbugs!'

Her son shuddered but said nothing. He seemed uneasy, she thought, and began to worry in earnest.

The back bedroom was very small. Douglas said, 'I might use this as a storeroom for the moment.'

Alarm bells rang in Marion's head. What would it be used for later?

'I shall buy a new bed and mattress, a second-hand chest

of drawers and wardrobe,' Douglas said. 'Maybe a cheap rug. What do you think, Mother?'

'It all sounds very . . . nice, dear, but won't it be awfully expensive?'

He took a deep breath. 'I'm going to suggest to John that we give ourselves a rise. I think we should both pay ourselves a little more. Business is good. Why should we scrimp and save? When are we going to enjoy ourselves?'

'And do you think he'll agree?'

'Why shouldn't he?'

Frowning, she looked around the empty room. 'Is there a chair anywhere, Douglas? I need to sit down. I have to talk to you about this. I really do wonder if—'

'Mother, it's too late! It's done. I've signed the agreement and have paid the rent in advance. Three months.'

In silence they began to go downstairs, but halfway down Marion suddenly sat down on the stairs.

'What is it, Mother? Aren't you well?'

'I'm anxious, that's all, dear. Do sit down with me. I have to ask you something. I need to be reassured. Your father and I . . .' She saw his expression change and her hopes faded. 'We're wondering if all this is . . . is about a woman?'

After a moment's hesitation, Douglas sat on the step below hers and turned to look up at her. She saw the colour flood into his face and knew she was right. Dear God! She felt faint and was glad to lean back against the banisters. 'Tell me, Douglas.'

There was a moment's silence and then, as though a dam had burst, the words came flooding out. It seemed the woman was older than him which was of no real importance but – oh horrors! – she was already married. But, naturally, she was married to a cruel heartless beast who made her life a misery and only Douglas could rescue her from this grim situation. Like a white knight, her precious son was riding into the fray and intended to bring the woman to live with him in this house – and in sin! Marion felt faint with shock. It was so much worse than she had expected.

A groan escaped her. 'Oh, Douglas! What have you done?'

'I knew you'd be like this!' His eyes darkened, hurt by her obvious disapproval. 'I knew you wouldn't understand.'

'Well, of course we don't understand. We wanted you to find a nice young woman and get married and—'

'I don't want that! I want Hermione!'

'Hermione? Is that her name? Hermione who? Should I know her?'

He hesitated. 'Possibly. I don't know.'

'What's her surname?'

A further hesitation alarmed her.

'Her husband is Oscar Fairfax.'

'The Oscar Fairfax who owns the ironmonger shops?' She stared at him in disbelief. 'Oh, no, Douglas!' Her voice rose and her eyes widened. 'Hermione Fairfax! Douglas! She's a member of our sewing circle! You can't . . . Oh Lord! How will I face her?'

'To hell with the sewing circle!'

'Douglas!'

'I'm sorry!'

At least he had the decency to look abashed, she thought.

'This is about me, Mother, not about you! Give up the sewing circle if you can't face her.' His expression was stony. 'She loves me. Loves me! Don't you understand? Don't you care?'

He shrugged, a habit she hated.

But her mind was still running ahead, listing the awful consequences of her son's action. 'Your father used to play golf with Oscar Fairfax!' She regarded him fearfully. 'Do they know? I mean, does Mr Fairfax know about you and . . . and his wife?'

'Not yet, but she has to tell him. Mother, there's more to it. You have to be resilient.' He held his breath.

'More? Resilient? What do you mean? What more can there be, for heaven's sake! I can't take this in. It can't be happening! Oh . . .!' Distraught, Marion clutched at her beads, twisting them round in her fingers.

'Hermione has just had a baby boy. My son.'

Marion gasped, grateful that she was already sitting down and could not fall down. Surely she hadn't heard him aright.

There was no way her son Douglas was the father of Hermione Fairfax's child. No. No. It was quite impossible.

'Never!' she whispered. 'I don't believe it.' But she did believe it, and she longed to faint clean away and wake up somewhere else. She hated this awful little house and the reason behind it. She almost hated her son. She certainly hated Hermione for stealing her son away and leading him into wickedness. She closed her eyes and began silently to repeat the Lord's Prayer, in the faint hope that He might hear her and do something to help.

'Mother! Are you all right?'

'No I'm not all right. And neither will your poor father be when I tell him!' Since the oblivion she craved did not arrive, she knew she must react somehow. *What could she say? What could she do? Was there anyway to undo this tangled skein?* 'You can't go through with it,' she said desperately. 'You must see that, Douglas. It's impossible. Tell her you've changed your mind!'

'And the baby?'

Good grief! She had forgotten. 'It can't be yours,' she told him. 'For heaven's sake – she has a husband. Nobody can prove that the child is yours. It's most likely a trick, Douglas, to make you go through with . . . with whatever you're planning. All you have to do is demand proof – and she won't be able to give it!' Hope flared. She had saved the day! A smile flitted across her pale face as she realized how close they had come to disaster. Thank goodness for the husband.

'It is my child,' he insisted coldly. 'You have a grandson, Mother, whether you believe it or not. I shall see him tomorrow. I'm going there on business. Hermione wants her husband to change his will to favour the boy. He believes that my child is his.'

'On business?' Marion's whole body stiffened. 'You surely don't mean . . .? Oh, Douglas . . .' She pressed a hand to her heart. 'Don't say she's a client!'

'She is.'

'But don't you know what that means?' Her voice rose hysterically. 'You've broken the firm's code of ethics! You're a solicitor. You can't misbehave with a client! What's John Granger going to say? My God, Douglas! Don't you realize what you've done? Hermione Fairfax will be the cause of your undoing!'

# Three

The following morning Hermione prepared herself for Douglas's visit by pampering herself with perfume, powders and cream. As she rubbed glycerine and honey into her neck and hands, she watched herself in the mirror and was satisfied that he would be totally bowled over. She wore her newest nightdress and matching negligee in a deep coral colour which threw a warm glow on to her face and softened it. She brushed her hair with long slow strokes, smiling at the picture she presented. It was a shame he couldn't see her getting ready, she thought. He would certainly find her irresistible.

'Oh, Douglas!' she murmured. It still felt like a minor miracle. After all these years of rejection someone adored her. After all these years pretending that Elena was her adopted child, she now had a child of her own. And someone who believed she was wonderful. Douglas had changed her life, he had given her a child and was going to take her away from Downsview and marry her.

'To be a proper family.' She smiled at her reflection. 'I love you, Douglas.'

Abandoning the mirror, she walked the few yards along the passage to her husband's bedroom. The bed had been made, his clothes tidied away, a pair of shoes placed carefully together beside the bed. There was faint smell of his cigarettes and a trace of the pomade he used to smooth his hair.

'Oscar!' she said. 'What will you say when I tell you I'm leaving? Will you even care?'

It was so long since he had been interested in her and even longer since he had appreciated her in the way that Douglas did. Not that she cared, she reminded herself quickly. If Oscar's vision of the ideal woman was a pathetic nanny then he was welcome to her. Hermione swallowed hard and blinked back tears. No time to feel sorry for herself, she thought, dabbing at her eyes and forcing a smile. It would soon be Oscar's turn to feel rejected. It would be his turn to suffer.

Forty minutes later she was in her lover's arms and nothing else mattered. For a long time they clung together and Hermione's heart was full of joy as he pressed her back against the carefully closed door of the drawing room.

'Oh, Douglas!' she said softly when at last they drew apart and she could draw breath. 'I kept imagining that you wouldn't come. That something would prevent you.' She kissed him again then took him by the hand. 'Come and see him – our little son. I asked the nanny to bring him down here so that you could see him without having to go up to the nursery. We have more privacy here. Come and see our little boy. Our little James.'

'James?' He was startled. 'But that's my second name.'

'No one has queried it. If they do I shall remind them there was a grand-uncle named James. Actually it's James Oscar Gerald Fairfax. Gerald after my father, God rest his soul.'

He put an arm round her as they leaned over the cot together to admire the sleeping child. 'One day he'll be James Oscar Gerald Hatton!' she reminded him. 'What do you think of him then, Douglas? Isn't he just perfect?'

'He is. Just like his mother – perfect in every way!' He stroked the sleeping baby's head. 'What will you say if his hair is ginger?'

'I'll say he takes after my grandfather. He's long dead and who will know? He certainly won't be able to call my bluff!'

They both laughed. His arms went round her again and they kissed for a long time, until Hermione gently pulled back.

'Business first,' she told him. 'Let's look at the draft. If it's fine I'll put it back in the folder before Millie or Cook comes in with the refreshments.'

Minutes later they were poring over the new will which Hermione intended should be signed by her husband.

The will leaving much of the estate to Elena would be replaced by one leaving most of it to baby James. As they read it through, Douglas said nervously, 'He won't like it, will he?'

'No, he won't.' She turned to him. 'But then I didn't like the first will.'

'You didn't? Ah!' He looked puzzled. 'Is there something . . .? That is, am I missing something? I'm not sure that I understand.'

'You don't have to, Douglas.' She hesitated then reached for his hand and laid it over her heart. 'You have to trust me, Douglas. What I'm doing is for the best – for the three of us. You, me and our son.'

He was staring at her. 'The three of us? Surely you mean the four of us. Elena . . .?'

Hermione shook her head. 'Three,' she repeated. 'Elena will be happier here with her father and her nanny. Believe me. If you love me you must trust me to do what's best.'

'I do trust you and I do love you, Hermione, but I don't understand why you want to . . . how you could possibly leave Elena behind? I'm quite willing to—'

'But I'm not!' Hermione struggled to soften her tone. 'The truth is – and you've forced it from me – Elena is adopted. We have never bonded and . . . I tried to love her but it just didn't happen. Isn't that terrible? I feel so guilty because . . . well, the truth is that she loves her nanny more than she loves me!'

Tears pricked at Hermione's eyelids and her mouth trembled. Putting the past into words – hearing them spoken like that – had hurt as much as she had known it would. Suddenly she felt faint and slightly nauseous. Don't you dare cry, she warned herself. You have to be strong and you have to see this through.

'Forced it from you?' Douglas cried, anguished now in his turn. 'Darling Hermione, I never meant to force you to do anything! What must you think of me? Believe me, Hermione, I just needed to know. To understand.'

'Well, now you know and you must think what you will of me. You think you know me, but you don't. I'm not the perfect woman after all.' Despite her intentions to be strong, she felt the first tears run down her cheeks. 'Can you live with that, Douglas?'

'Of course I can. I can't live without you – you know that! Please don't cry, sweetheart! I simply need to understand.' He pulled her into his arms. 'I'm so sorry. What a bully I am. Forgive me, dearest girl. Forgive me for being such an insensitive idiot. I do understand. Really I do.'

'You don't! You'll never understand.' She was crying in earnest now, unable to hold back the tears as years of self-restraint crumbled and her sense of grief and loss re-emerged to overwhelm her. There were things of which she could never speak. Humiliations of which she dare not even think. Now Oscar complained of her continued depression little realizing how close she had come at times to losing her sanity.

There was a knock at the door and Douglas, still holding Hermione, called out, 'Not yet! We're not quite ready! Give us ten minutes, please.'

But he was too late. The door opened and Millie stood in the doorway holding the tea tray. She stared at them wide-eyed. Hermione gasped. Frantically dabbing at her eyes, she stared fixedly out of the window.

'Ten minutes?' Millie glared at him. 'The tea will be stone cold by then!'

Douglas hesitated. Since Hermione was still trying to compose herself, he said, 'Then bring it in . . . and then leave.' Millie set down the tray on the table. 'Your mistress is feeling unwell . . . Overtired . . . Business can be very worrying.'

Millie narrowed her eyes. 'Is the mistress crying?'

'No . . . At least she . . .'

'She is crying!' Her voice rose accusingly. 'I saw the tears.'

'Well, she is, but—'

'You've upset her!'

'No!'

Hermione turned, looking flushed, and said firmly, 'Please, just leave us, Millie.'

Millie regarded Douglas suspiciously. 'Should I tell Cook, Mrs Fairfax?'

'No. And don't you dare argue with Mr Hatton! If you don't go this very moment, Millie, I shall sack you! I mean it. I may sack you anyway. It's no less than you deserve.'

There was a long silent confrontation and then Millie's defiance wavered, giving way to the need for self-preservation. She spun on her heel and went out, but she couldn't resist slamming the door behind her.

The baby woke and started whimpering. Douglas immediately pulled Hermione to him and said, 'You're overwrought, darling. I'm going to go and let you go back to bed.'

'No. Stay, Douglas. You can't go yet. I need you.' She looked at him beseechingly.

'Then I'll stay,' he amended quickly. 'I'm sorry I've upset you. Say you forgive me.'

'I do. Of course I do.'

'I suppose I'm a bit of a novice at this sort of thing. I mean women and their emotions – I don't have a lot of experience.'

She nodded. It was true, she thought wryly. He had probably expected love to be all joy and red roses. Poor Douglas. She smiled through her wet lashes. 'You have no idea, my dear Douglas, just how hard love can be.'

'But you do still love me?'

'Of course I do! And only you – for ever.'

He smiled back at her. 'How would you like a surprise? I mean it, dearest. I'm planning something that will excite you. Something wonderful that we can share. Shall I tell you? It might cheer you up.'

'But then it won't be a surprise.' She took the handkerchief he offered and wiped her eyes. 'I must look a mess.'

'You look as beautiful as ever!' he assured her. 'It's something for me and you and little James! Can't you guess?'

Hermione shook her head and moved towards the crying baby. She picked him up, soothed him and laid him down again. Returning to the table she attended to the tea. 'Let it be a surprise, Douglas. You know how I love surprises.'

She poured the tea, thankful to have something to occupy her hands while she regained her composure. She was worried. What was that awful Millie telling Cook? She would have to say that she, Hermione, had felt obliged to come down and deal with the will, but had felt weak and tearful even before Douglas arrived. Maybe she could blame it on recently giving birth. It was well known that new mothers were often very emotional at such a time, even without all the extra stresses that affected Hermione.

They drank their tea, making small talk and avoiding anything that might bring about more tears. Fifteen minutes later Douglas left the house to return to his office, and Hermione went back to bed, badly shaken by her loss of self-control and anxious about the possible consequences.

Downstairs, the door to the drawing room was open and Toby padded in, sniffing the air enquiringly. He went straight to the table and pushed his head under the trailing edges of the chenille tablecloth.

Elena threw her arms round his neck. 'I'm a doptid,' she told him. 'Is that good, Toby? I'll have to ask Papa.' She crawled out and stretched her stiff legs, grateful that she had not been discovered. She had occasionally been banished to the nursery for far lesser crimes.

'What are doptids?' she wondered aloud. 'No good asking you, Toby. You're only a dog and if you did know you couldn't tell me. Unless I learned to speak dog language . . .' She hugged Toby, comforted by his warmth. Whatever doptids were it meant that she could not go and live with Mama and Mr Hatton because she was one of them. So . . . probably she would stay in Downsview and live with Papa, and Nanny would look after them. Her frown faded. That would be nice because she would still have Toby . . . but then James would be gone. 'I don't want to lose my brother,' she said to Toby, beginning to feel anxious. 'I'll ask Nanny about it.' Her frown reappeared. She couldn't ask for help from anyone without revealing what she had overheard – and how she had overheard it.

★　★　★

In the kitchen Cook sighed with exasperation. 'If you ask me once more if you're going to be sacked, I shall scream!' she told the maid. 'You should have shown a bit of common sense. A bit of discretion. Seeing it was an awkward moment you should have kept your mouth shut. Set down the tray on the table and left.'

'But she was in tears. I dunno what he'd done.'

'It wasn't your business, Millie. You didn't have to inter-fere. If you're going to keep this job you'll have to learn to understand these things. There was something going on between them. OK. But they obviously wanted to keep it private.'

'He looked very guilty,' she insisted, resuming her familiar sullen expression. 'He might have been hitting her.'

'Don't talk so daft, Millie! You made it worse for them, whatever it was, so Mrs Fairfax was angry with you. What did you expect?'

'How was I to know? He was making her cry.'

'You don't know that, Millie. She might have been crying anyway. She may have been feeling a bit weepy. And as for slamming the door. Well, that might have been the last straw.' She stared at the list she was making of items needed for the store cupboard. 'She should never have come downstairs so soon after the baby being born. But it was business so I suppose she had to.' Cook scribbled out one of the items and said, 'How am I supposed to concentrate with you standing there, wittering on in my ear? Do something useful, Millie, for heaven's sake.'

'Like what?'

'Like start on the potatoes for tonight's meal and then dry those things on the draining board and put them away. In other words, Millie, look around and see what needs doing.' She gave an exaggerated sigh and added mustard to her list.

Muttering under her breath, Millie obeyed but gave vent to her anger by viciously gouging out every small blemish on the unfortunate potatoes. When Cook left the room for a few moments, she stole a handful of currants from the jar in the larder and stuffed them all into her mouth at once.

When Cook returned she said, 'Look, Millie, I think the best thing you can do is go to Mrs Fairfax as soon as she's on her own again and apologize nicely. And I don't mean a grudging sorry, I mean something like "I'm sorry, Mrs Fairfax. Could you please give me another chance?" Something like that. And look sorry. Don't glare at her. She might be pleasantly surprised and give you another chance.'

'I can't remember all that!'

'Of course you can. But first you go and tidy yourself up. Comb your hair and splash some cold water on to your face. And straighten your stockings – they're all wrinkled.' She shook her head despairingly. It seemed that despite all her well-meant advice, Millie was beyond help. It seemed very likely that this latest episode might lose her the job. She was her own worst enemy. 'Make an effort, Millie,' she pleaded. 'How many times do I have to tell you?'

Millie hesitated. 'I've already forgot what I have to say to her.'

Cook frowned. She, too, had forgotten. Now she tried again, concentrating on searching for the right words. 'You should say, "I'm terribly sorry for bursting in like that." No, better still say, "I'm terribly sorry for intruding and it won't happen again. I hope you will overlook it."' She smiled with satisfaction. 'That should do it. Now use the mirror behind the back door and come to see me when you're presentable.'

'I'll forget it. I know I will. Can't you tell her for me?'

'No, because it will be better if you do it. And whatever she says to you just nod your head politely and say "Yes, ma'am," and come out and close the door quietly. Ten to a penny she lets you off.'

Five minutes later Millie returned beaming with relief. 'She was really nice. She actually smiled! So I can stay but I have to improve my performance.'

'What did I say?' said Cook, pleased with the result of her strategy. She handed Millie the shopping list. 'Right then, time for you to make yourself useful.' She looked hopefully at the girl, delighted by her success. Perhaps, after

all, she could make something of this awkward, prickly girl.
'You can learn something new, now. I'll show you how to
make a telephone call and you can dictate this list to the
grocer and ask him to deliver the stuff tomorrow before
ten a.m.'

Marion Hatton pulled a chair closer to her husband's bed
and watched him take the first tentative sip of his tea. His
first cup of the day. Ivor liked to be spoiled and Marion
always took him a cup of tea in the morning to drink in
bed. Something she insisted was a great luxury. In fact, it
kept her husband from getting under her feet for the first
hour of each day – a precious hour when she had the house
to herself and could potter undisturbed.

Ivor liked to believe he was something of a connoisseur
when it came to tea and she was expected to obey strict
rules when preparing it.

'Perfect, dear,' he told her. 'I've taught you well.'

'You have, Ivor.' Her smile was sweet, bordering on dutiful,
but mentally she chalked up a secret tick in her imaginary
column. She had not warmed the teapot before adding the
tea leaves but had got away with the omission.

'So, when are you going to talk to Douglas about this
ridiculous house business?' he asked. 'The longer you leave
it . . .'

'Ivor!' she exclaimed. 'You must be reading my mind. I
was just about to tell you about the conversation I have had
with him. I spoke to him about a week ago, but you were
a bit poorly with that nasty cold and I thought I'd wait.'

'Wait?'

'Until you felt better.'

'Good Lord! Is it that bad?'

'Yes, dear, it is that bad. Worse than that bad, if the truth
be told.'

Slowly he lowered the cup to the saucer and stared at her
fearfully over the rim.

'It seems, Ivor, that he has rented the entire house – rent
in advance. There is no undoing it, Ivor.'

'But why? That's what I want to know, Marion.'

'There is a woman involved. A woman who should have known better! A woman we know socially.'

'Good God! Has the boy gone quite mad?'

Marion had originally decided not to tell him the worst until he had had a chance to come to terms with part of it, but now she threw caution to the wind.

'It's Hermione Fairfax!' She waited for his reaction.

As his hands began to tremble she quickly reached forward and took the cup and saucer from him. His face had paled and his eyes were wide with shock.

'Hermione Fairfax?' he said. 'Oh my God! My God! But she's much older than him! What on earth . . .?'

'I'm seven years older than you, Ivor!' she snapped crossly. 'It hasn't done you any harm!'

'Of course not dear,' he said hurriedly. 'I'm sorry. That was stupid of me.'

She took a deep breath. 'There's more, Ivor. She's going to leave her husband and move in with Douglas and . . . and they . . .' It was difficult to say the rest, but she forced the words out. 'They have a child!'

It took a few seconds before the reality dawned and then, with a gasp, he fell back against the pillows. He was now ashen, trembling and gasping for air.

'Ivor!' She leaned over him. 'Deep breaths, Ivor! We have to be brave, dear! We can survive this somehow. I know we can. Ivor! Open your eyes and look at me. We can survive this. Do you understand? We can deal with it.' She regarded him anxiously and felt her own anxiety level rising also. 'There's always a way, dear. Breathe!' She snatched up one of his hands and rubbed it frantically although now she was not feeling too well herself. Shocked by his reaction she felt her own knees tremble. Please God don't let him have a heart attack, she pleaded silently, watching his eyes roll aimlessly. If only Douglas were still at home, she thought, he would know what to do – but then if he were at home maybe none of this would be happening. Perhaps she should have asked him round while she broke the news – it was his fault, after all – but she hadn't done so and now she would have to cope on her own.

'Try to relax, Ivor,' she begged. 'Take deep breaths and think of something else. Something pleasant. That day we spent at Bognor Regis three years ago for your birthday.'

He glared at her. 'Think of something pleasant! Marion! All I can think of is that woman with my son . . . producing a child! How dare she! He's little more than a boy.'

'He's in his mid-twenties,' she argued. 'You can't blame it all on to her. He must have known what he was doing.'

'I can blame her and I do! This is impossible!'

He was recovering, she thought thankfully, seeing him struggle back to a sitting position. Wordlessly she handed back the cup and saucer.

'I blame her husband,' she told him. 'He should have been nicer to her then she wouldn't have felt the need to stray. She may have felt neglected or—'

'Don't take her side, Marion!' He considered her comment. 'Though Fairfax should have seen what was happening and put a stop to it.'

'Perhaps he doesn't care, Ivor. Perhaps he's glad to get rid of her.'

Ivor, his eyes closed, sipped his tea. 'Thank God I don't have to see him any more on the golf course. Being a bit of an invalid does have its uses! Oh, Douglas, my dear boy, what a fool you are! A child! I can't imagine a more shocking idea, can you?'

'I certainly can't imagine him living in that cottage on Highgate Hill with that woman.' She shook her head. 'I'd like to go round to their house – the Fairfaxes' house, I mean – and tell her just what I think of her.'

Ivor looked startled. 'I thought you were on her side?'

'Not entirely. I just object when everyone blames the woman first. It isn't always so. Just as often the man is to blame.'

'I don't know who's to blame but . . . Maybe it is her fault. Women can be very subtle. Flattering him. Leading him on.'

'You think she seduced him?'

He came to a sudden decision. 'Yes, that's exactly what I think.'

Neither spoke for a while and their anger slowly cooled into a deep depression.

Ivor said slowly, 'But how do we know for sure it's Douglas's child?'

'We don't. But he insists that it is.'

Ivor handed back the empty cup, still dazed by the suddenness of the disaster. 'Suppose we refused to see her – or even to speak of her – would that bring him to his senses? Maybe make him think again about her. Make him see her in a less glamorous light?'

'I don't think so, Ivor. It might drive a wedge between us and then . . .' The consequences appalled her. 'We don't want to lose our son,' she said shakily.

He groaned.

Marion had planned to rally her husband by a brisk and positive account of the situation, but she had failed abjectly. Instead she now felt crushed with apprehension and the sense of growing calamity she had hoped to avoid. Helplessly she reached for Ivor's hand and clung to it. 'What on earth are we going to do?' she asked.

The following day, the twelfth of December, Winifred took the children for a walk. It was only two weeks till Christmas yet it was a bright, sunny day with almost no breeze, though today she took no pleasure in the weather. She was worried by news of a plan by Hermione to send Elena away to boarding school. It seemed that Oscar disagreed at first, but recently Hermione appeared to be winning the argument. Winifred was also against the idea, convinced that Elena was too young to be separated from the family. No one, however, had consulted her on the subject and she felt it necessary to prepare Elena for the prospect in case it might happen. She could soften the blow by pointing out the positive aspects of going away to school. If Hermione won the argument, Winifred wanted to lessen the shock for the child.

Oblivious of this, Elena marched happily along, her hands gripping the handle of the baby's perambulator. It was dark blue with a matching hood, well-sprung, with two large and two smaller wheels and it took very little effort to propel it along the lane. Normally on their walks it had been Elena's pride and joy to hold Toby's lead, but that was then. That was before the arrival of her baby brother.

Elena, in her element, called out at intervals to the dog. 'Mind out, Toby! You'll get run over!' She turned to Winifred. 'He's a silly old dog. He keeps getting in the way of the pram.'

She stopped abruptly to move round and lean over the sleeping baby. Carefully she tucked him in for the third time in five minutes and smoothed down his pale blue quilted cover. 'I wish he'd wake up,' she said plaintively. 'He's missing everything – the sky, the trees. We might see a squirrel or a horse and he'll miss that too.' She glanced up as a man approached on a bicycle. 'Oh, look! Here comes a man on a bicycle. I think it's Mr Potter from the dairy. James has missed seeing Mr Potter.'

Winifred, paying no attention to her words, drew a large breath and broached the subject of the boarding school for the first time.

'I knew a little girl once, Elena, who went to a very big, very nice school and lived there for some of the time. She had a lovely time, playing with all the other girls.'

'I could wake him up,' Elena suggested. 'Would he mind, do you think?'

'Yes, I think he would mind. Babies need their sleep.'

'But he sleeps at night.'

'But he's very young and he needs lots of sleep. Elena, the schools where you go and stay are called boarding schools. Girls who go to boarding school make lots of nice friends and they are never lonely.'

'Toby! Mind that puddle!' Elena manoeuvred the pram round a puddle while she beamed cheerily at Mr Potter who was slowing down. 'Mr Potter, this is James, my new brother. The stork brought him, but he came and went so quickly I didn't see him.'

Mr Potter, tall and thin, wearing plus fours and a waterproof jacket, stopped the bicycle and steadied it. 'Good morning, one and all!' He raised his hat to Winifred and said, 'A new brother, Elena! How exciting!' He peered short-sightedly into the pram.

'How's your wife, Mr Potter?' Winifred asked.

'Not good, I'm afraid. The old ticker, you know. She's a martyr to her heart, you know. The doc gives her this and that, but it makes no difference. Poor Mary. She suffers in silence, but I know it wears her down. She's very depressed.'

Elena said, 'When she's better she could come round and see James. He's a very friendly baby. That might cheer her up.'

'Friendly? Is he really? Well, bless my soul! A new baby brother for young Elena. How splendid!'

With a vague smile in Winifred's direction, Mr Potter set the bicycle in motion and moved on. Elena rearranged the baby's covers and the walk continued.

Eventually, Winifred tried again. 'At boarding school you would learn to play rounders, that's a game, and—'

'Did you go to a boarding school?'

'No, but I wanted to.' A small lie, she told herself, but necessary.

'Papa wants me to have a governess next year. I like governesses.'

'How do you know you do? You've never had one.'

'I just do. She's going to teach me to play the piano and when James is old enough he can learn the lessons as well, and we'll – Oops!' She stopped the pram suddenly. 'Toby! Oh, dear, he's found something dead! Is it a rabbit? Oh, no, it's a squirrel! Ugh! I hate dead things. Toby, leave it alone!'

Ignoring her shrieks, the dog sniffed excitedly at the furry body.

'Don't look at it, Elena,' Winifred told her. 'It's time to turn back, anyway. Let me help you with the pram.' They turned it and set off towards home. Toby lingered over his interesting find.

'We'll leave Toby behind,' Elena decided crossly. 'He's a horrid dog, and I shall . . . Oh, look!' She brightened. 'James is awake! Thank goodness he missed the dead squirrel! He wouldn't like that, would he?'

'No, he wouldn't. So, Elena, what do you think about boarding school? It sounds fun, doesn't it?'

'Yes, it does, but I can't go because I can't leave James. He'd miss me.' She stopped the pram and bent down, smiling radiantly. 'You'd miss me, wouldn't you, James? Look, Nanny, he's moving his lips. And he's moving his head. I think he's trying to nod. He can't talk yet, but he's trying to say yes!'

After their evening meal, Oscar and Hermione sat by the fire in silence. The clock in the corner – a large grandfather clock passed down through the Fairfax family – struck nine and Hermione decided she could delay her bombshell no longer. A part of her dreaded the inevitable battle, but a small, mean part relished the chance to hurt her husband the way he had once hurt her.

'I need to show you the draft will that Douglas Hatton and I have prepared,' she said, annoyed by the telltale quiver in her voice. 'The sooner we agree and it can be signed and witnessed, the better I shall be pleased.'

As she had anticipated, he was looking at her with alarm, his eyes narrowing with suspicion.

'You and Hatton? I don't understand. Surely any new will should be drafted by both of us. Hatton is only the solicitor.'

'He is also an adviser, Oscar. Now that we have another – a son.' For a moment she was flustered by the slip but quickly controlled her nerves. 'Now that we have James, you must rewrite your will leaving the businesses to him. Leaving most of your possessions to him, in fact. Your daughter . . .'

He leaned forward, his hands gripping the arms of the chair. His face was white with shock, but Hermione prepared herself for the furious colour that would soon rush into his face.

'How dare you presume – you and Hatton – to revise my will without even informing me!'

'Oscar!' She feigned surprise. 'I hardly needed to inform you. You must have known that if the child were a boy you would have to make certain changes. You cannot leave everything to your daughter, now that you have a son to carry on all that you have worked for! James would have to run your businesses. Anything else would be ridiculous and you know it.'

She held her gaze steady, but inside her stomach churned with apprehension. She must be careful. She didn't want to make him so angry that he refused what she was suggesting. 'I simply mentioned to Mr Hatton that I assumed we would be making changes and he offered to help. I thought you would be grateful. I know how busy you are, Oscar.'

'I'm not so busy that I can't find time to . . .' He swallowed hard. 'For goodness' sake, Hermione, the boy's only a few weeks old! What's the hurry?'

'Mr Hatton said that the sooner you started to consider the matter, the sooner . . .'

'Mr Hatton? Damn Mr Hatton and damn his interference.' He glanced round, his face darkening with anger. 'So where is this draft will he's had the nerve to prepare?'

Hermione produced the three sheets of paper on which the solicitor's secretary had typed a few suggestions. As she held it out, her husband snatched it from her and, without reading a word, tore it in half and thrust it into the fire.

He leaned back, breathing rapidly, trying to subdue his anger.

'That was very childish, Oscar!' Hermione, still attempting to appear calm in the face of his reaction, sat erect, watching him. 'Why are you behaving like this?'

'Because I know you, Hermione, and I don't trust you. You're up to something and I think I see what it is. You can't wait, can you, to see Elena disinherited? You've produced a son and you want to use him to spoil Elena's future prospects. Well, I won't let you. Of course the business will have to go to James, but I shall see that Elena is left well provided for in the case of my death.'

'James must have the larger share.'

'I will decide that, not you!' He watched the last of the burning papers twist into blackened flakes. 'Why are you determined to bring this up – now, of all times – when we should be so happy?' He turned from the fire. 'We now have a son. We have a child of our own. I thought you would be happy but . . . You're in a strange mood, Hermione. Perhaps the doctor . . .'

'Leave the doctor out of this, Oscar!'

'But why the sudden hurry? Hopefully I shan't die just yet.'

'Why the sudden hurry when Elena was born? You couldn't wait to revise your will in her favour despite the fact—' She broke off as a steely glint came into his eyes.

He said, 'We had an agreement, Hermione. Never to look back. Never to rake up the past.'

'That was before we knew we could have another child.'

'You mean before you decided that we could try again. It was you that decided Edward was our last chance – if you remember. Two miscarriages, Hermione!'

'I don't need you to remind me.' Her breath caught in her throat. She had not expected the conversation to take this turn and it put her at risk of emotions she had spent years trying to overcome. 'You can't blame me for Edward's death!' she whispered.

'I never did blame you, but I can blame you for refusing to try again.'

She protested at once. 'The doctor said . . .'

'He said what you wanted him to say, Hermione!'

She closed her eyes, suspecting for the first time, that she might lose this argument. It was true, what he had said. After their son died at the age of thirteen weeks, she had been afraid. Despite the doctor's reassurance that she was in no way to blame, she felt responsible for his death, believing that she had somehow failed as a mother and terrified that if she gave birth again that child, too, would die.

She abruptly changed the subject. 'Mr Hatton has another copy. I shall tell him that you have destroyed the first one.'

'Tell him anything you wish – but also tell him to speak to me first in future. I pay him, not you.'

They stared at each other defiantly.

Hermione changed direction yet again. 'You think so little

of me, Oscar. I can see it in your eyes.' Before she could
stop herself she cried, 'Do we have a marriage any more?'
As soon as the words were out she was terrified. She had
not intended to raise this particular question until the question of James's inheritance was settled to her satisfaction.

'Don't be ridiculous.' He stood up, looked round uncertainly then sat down again. 'We agreed, Hermione. We
had a pact. We all three promised to try and forgive and
forget. You haven't kept your part of the bargain.'

Her eyes blazed. 'We also agreed never to speak of it and
you're doing just that!'

'You promised to try and love the girl but you didn't try
very hard. You don't love her and she knows it. If it were
not for . . . for her nanny she would have no affection except
from me – and now you want to send her away to school!
I know why you're doing it, Hermione. You want to punish
her! And me!'

'That's nonsense. Now you're being ridiculous. You
smother her with affection. You both spoil her! You do it
to hurt me and she is becoming a precocious brat! Boarding
school will give some discipline.' Her voice broke suddenly
and she fell back into the chair with her hands over her
face. She had thought she was prepared for a battle but now
she was trembling, cold with fear.

She heard him get up and walk to the door. When he
slammed it behind him she realized she could hardly breathe
for the pounding of her heart.

Moments later she was on her knees, hands clasped, eyes
closed, praying hard. 'Dear God, if you have any compassion see my plight and help me. Poor Elena is such a
distraction – she would be happier away from me. She will
learn to stand on her own two feet . . .' She hesitated, trying
to convince herself of the truth of what she was saying.
'If she goes to boarding school Elena will make friends and
she will thrive. She is that sort of girl. Confident and . . .
and sociable. And I will be able to pay more attention to
my son. I mustn't let him die! Please God, watch over us.
Don't let me make any mistakes. Punish me for my failings,
Lord, but let my little son live!'

# Four

Upstairs in his study, Oscar stood behind his desk and poured himself a large malt whisky with hands that trembled. How, he asked himself, had the situation deteriorated so quickly? They seemed to have reached an impasse in the relationship and he blamed himself for believing that it could have ended differently. If only Edward had lived . . . but he had been found dead in his cot one morning and no one was to blame. The doctor had been very certain of that and the coroner had agreed. 'These things happen,' they had both said, but Hermione had taken no comfort from the words. Poor woman. The grief and guilt had remained to haunt her.

He sighed heavily. The recent pregnancy had promised a reprieve for all of them, but the new baby seemed to have changed his wife. For years she had been withdrawn and moody, often depressed, but he had learned to cope with that. Now she was suddenly charged with a kind of wild energy like a dormant volcano threatening to erupt. True, she seemed happier at times, but he also felt that he was living with a stranger. She was stronger and more unpredictable. He could no longer read her mind and it worried him. Her behaviour threatened to change all their lives yet again.

He swallowed the whisky and poured himself another which he downed in three large gulps. 'Damn you, Hermione! Can't you see what you are doing to us?' If he could not quickly retrieve the situation they were heading for disaster. He stared for a moment into his empty glass. He had always had a contempt for men who turned to the bottle for solace, but now he muttered, 'Why the hell not?' He reached for the bottle again. 'It can't make things any worse!'

Two days later John Granger was searching his filing cabinet for a copy of a land exchange which had been temporarily mislaid. Normally a very organized person, he hated to be proved careless and the missing file bothered him. He was in no mood for an interruption from Miss Terry.

'What is it? I'm rather busy.'

Miss Terry, middle-aged, reliable, and usually unflappable, had been with them from the beginning. Now she looked a little less unflappable. In fact, she blinked nervously. 'It's a woman – it's Mr Hatton's mother!'

'Mrs Hatton? Then why tell me? Isn't Douglas . . .?'

'She doesn't want to see her son. She insists on seeing you. She seems rather upset but won't say what it's about.'

'Hmm . . . I suppose you'd better show her in.' Reluctantly he abandoned his search as a frisson of alarm crept through him. He hoped this visit was not about what he privately thought of as 'the other matter' – that is, Douglas's involvement with a married woman. If it were, then he would lie through his teeth to protect his friend, but he would feel very uncomfortable doing so. His family had been friends with the Hattons for many years, ever since the two men met at Oxford. Their fathers had played golf together until Ivor's health deteriorated and, until recently, on the last Sunday of July each year, the families had picnicked together on Camber Sands. It had become something of a summer ritual. Douglas had also been best man at John's wedding.

'Mrs Hatton, how nice to see you.' John smiled as they shook hands. 'Do sit down and tell me how I can help you.'

She remained standing, however, and his hopes faded. 'I don't know how much you know . . .' she began, her clutch bag held close to her chest as though she half-expected to be robbed. 'About Douglas, I mean. About this woman but . . . I expect he's confided in you. Men do confide in each other. I've only just found out and I don't know what to do. It's making my husband ill, all this anxiety, and recently his heart's become something of a worry.'

John tried his best to look puzzled. 'I think you should sit down, Mrs Hatton.' He moved round from behind his desk and urged her into a seat. Poor woman. Discovering her son was about to move a married woman into his rented cottage!

Despite their friendship, John had always envied Douglas his looks, and since his own marriage to Moira there had been times when he envied his friend his carefree single status. Never, by word or deed, had he ever suggested that marriage was less than perfect or that there were times of misunderstandings and even brief conflicts. He believed that Douglas envied him.

Although Douglas was two years younger than him, John had constantly tried to find him a partner but without success. Douglas was undeniably shy and now it appeared that it had taken a married woman to reach him.

Returning to his own side of the desk he said, 'I'm afraid you have me at a disadvantage, Mrs Hatton. I'm afraid Douglas hasn't confided in me. What exactly are you worried about?'

As the familiar details poured out, he managed to show surprise and disappointment while he allowed his mind to drift as he considered rather smugly his own choice of a wife. Moira had been introduced by one of his mother's friends and it had been love at first sight. An engagement followed. Both sets of parents were in favour of the match and had been generous to a fault to the young couple. He and Moira were happy most of the time and eventually he was sure they would have a child or two – or three, if Moira had her way! He hid a self-satisfied smile. No heartache, no recriminations, no scandal. Poor Douglas on the other hand . . .!

When Mrs Hatton paused, he said, 'But will it last, Mrs Hatton? The affair might burn itself out. You know, a wild fling, quickly forgotten. Perhaps you are worrying unnecessarily.'

Mrs Hatton stared at him. 'A wild fling? Is that how you see it? He's taking her away from her husband! And there's the child? Have you heard a word I've said?'

A child? Douglas had said nothing about a child! He tried to rally his thoughts. 'Of course I have but . . . I'm sorry, but I don't feel I should interfere.'

Ignoring him, she went on distractedly. 'There'll be nothing but trouble. It will be in the papers! Everyone will be talking

about it. You know how people talk in small villages and
Hawkhurst is no exception. I was hoping, if it's not too late,
that you might talk him out of it. There! That's why I've
come to you. He just might listen to you.' When he didn't
immediately answer, she said, 'I'm sorry to burden you with
the news, but you would have to find out sometime and
better now than later.'

'I'm so sorry, Mrs Hatton, but I can't quite see what I
can do. Perhaps your vicar might talk some sense into him.'

'I thought – or rather I hoped – we could help each other.'

Something in the words chilled him suddenly. 'Help each
other? In what way?' he asked. 'That is, how can you help
me?'

Surprised, she said, 'Well, it won't do the business any
good, will it? A solicitor having an affair with the wife of
a client. That sort of thing is surely unethical and might
upset some of your clients. I thought you would want to
talk him out of it.'

Through the silence, John heard only his own heartbeat.
'A . . . a client?' he whispered. 'Oh my God!' He covered
his eyes. 'Who is it?'

'I told you. Aren't you listening? It's Mrs Fairfax.'

For a few seconds a merciful fog seemed to fill his mind
so that nothing was quite real but then it lifted, leaving his
mind agonizingly clear and the future problems in sharp
focus. When he felt able to speak he said hoarsely, 'I shall
certainly have to try and make him see sense, but knowing
Douglas I don't feel too hopeful.' Thinking frantically, he
suddenly decided to take the initiative. 'Perhaps we should
ask him to join us right now. Then we can thrash this out.'

'Thrash it out? Oh dear.' Her face paled.

John swallowed but his mouth was dry. He rang for Miss
Terry who told him that Douglas was on his way to visit a
Mr Fisher who lived in Iden.

'Then he'll be going straight home,' she added. 'And he
is taking the day off tomorrow as he has something important to attend to in London.' She gave a disapproving sniff.
'He wouldn't say what, but he tapped the side of his nose
and said it was private business.'

In spite of his earlier intention, John breathed a sigh of relief. For the time being he was spared a major confrontation. 'Then please bring us a tray of tea, Miss Terry, and don't interrupt us unless it's something urgent.'

When she'd gone he ran his fingers through his hair and looked soberly at his visitor. 'This is really most serious, Mrs Hatton. I think you'd better start again at the beginning,' he said and this time she would have his full attention.

That same evening Millie was drying her hands, thankful that the day had ended, the weekend beckoned and she could go home.

Cook came out of the pantry, shaking her head. 'I don't know what's got into that woman,' she grumbled. 'Christmas in less than two weeks and will she talk to me about the food? No. She's too busy or she's rushed off her feet or she's going to give me the menus, but she hasn't done it! I should be making mince pies. What am I supposed to do? Food doesn't grow on trees! It has to be ordered.'

'Some of it does. Grow on trees, I mean.' Millie reached behind the back door for her coat and slid her arms into the sleeves. 'Apples and pears and—'

'Thank you, Millie! I mean if you don't get the order in early they might not have what you want. The shops run out of things. I mean, does she want a goose this year or not? Last year she moaned about the turkey. Said it was dry.'

'Ask her again,' Millie suggested helpfully, buttoning her coat. She pulled down her scarf and wound it around her neck. 'I love Christmas. We have our dinner late when I get home from here. We have sprouts with bits of bacon and I love that and we have a big chicken but one year the man down the lane was taken into the hospital so he gave us his duck because he couldn't eat properly because of his throat. Duck's lovely and all fatty.'

Cook sat down heavily. 'We haven't even ordered the dairy foods yet!'

Elena came into the kitchen. 'Nanny said I was to ask if I can help with the mince pies like I did last year. May I?' She glanced at the empty table. 'Oh!'

Cook shrugged. 'You'd best ask your mother. She's all at sixes and sevens this year and I don't know how many to make, if any. Good thing I did the pudding in October.'

Millie searched her pockets for gloves. 'I expect she's forgotten the date – too busy looking after that brother of yours.' She smiled at Elena.

'No, she's not. I look after him,' Elena said proudly. 'And Nanny does too. But he loves me best. I push the pram when we go out.'

Millie regarded her slyly. 'He'll miss you when you go away to school.'

'I'm not going away. I told Mama and Papa says I needn't go so I won't.'

Millie and Cook exchanged looks but just then the door opened again to admit Winifred.

She said, 'James is going to bed now, Elena, if you want to . . .'

'Oh, yes! I do.' She beamed. 'I tell him a bedtime story and it makes him fall asleep.' Forgetting all about the surprising lack of mince pies in the making, she wriggled past Winifred and ran along the corridor. For a moment the three women eyed each other.

Cook said, 'It'll break her heart if they send her to boarding school.'

Winifred said grimly, 'Over my dead body!' and hurried after Elena up the stairs, in the direction of the nursery.

Friday morning found Douglas, warmly dressed, waiting on the windswept platform at Hawkhurst Station, humming cheerfully to himself as he waited for the train to London. He had bought *The Times* and was glancing at the headlines.

'No good news!' he muttered cheerfully, totally undeterred. Nothing was going to blight his day. Opening the paper he scanned pages two and three. 'Ah! The Irish Question.' He tried to read on, seeing the words but making no sense from them. It was simply a way to pass the time until the train arrived that would whisk him to London and his planned shopping trip.

He had a list in his head of the stores he would visit and it included Harrods where he wanted to buy Hermione a ring. He knew she wouldn't dare wear it until she had divorced her husband, but at least she could keep it safely hidden and look at it from time to time. It would be proof of his commitment to her; a reminder that when all the fuss had died down, they would be happy together.

Carefully, he folded the newspaper and tucked it under his arm. After buying the ring (maybe a diamond solitaire) he would make his way to Heals' furniture department where he would buy a beautiful double bed and a silk-covered mattress. At least his mother would find no fault with their bed! It would take most of his savings to buy the ring so the bed would have to be a 'hire purchase' transaction but who cared? Wrapped up in his cheerful thoughts, he nodded at the glittering prospect ahead of him.

A man next to him gave him a suspicious glance and was rewarded by a radiant smile.

Douglas said, 'Nice morning!'

'Is it?' To prove his point he hunched his shoulders and rubbed his bare hands together.

His trousers, Douglas noted belatedly, were unpressed, his raincoat shabby and his well-fingered cap grimy with age. Illogically, Douglas remembered the leather gloves in his raincoat pocket.

Impulsively Douglas offered him the folded newspaper. 'I shan't have time to read it,' he explained. 'Don't know why I bought it really.'

'I never read *The Times* – but thank you.' He took it, folded it even smaller and shoved it into the pocket of his raincoat. Adopting a high-pitched voice he mocked, 'Might do the jolly old crossword, what!'

Douglas registered the false voice but he ignored the sarcasm. As the train steamed alongside the platform, with the usual screaming brakes and shuddering halt, he hurried further along before pulling open a door and climbing inside.

He sat between an elderly woman who was intent on her knitting, and a very young man who looked like a clerk of some description.

He had seen three beds advertised in *Tatler* and would choose one of them. Possibly the traditional design with brass rails and knobs and elegant curves . . . although the mahogany bedhead was also a possibility. Which one would Hermione prefer, he wondered, his excitement rising. In his imagination he saw them enter the bedroom, saw himself sweep her off her feet and lay her on the bed. Then he would tell her to close her eyes and he would produce the ring in its small leather box and go down on one knee . . .

The train pulled in at Charing Cross nearly two hours later and dozens of doors crashed open as the passengers abandoned the train and scurried towards the barrier. They always reminded Douglas of rats leaving a sinking ship but today he went with the flow, happy to be swept along in the general hurry. Suddenly he caught up with the man in the grimy cap and, on impulse, Douglas pulled the gloves from his pocket and held them out. 'Here! Let's hope they fit you!'

Fearing another insolent remark instead of a 'Thank you!' he avoided eye contact and rushed ahead through the crowd. Once clear of the station he headed straight for the taxi rank – and Harrods!

By eleven o'clock the same day John Granger was beginning to feel rather feverish. He felt sure his pulse rate was rising and he blamed Douglas. If he died prematurely of a heart attack, he reflected bitterly, it would be Douglas's fault for throwing such a large spoke into the wheel! He stared at Miss Terry, who had appeared in the doorway, and tried desperately to hide his fear. He said, 'Not another phone call?'

She nodded. 'Miss Marriot. Leigh Green.'

'Oh Lord! Did she have any details? I mean, how much she does know?'

'She said she's heard a rather odd rumour that Mr Hatton has moved into a house on Highgate Hill and might be getting married. Her son is a friend of the people next door to the house.' She hesitated. 'I also heard from a friend of mine that the Fairfaxes' daughter Elena is being sent to a boarding school – rather unexpectedly. My friend has the same butcher and they're saying the family is in "a bit of a state" – whatever that means. It seems the maid has been talking out of turn, saying Mr Hatton is a regular visitor and a bit too friendly with the wife . . . but she could be exaggerating.'

She eyed him hopefully.

John rolled his eyes. 'Oh Lord, it only takes one or two rumours. They spread so fast. Like a damn bush fire! Oh, sorry!' He glanced at her apologetically.

'That's all right, Mr Granger. I understand how you must feel. I mean, who would have expected such a thing. Mr Hatton's such a gentleman.' She shrugged. 'That's the drawback to living in a village – everyone knows everyone else and they do love to gossip.'

John found himself longing to confide in her – it would be useful to get a woman's view – but he restrained himself. 'It's certainly out of character,' he said weakly.

She said, 'I walked Pixie – that's my dog, of course – down the hill this morning – she has to have a bit of exercise first thing – and went right past the house, but there was no sign of habitation. I glanced in and there are no curtains and you can see right in and it's empty at the moment. No furniture. Nothing.' She fiddled with her mother's wedding band. 'Do you think there could be a mistake of some kind?'

'I'm afraid not. Douglas has told me a little. In confidence, naturally . . .' His voice trailed off.

Her mouth fell open. 'Oh, dear! I was hoping against hope. His poor mother will be beside herself, what with an invalid husband and now this.'

They regarded each other soberly.

'I hope you don't mind me asking you this, Mr Granger,' Miss Terry asked, frowning, 'but could this affect my position? I mean, can the firm carry on?'

John stared at her, appalled by her question. 'Of course we shall carry on, Miss Terry! Oh, you mustn't fret on that account.'

'I just wondered if he might, you know . . . resign or something and this being a small firm . . .'

John's mouth went dry and the words he might have used to reassure her remained unspoken. He had never considered that the firm might not survive. If Douglas resigned what would happen next? He, John, could find a new partner but the money situation would be different and possibly difficult and without a doubt it would cast an unhealthy shadow across Granger & Hatton. He groaned aloud. Was it still possible to stop the affair, he wondered with sudden hope? Suppose he talked some sense into Douglas and he agreed to break off the relationship. Or was it already too late? Miss Terry was right. People loved a good gossip and a juicy scandal would seem heaven sent.

He closed his eyes, opened them again and stared helplessly round his office as his thoughts whirled faster. How long would it be before the Fairfaxes' new baby's parenthood was questioned? he wondered. So far that had not been part of the equation – at least, not as far as anyone knew. A wife taking a lover was bad enough, but a wife giving birth to her lover's child was going to raise more than a few eyebrows.

His gaze finally focused on his secretary's face and he saw panic in her eyes. 'You mustn't worry, Miss Terry,' he told her, somewhat unconvincingly. 'I'm sure we shall survive this rather unfortunate episode and you will still be with us.'

'But if the worst happens . . .?'

'Then I would give you a wonderful reference and would do my utmost to find you another similar post. You have no need to worry on that score.'

Brightening, she gave an audible sigh of relief. 'Shall I make you a cup of tea, Mr Granger? And how would you like a slice of angel cake?'

'Angel cake? Goodness! It's not your birthday, is it?'

'No, Mr Granger. That's next month but I made it last night. Maybe a cake might cheer us all up, things being . . . a bit haywire!'

Poor soul, he thought, with sudden compassion. She lives alone with her scruffy old dog and now we are threatening her fragile security. 'Angel cake sounds terrific, Miss Terry.

How kind of you to think of it.' He gave her a warm smile. 'I'm beginning to think you are something of an angel yourself!'

A warm flush brightened her cheeks as she hurried off to the tiny kitchen, but John's stomach still churned uneasily. It would take more than angel cake to solve his problems.

That afternoon a large van drew up outside the house and Elena watched excitedly as the new Christmas tree was unloaded. Her father had come home early to be there when it was delivered and now Elena and Nanny regarded it critically.

Her father said, 'It's a foot shorter than the last one. Last year's tree was too big and rather overpowered the room.' He looked fondly at his daughter. 'What do you think, minx? Nanny has found a nice pot for it to stand in. Then next week we can decorate it.'

That was a task Elena loved. The baubles were stored in an old hamper which was kept in the attic and there would be paper chains to make and thin gold ribbon to drape around the tree. Christmas was finally coming and she had tried to be extremely good so that if Father Christmas asked for a report, it would be a good one. She was preparing a note to send up the chimney on Christmas Eve, when she knew there would be elves about to collect them and carry them to Father Christmas. She had already written three notes but had discarded each one in favour of something more spectacular that was bound to catch his eye. The latest had an edging of holly leaves carefully painted with three different shades of green from her paintbox.

Between them they carried the tree into the house, along the passage and into the sitting room. Primed for the occasion, Nanny had a large terracotta pot for the tree's roots and a bag of soil to go round them to keep the tree alive. Even Cook and Millie approved of the Christmas tree although they had the unenviable job of sweeping up the pine needles which fell relentlessly on to the polished floor on a daily basis. For them Christmas meant extra work but it also meant a break from the monotony of everyday life and for that reason they cherished it. They both appeared to admire it in its natural state then returned to the kitchen. Once it was decorated, they would be invited in to celebrate the moment with a glass of sherry.

Elena said, 'We must keep the tree a secret from James until it's decorated because then it will be a most wonderful surprise. Who is going to write a letter to Father Christmas from James? I could do it because he can't write yet.'

Her father smiled at her. 'What a good idea, Elena. Then you can pop both letters on the fire at once.'

Elena stood back to watch as he steadied the tree in the large brass pot and Nanny patted in handfuls of soil.

'Poor tree,' said Elena. 'It looks miserable without its candles and pretty things.'

'We'll decorate it after work on Friday evening,' he suggested. 'I'll come home early and we'll all do it together.'

'And James can see it afterwards!' Elena said hopefully.

'He'll be in bed and fast asleep by then,' Nanny reminded her. 'He'll see it the next day and be very excited!'

Elena decided to sulk and produced a forlorn expression, but at once remembered that she was supposed to be on her best behaviour and hastily replaced it with a cheerful nod.

She gazed at Papa. 'What do you want him to bring you?' she asked. 'Father Christmas, I mean.'

'I've told you, minx. He only brings presents for children. The grown-ups have to give each other presents. I don't know what your mother wants, but I shall ask her in good time.'

'And Nanny?' Elena asked.

After a moment's hesitation, she said, 'I want a happy year for every one of us.'

Elena screwed up her face. 'That's not a proper present because you can't wrap it up.' She turned to her father. 'I know what Mama wants because I heard her telling Douglas. She wants . . .'

'Douglas?'

Nanny said quickly, 'She means Mr Hatton. Elena, you've been listening again to other people's conversations! How many times have I told you – it's bad manners!'

To make matters worse her beloved Papa was looking at her strangely. 'So what does your mother want for Christmas, Elena?'

'She wants a new will.'

Her father and Nanny exchanged one of those looks which always made Elena feel left out.

Her father said, 'Well, she'll be disappointed!'

There was an awkward silence and then Nanny said in a very quiet voice, 'He phones too often for my liking.'

In an attempt to make them include her, Elena volunteered, 'I don't like Mr Hatton. He made Mama cry.'

At once she had their attention and that pleased her so much that she quickly raked her memory to recall anything else that would interest them.

She went on. 'Millie came in and said, "Are you crying?" and Mama said she wasn't, but she was, and it was because she doesn't like doptids, and then he said that . . .' She faltered. They were both staring at her in an unfriendly way.

Her father said hoarsely, 'They said all this in front of you? My God!'

'Wait!' said Nanny. 'Were you under the table again, Elena?'

'Under the table?' he demanded. 'What on earth do you mean?'

'I mean that a certain young lady sometimes sits under the big table reading, and sometimes hears things she shouldn't! I'm always telling her not to do it.'

'Eavesdropping! That really is very naughty, Elena. I'm surprised at you.' Her father rubbed his eyes wearily. 'I sometimes think this family will drive me out of my mind! Douglas Hatton and Hermione? It's ridiculous! What is she thinking of?'

Elena was now regretting her revelations but it was too late. Papa was cross with her, and Nanny was also frowning at her.

Suddenly Nanny took hold of both her hands, but she didn't look so angry any more. 'What was that you said, Elena, that your mother doesn't like?'

'Nothing.'

'Elena! What was it?'

Elena didn't want to repeat what she had heard because for some reason she felt that Papa was going to be upset about it, but after a long silence she could stand it no longer. 'Doptids. It's because I'm a doptid.'

'Goddammit!' he cried, visibly shocked. 'Confiding in that puffed-up puppy! Is she that desperate? Saints preserve us! That really is the last straw!' He caught sight of Elena's stricken face. 'And you – go upstairs at once! And don't ever do that again. D'you hear me? Nice little girls do not listen in to other people's conversations!' Without another word he stormed from the room leaving them both badly shaken.

They regarded each other soberly.

Nanny said, 'I think the safest place for you, Elena, is the nursery. Go!' She pointed to the door. 'And get yourself into bed. I'll be up directly.'

'But I haven't had my tea.'

'Just go, Elena. You've upset your father.'

'Will you brush my hair?'

'No! You can do it yourself, just this once. Now go along!'

Ashamed, Elena tried to produce a few tears but nothing happened. A dreadful thought occurred and she howled, 'Are you going to tell Father Christmas?'

'I'll think about it!'

Elena did cry then, wailing, sobbing and hiccuping as loudly as she could as she made her way up to the nursery.

Oscar found his wife sitting in the conservatory with a rug over her legs. She was reading a book but glanced up as her husband entered the room. One look at his thunderous expression made her fumble for her bookmark and then, from sheer nervousness, drop the book.

'What's all this I hear, from Elena of all people, about you telling Hatton that she was adopted?' His face was pale with anger and he spat the words at her. 'Tell me, Hermione, that it isn't true! That you didn't.'

She shrank from his anger, feverishly searching for an explanation that would satisfy him while part of her relished his distress.

Gathering her courage she managed a defiant look as she

answered. 'I did, as it happens. It was necessary. But I didn't tell him in front of Elena. I have too much sense for that, Oscar, whatever you may think of me.'

'She was under the table! She heard everything.'

'Under the table?' Her face paled. 'Under the table? For heaven's sake, Oscar. That child is beyond the pale. Spying on—'

'What else did you tell him?'

'Nothing else. He was asking questions connected with the new will and I simply . . .'

He towered over her, his face furious, his manner threatening and for the first time she felt a frisson of alarm.

'How many times do I have to tell you there is not going to be a new will until I say so? You can plot with Hatton all you like, but I shall be the one to decide the new will! And all these phone calls from Hatton – what is going on between you, because I warn you, Hermione, if there is anything . . .'

Throwing restraint to the winds, Hermione shouted, 'What would you care if there was something between us? You don't care a jot about me as a person. You don't love me so why shouldn't I find someone who does?'

Abruptly he sat down and she saw how shocked he was. So he hadn't guessed, she thought in surprise. He had had no idea. Well, that was familiar to her. There had been a time when she had been unaware that he had found someone else; a time when she had needed him quite desperately and when he and Winifred had deceived her.

She drew several long breaths and tried to compose herself before the expected onslaught of accusations and reproaches.

He said, 'So it's true! You and Hatton!' His expression was bleak, his voice was flat and she understood exactly what he was feeling because she had gone through exactly the same agony years before.

'It's not pleasant, is it, Oscar?' she said bitterly. What could he say to her, she wondered, that she had not said to him in the not so distant past?

'Let's hope Elena doesn't want an explanation of adopted,' she went on. 'If she does, Oscar, I think I shall have to leave that to you.'

'You're a bitch, Hermione!'

She flinched at the spiteful word. 'Perhaps I'm what you deserve, Oscar.'

He was rallying, she noted. Pulling himself together in an attempt to take the high moral ground, trying to assess the situation and wondering how many people knew of her infidelity.

'So am I the last to know?' he demanded.

She had read his mind but it gave her no satisfaction. She shrugged.

He said, 'How far has this gone?'

'He's asked me to marry him.'

'My God!'

Hermione saw the disbelief in his eyes and felt a small frisson of satisfaction followed at once by a sense of hurt that he should assume her to be of no interest to another man. Did he find her so unattractive? she wondered.

'The nerve of the fellow!' he said grimly. 'And what did you say?'

She paused before answering, suddenly cautious, afraid to say too much. 'I said I'd think about it. It depends on you, really, Oscar. If you want to keep me there are ways I suppose. If not, I have someone to go to and I shall leave you. I shall take James and you will have your precious Elena.'

The room felt unnaturally quiet until the clock suddenly struck five.

After a long silence he said, 'If you leave me, Hermione, I shall sue for divorce, you will be the guilty party and both children will remain with me. You will not be allowed to take James. Get that into your head before you do anything rash.'

His voice now was slightly laboured, she noticed, and his breathing was shallower. Was that anger or grief?

Hermione hardened her heart and prepared to shake him to his bones, but even as she opened her mouth, something made her hold back. If she told him that James was not his son, there was no way of predicting what he would do – except to deny it and he would certainly do that. She had to be careful, she reminded herself, and wished that she had not been catapulted into this confession. Thanks to Elena, she had not had time to think the matter through properly or come to a definite decision.

In her heart, she didn't really want to be a divorced woman with all the stigma that entailed, although it might have been nice to marry Douglas. He was young and he adored her and she was in love with him but she didn't want her heart to rule her head. It was exhilarating to know that Douglas loved her but he was poor compared to Oscar and she was used to luxuries. Also, if she ended up as a divorced woman she might be shunned by some of her erstwhile friends. She and Douglas would have to move away and that meant he would have to leave the business . . .

She sighed. She did love Douglas but they had no prospects together and little real chance of happiness. Of course he would be bitterly disappointed but he was young and resilient and wasn't the first young man to nurse a broken heart. He would survive the disappointment. What Hermione wanted more than anything else was for her son to inherit Oscar's money and for Elena to have very little. She knew that was spiteful of her and it shamed her, but she had suffered so much from Oscar's infidelity that the thought of revenge was inevitably sweet. Once Oscar knew that James was not his child, he would probably leave him nothing and she could hardly blame him for that. Oscar would now wonder who the boy's father was.

Hermione stood up on legs that trembled. 'It's quite simple, Oscar. If you want me to stay, make a new will in James's favour. If you want me to go, divorce me and take all the unpleasant consequences.' She would keep the fact that James was not his son until later. Maybe he need never know.

Without glancing at Oscar, Hermione walked past him to the door with her head held high, but once outside her strength abruptly deserted her and she fell back against the wall feeling dizzy and almost nauseous with the powerful aftermath of her emotions. Feeling dislocated from every-thing around her, she needed to be in her own bedroom away from prying eyes; she needed to feel safe. That was her aim as she stumbled blindly along the passage in the direction of the stairs. Suddenly she was crying but went on, clinging to the banister, hauling herself up one step at a time. She was halfway up the stairs when her husband came out of the sitting room, snatched his coat from the hallstand and went out of the front door, slamming it violently behind him.

# Five

Upstairs in the nursery Winifred heard the front door slam and guessed that Oscar had stormed out but had no idea what they had argued about. She had resisted the temptation to eavesdrop and would have to wait for enlightenment. She hoped quite desperately that he had not left for good but had simply removed himself from the arena and would eventually return.

As though reading her thoughts, Elena said, 'I want to see Papa!' She had bundled herself into bed and now sat up, clutching an armful of teddy bears and a rag doll, peering over them wide-eyed with anxiety.

'I think he's gone out, Elena, and even if he hadn't, I don't think he'll want to talk to you. You're a naughty girl and you've caused all this bother and all because you don't do what you're told.'

'What did I do?'

Her voice trembled, but Winifred hardened her heart. Elena had let slip damaging information and Oscar was suffering. She loved the child but she also loved Oscar and her loyalties were divided. She chose her words carefully, unwilling to confirm or reveal anything Elena had not already understood from the exchange. 'You told them you had been spying and that's not a nice thing to do. How many times have I warned you?'

Elena's head drooped and she hid her face in the toys. 'I want to see him!' she insisted, her voice muffled. 'When is he coming back?'

'How do I know? Now lie down and go to sleep. There will be no story tonight.'

'But it's not bedtime. I'm not sleepy. I want some tea.'

Relenting slightly, Winifred said, 'You'll see your father in the morning.'

'Will he tell Father Christmas?'

'I don't know that either. I don't know anything, Elena. I wish I did. Now I don't want to hear another word out of you. Good night.'

After a long moment Elena said, 'I want to see Mama!'

'I'll ask Cook to find you some bread and butter and a glass of milk, then you must go to sleep.'

Later, Winifred sat beside James's cot and shook her head.

Who are you, little one? she wondered silently. Who is your father? Are you James Fairfax or James Hatton? If the latter then Hermione had turned the tables with a vengeance – and who could blame her?

'Not me!' she said with feeling. The fingers of her right hand crept up to cover her mouth, to try and stop the trembling. Her heart seemed to be racing and she closed her eyes. This might be the night all their lives were changed for ever.

It was midnight and Oscar had not returned. Hermione was trying to pretend to herself that she did not care, that he could stay away for ever for all she cared, but she was worried. Had he done something desperate? Had he gone to challenge Douglas? The idea chilled her. Or had he decided to kill himself? Knowing her husband, she thought that unlikely and pushed the idea to the back of her mind.

'Just come home,' she whispered to herself, peering out into the darkness. She leaned forward in the chair, pulled the blanket round her shoulders and pressed her face against the window in a vain attempt to see the headlights of his motor car when he returned. The moment he came into view she would rush back into bed and pretend to be asleep. She would not admit to having been at all distressed by his long absence. He was probably trying to frighten her and she certainly was frightened, but he must never know that.

If he had gone to the Royal Oak he would be back by now because they called last orders at ten o'clock and turned their customers away soon after. The idea came to her that perhaps there was yet another woman in his life. That wouldn't surprise her.

'A leopard can't change his spots!' she murmured angrily.

It came to her abruptly. She would ring Douglas and tell him what had happened. He would reassure her . . . but it was very late. Would Douglas be upset by a late-night phone call?

Without thinking too hard about the possible consequences she threw off the blanket and hurried downstairs in her nightdress. No sign from the nursery. The baby wasn't awake – at least, he wasn't crying – which meant that the nanny was probably also asleep. With feverish hands she clutched the receiver while she gave the number and waited for the operator to connect them. She had not turned on the hall light and sat in the dim light of the moon which filtered through the stained-glass window of the front door.

'Hullo?' It was a woman's voice. 'Er . . . This is Hawkhurst three-seven.'

'I need to speak to Douglas, please. It's very—'

'Speak to Douglas? At this time of night. Who is this?'

Hermione's heart sank. This must be his mother! Her first instinct was to hang up but something compelled her to carry on. 'I'm a friend of his,' she said as firmly as she could. 'It's very important that—'

'Why can't it wait until the morning? It's gone midnight, in case you were unaware of the time.'

*Wretched woman!* Hermione pressed on. 'Would you be kind enough to bring him to the phone? I need to speak to him.'

There was a pause and Hermione sensed a suspicion forming in the other woman's mind.

'I hope your name isn't Hermione Fairfax!'

'It is, though I fail to see what that has to do with my needing to speak to him. I can assure you he will want to speak with me.'

'He's asleep and I refuse to wake him. Perhaps you would have the decency – if you have any, that is – to ring back in the morning at a more appropriate time.'

'He's going to be very angry when I tell him how you've spoken to me.' Hermione glared into the darkness.

'Not as angry as I am, that you are trying to ruin his life and very likely you'll succeed!' Her voice was rising. 'You may want to drag him down to your own level, but he's my son and my advice to him is to finish with you as soon as possible. You're nothing but a whore and you should . . .'

Another voice intervened – a man's voice – and Hermione guessed that it was Douglas.

The mother cried, 'It's her! No, I . . . Give me that phone, Douglas!' The voice was quieter now because it was further away and Hermione assumed Douglas had snatched it from her.

'Go back to bed, Mother. You don't understand anything!'

Hermione groaned as the argument continued at the other end of the line. She waited impatiently and was at last rewarded by hearing Douglas's voice.

'Hermione! Darling! I'm so sorry. Just ignore . . . Mother, let go of the phone. You can't stop me receiving a phone call!'

While Hermione struggled with her emotions, she heard another voice – male and deeper. Was it Douglas's father? Whoever it was he was protesting about the noise, and then suddenly the line went dead. Someone had hung up. Hermione stared at her own phone and then returned the receiver to its rest.

She whispered, 'Oh God!' and sank down on to the bottom stair, imagining the three of them arguing hysterically over her. What should she do? Wait for Douglas to ring her when his parents had given up and gone back to bed? If they went back to bed. His mother might refuse to go back to bed if she knew Douglas was going to return her call. Poor Douglas! By the time he was free to call her, and she was sure he would try, Oscar might have returned.

Slowly she stood up, shivering. Time to go back to her vigil at the window in the bedroom. She was about to retrace her steps up the stairs when she caught sight of a shape on the front steps. A man's figure, she guessed, and her pulse quickened once more. How had Oscar returned without her hearing the car?

The visitor rang the bell. For a moment she froze in panic. It might be Mr Hatton, senior, sent by his furious wife, to impart a few home truths. To warn her, perhaps, from any future involvement with their son! Nervously Hermione tried to swallow but her throat was dry. She tried to summon anger but fear had taken hold and she was stricken with indecision.

'Police!'

Hermione hesitated, aware that she was not dressed suitably for the occasion – whatever it might be. A man's voice shouted, 'It's the police. Please open the door.'

She took a few steps along the hall but heard footsteps on the landing above. Turning she saw the nanny hurrying down the stairs and for once, was pleased to see her. At this moment she desperately needed an ally.

'It's the police,' she said helplessly.

'I'll see to it, Mrs Fairfax. You go back to your bedroom and fetch a dressing gown.'

Hermione fled upstairs, grateful to put off whatever bad news the police had brought. At least Oscar hadn't been arrested for attacking Douglas because she had heard Douglas's voice not too many minutes ago and he was safely in his own home albeit in the middle of a family row.

Snatching up her dressing gown, she tugged it on and rushed downstairs again. Winifred was talking to a policeman. Hermione noticed that he was wearing bicycle clips.

'It's your husband, Mrs Fairfax,' the sergeant told her as she rejoined them. 'He's in the cottage hospital. If you've no transport, you'd best call a taxi.'

'What happened?'

Winifred said, 'He . . . He collapsed.'

The sergeant gave her a caustic glance and elaborated with scarcely hidden satisfaction. 'He drank too much in the Royal Oak, refused to leave, there was an altercation, he was thrown out on to the forecourt. When he tried to get up he collapsed.'

'You get dressed, Mrs Fairfax,' Winifred said. 'I'll call for a taxi.'

The sergeant said, 'You could walk it in fifteen minutes!'

Hermione hesitated. 'Walk? I don't know . . .'

'You can't be expected to walk all that way alone in the dark.' Winifred gave the sergeant a frosty look.

Hermione hunched her shoulders defensively. 'Perhaps you should go,' she said to Winifred. She had no wish to face her husband after what had happened and shrank from seeing the damage she had inadvertently caused him. 'Tell him I'm too upset.'

The sergeant shook his head. 'It needs to be a relative,' he told them.

Winifred said, 'Then you must go, Mrs Fairfax. Stay with him. He'll be very frightened and will need someone. I'll be fine here with the children.'

'Thank you.' Hermione gave in unwillingly and, pulling herself together, tried to assess the situation. 'Don't frighten Elena when you break the news. You know how she adores him. Let her think it's not serious. I'll leave it to you.'

When she came downstairs again the taxi was at the door and as they drove away, they overtook the sergeant pedalling back to the police station.

The next morning the staff were told by Winifred that Mr Fairfax was in hospital and had suffered a heart attack and that Mrs Fairfax was going to spend the day in bed catching up on her sleep and was not to be disturbed, not even for a telephone call. Winifred would deal with everything in her stead. All other details relating to Mr Fairfax's condition were withheld. While Winifred bathed James and waited for Mrs Fairfax to return, Millie went into the dining room as usual to lay the breakfast table and found Elena curled up with a teddy bear in Oscar's chair at the head of the table.

'Oh, Elena! Your poor Papa!' she exclaimed. 'Let's hope he doesn't die! My grandpa died of a heart attack.'

'Is he mouldering bones?'

'I 'spect so. He's been down there long enough. Years and years.' She set out two place mats and the corresponding cutlery. 'He died before I was born, but he's buried near Canterbury because that's where they lived.'

'What is a heart attack?'

Millie paused to consider. 'It's when your heart gets worn out and doesn't work properly any more. It hurts a lot when you have it. You fall down and keep groaning. Groan, groan, groan – in agony. That's what my grandma said. And you can have little heart attacks and bigger ones. Then when it's too worn out you just die.' She found the napkins in the sideboard drawer, each in its own silver ring, and put one beside each place mat.

'But Papa's not going to die,' Elena told her. 'His heart is only a little bit tired because he's been working so hard. Nanny told me and I told James so he won't worry.'

Millie laughed as she added salt and pepper pots and a tea strainer to the table. 'Babies can't worry, silly! They can't even talk so how can they be worried? That's just plain daft!'

Elena considered the argument. 'He looks worried sometimes. He frowns so he must be worried. And James thinks a lot. He can't say that he loves me, but he thinks it. Nanny said so.'

'Nanny, Nanny, Nanny!' She tossed her head. 'If Nanny said so then it must be true!'

Elena gave her a suspicious look. 'I'm going to see Papa in hospital when the doctor says I can. I might go tomorrow if he's better and we might take some grapes. Grapes make you get better faster.'

'He won't get better that fast. It takes weeks and weeks when you've had a heart attack.'

'Then I'll write him a letter and the postman can deliver it or Mama can take it when she goes to visit him.'

'If she does!' Millie grinned. Then she tapped her nose. 'Maybe she won't.'

Elena wrinkled her forehead. 'What does that mean? Tapping your nose?' She tapped her own nose experimentally but nothing happened.

'It means that maybe I know something you don't know – like what your Papa did last night!'

Elena regarded her blankly.

'Like . . .' Millie raised her eyebrows. 'Like my dad was in the Royal Oak and saw your dad!'

'You mustn't call your papa "Dad". Mama says it's common!'

'Oooh! Common, is it? Well, common or not your father was—' She stopped abruptly and put a finger to her lips. 'Sorry! I nearly forgot – I'm not allowed to tell you. It's a secret. Not suitable for your young ears, but rather shocking! Naughty, naughty Papa!' She laughed, stepped back and surveyed the table with pride. She had added the teapot stand and toast rack from the sideboard. 'There! Cook won't be able to find fault with that.'

Elena thought sometimes that she hated Millie. Millie was what Nanny called too clever by half or a knowing little madam or too stupid for words or asking for a box round the ears. At this moment Elena preferred the last one, but instead she grinned and tapped her nose.

'Meaning?' Millie demanded.

'You've laid the table for breakfast!'

'So, Miss Clever Clogs?' She cast a quick glance at her handiwork to see if she'd forgotten anything.

Elena retreated to the doorway for her parting shot. 'Mama's sleeping and Papa's in the hospital. Nanny and I have had our breakfast. Nobody's having breakfast!'

Turning, she heard Millie's furious gasp but by the time Millie reached the door, Elena was halfway up the stairs on her way to the nursery, Nanny and sanctuary.

Monday did not start well for Douglas. He had hardly slept at all and felt frayed and unhappy. He was furious with his mother after the aborted phone call from Hermione and his unsuccessful attempts to return Hermione's call after his mother and father had finally gone back to bed. Sunday had been equally unproductive with nobody willing to help him. Today he had eaten no breakfast and finally reached the office in a state of fear mixed with confusion. To make matters worse, Miss Terry greeted him with a chilly 'Good morning,' and told him John Granger would be in soon after ten as he had a client to visit.

'And he would then like to speak with you urgently, Mr Hatton, so please keep your diary free.'

She did not offer to make him a cup of tea and he took that as a sign that things were serious. Damn! As if he didn't have enough to worry about. He went into his office, took off his coat and sat down. He then got up again and began to pace about the room, wondering how he was going to get in touch with Hermione. Presumably if he rang now her husband would have left the house on his way to work. But he would have to go through the secretary and Miss Terry would possibly recognize the number and might listen in. It was strictly against the rules but in the present circumstances . . .

'Damn her! I'll do it anyway.'

Miss Terry noted the number, made no comment and put him through.

'Hermione!' he cried. 'Oh, thank heavens! After last night . . . I don't know what to say. Just forgive me, darling!'

'This is Winifred Franks. Who is this?'

'Oh!' Shocked, he cursed his stupidity but rushed on. 'This is Douglas Hatton. I'd like to speak with Mrs Fairfax, please.'

'I'm afraid Mrs Fairfax is sleeping. She has had a bad shock . . .'

'A bad shock! Oh God! Is she all right?'

'Absolutely fine, but very tired. Her husband was rushed to hospital late last night and she sat up with him through the night. She has had very little sleep. Perhaps I could ask her to ring you later when, if, she gets up.'

Douglas said nothing, his senses reeling. Her husband had had a heart attack! Oscar Fairfax might die! Sitting back in his chair he clutched the receiver to his chest while he tried to think. What difference would this make to Hermione? Did it mean that if he didn't die she would be reluctant to leave him? Would it make her look heartless if she did?

'Mr Hatton, are you still there?'

To give himself longer to think, he asked, 'Are you the housekeeper?'

'No, I'm the children's nanny.'

'Oh. Look . . . I'm . . . I'm sorry to hear about Mr Fairfax. Was it . . .? Will he . . .? How serious was it?'

'I'm afraid I've been told not to give out details.'

'Is Mrs Fairfax going to visit him later today?' If she were planning to be at the hospital, Douglas could waylay her as she came out. They could sit in his motor car and talk.

'No. She isn't feeling up to it.'

'So no one will visit him?'

After a moment's hesitation the nanny said, 'I may go instead.'

Disappointing, but he told himself that this turn of events might play well with his parents. They might feel a glimmer of sympathy for her. Or they might see how near he was, if Oscar were to die, to being able to marry her without the scandal of a divorce.

'Mr Hatton, I have left the children unattended. I must go.'

'No, wait! Please. Is there a time when I could phone Hermi— phone Mrs Fairfax? Today?'

'I have no idea when it might be convenient, Mr Hatton. I'm sorry. I really have to go.'

The line went dead. She had hung up on him.

'So, Miss Terry, did you listen in?' he wondered aloud. If so there would be another rumour circling. But he had more important things to worry about. He had stopped caring about anyone but Hermione and an idea had come to him which made him sit straighter in the chair. He would park near Downsview and watch for Miss Franks to leave, then he would go to the house and insist on seeing Hermione. With her husband in hospital and the nanny visiting him, there might be nobody else around. Unless the cook kept longer hours than was usual. The maid would be long gone if he left it until about six or maybe seven, if he could bear to wait that long. A smile lit up his face. He would take the ring! He would give it to her and propose. Then he would go home and tell his parents. If they wouldn't wish him well he would pack a bag and move out. He would move into his rented house and wait there for Hermione and little James to join him.

Still smiling, he wasted the next hour in happy daydreams and was rudely awaken at ten fifteen when John Granger came into the office.

★   ★   ★

Sitting without being invited to do so, John glared at him, making no effort to hide his displeasure. Probably, thought Douglas, Miss Terry had listened in and had passed on the relevant information. His mood was so buoyant that he told himself, Take the bull by the horns, Douglas! Take the initiative here.

He asked, 'How much do you know, John?'

Obviously surprised by his attitude his partner replied, 'Enough to know that you are in deep trouble, Douglas, and although I'm sorry and we've been friends for a long time, I can't sanction the way you're behaving. It seems so out of character and if this is . . .'

'Don't say it!' said Douglas firmly. 'Don't blame Hermione! I won't hear a word against her. I suppose you realize that with Oscar Fairfax at death's door, Hermione is—'

'At death's door? What on earth are you talking about?'

Genuine surprise, Douglas noted. So he had maligned Miss Terry. Never mind. 'He's had a heart attack and is in the cottage hospital. Hermione was in a state of exhaustion this morning.'

John said, 'So she must care for him after all!'

'He's her husband. Even if she no longer loves him . . . Anyway, if her husband dies it would make our situation much easier. No messy divorce.' He tried not to sound triumphant.

John shook his head. 'Poor devil! An unfaithful wife and now a heart attack. But that wasn't what I came in to talk about. We've had a couple of subtle enquiries about you and Mrs Fairfax.' His voice was cold, his expression baleful. 'I seriously suspect that our good reputation is going to be damaged by your infatuation with that wretched woman. You have to give her up, Douglas.'

'And if I don't?' Douglas was surprised at how little he cared. Nothing mattered, he told himself, except being with the woman he loved. That woman was Hermione and suddenly their happiness together had moved closer. If Oscar died Hermione could hold up her head again and they could marry with their families' blessing. It all felt so inevitable – as though God was playing a part in the story.

As though, perhaps, it was meant to be. 'If I don't?' he repeated.

'Then you must rethink your position here. You may think you're vital to the firm's success—'

'I do think that! I know that! I have as many clients as you do and they—'

'You do have as many, Douglas, but if this affair continues you may start to lose clients.' He leaned forward. 'You must see what this affair is doing to your reputation.' He searched for another line of attack. 'Ask yourself if Mrs Fairfax wants to ruin your career for you.'

'That's a disgraceful thing to suggest!' he said hotly. 'All she cares about is me and all I care about is spending the rest of my life with her. If you've ever been in love, you'll understand what it means to us to face the future together, no matter what the cost. We're not the first couple to find ourselves in this predicament and we won't be the last!'

Douglas found himself wishing that somehow his parents could hear him now, defending the woman he loved with such passion and conviction. He felt that nothing in his whole life had mattered until this moment, and he could allow nothing to interfere with his plan.

John said, 'For God's sake, Douglas, you're not even listening to me! Your career may be on the line and I'm trying to help you!' Helplessly he regarded his partner. 'We have to be realistic and think this through. Look at the damage you are doing – not only to the firm but also to people you love. I can't imagine how your parents are coping.'

'They're my parents, John, not yours, so leave them out of it!'

Now Douglas was angry. He knew how much his parents were suffering and there would be plenty more to come when he moved Hermione into the house on Highgate Hill, but they would come round in time. They would love little James and they would, with time, forgive Hermione and find it in their hearts to love her. There would be other grandchildren. Douglas was their only child.

John was on his feet now and Douglas realized he had missed something.

'Are you listening to me, Douglas?'

'Of course I am!' *Whatever had he been saying?*

'So will you go away and think about it?'

'Yes.'

'I'd like your answer by the end of the week.'

'Answer to what?'

'To the question – are you going to give her up and remain part of this firm . . . or are you going to offer your resignation.'

Douglas stared at him with total incomprehension. 'Resign? I've put money into this firm.'

'I'll repay your share.'

'Jesus Christ, John!'

John got up abruptly, his face pale and anguished. 'I don't want to do it, Douglas. Don't make me do it.'

'You can't make it without me! We're a team. Always have been.'

'I mean it, Douglas.'

Before Douglas could think of a sufficiently cutting reply, his erstwhile friend had slammed out of the room, back into his own office.

# Six

When Winifred arrived that evening at the cottage hospital, she brushed the snow from her coat and made her way towards the men's ward where she hoped Oscar was recovering from his heart attack. The chairs lining the corridor were already filled with people waiting to visit sick relatives but a man gave up his chair to her and she sat down gratefully. She was dreading seeing Oscar and fearful of talking about Hermione and the recent revelations. In her coat pocket she carried a letter from Elena and the will which Hermione had insisted she should bring for his signature.

A nurse appeared from the ward at the end of the corridor and rang the handbell to announce the beginning of visiting time. Carried along by the flow of eager relatives, Winifred stopped at the ward's entrance to explain that Mr Fairfax's wife was unable to attend as the shock had made her unwell and she was confined to bed.

'I have come instead of her,' Winifred explained. 'Is that all right?'

'I don't see why not,' said the Sister and allowed her to continue. 'Third bed on the left,' she called after her. 'Try not to tire him. Probably ten minutes will be more than enough. Mr Fairfax is very weak.'

Although Winifred had tried to prepare herself, she drew in a sharp breath when she saw him. Oscar, pale and drawn, was laid back on the pillows like a discarded doll. His eyes were closed and even his hands on the blue bedspread looked thinner and somehow helpless. For a long moment she stood silently beside the bed, trying to come to terms with the revised version of the man for whom she had once risked everything. But that was in the past. They had both been punished for that misjudgement and they had pledged never to speak of it again, but it had not prevented Winifred from years of remorse and regret.

But I still love you, she thought wistfully. I suppose I always will.

As if reading her mind, Oscar opened his eyes and, seeing who it was, gave a tired smile. 'Winifred!'

Instinctively Winifred pulled herself together and tried to look cheerful, unwilling to let him see how shocked she was by his appearance.

'You gave us a terrible fright, Oscar,' she said, trying not to reveal just how much it meant to hear him use her Christian name after so long. Pulling up a spare chair she sat beside him. Impulsively she picked up his hand and kissed it. For a moment her gaze met his, but he made no comment and she almost regretted her action. But not quite. It brought back emotions she had believed forgotten – or at least thrust to the back of her mind – and she felt a momentary glimmer of hope which, from habit, she promptly quashed.

'So how are you today, Oscar? Your wife sends her—'

'Love? No, she doesn't!' He closed his eyes. 'Let's not pretend.'

'Her best wishes,' she ended lamely.

'Oh! I thought you were going to say her love.'

Winifred shook her head. She had known this would be difficult, but she had steeled herself to say certain things, in case the opportunity did not arise again. 'Oscar, I'm so sorry for what has happened. I don't know how to help you. I wish I did. She's a fool!'

'Perhaps I deserve it.' He tried to smile. 'She's turned the tables on me with a vengeance! Who'd have thought it? How's she taken it? Has she taken to her bed?'

'Yes.'

'Any sign of Hatton?'

'Not so far, but he telephoned later – while Mrs Fairfax was here with you. I told him the bare facts, nothing more.'

'Is Elena all right? Poor child. I hope she doesn't realize that she let the cat out of the bag!'

'I don't think she realizes the seriousness of her revelations. That reminds me.' She pulled the letter from her coat pocket. 'She has written you a letter decorated with flowers and a picture of the dog. Shall I read it to you?'

'Please.'

> Dear Papa,
>     We are sorry you are not well and hope your heart is soon better.
>     Love from Elena, James and Toby

'Elena was most insistent that James be included,' said Winifred. 'I wrote it and she copied it. It took her three attempts because she wanted it to be perfect!' She opened the top drawer of his bedside cabinet and tucked the letter inside. He was looking tired already and the nurse had warned her to be careful. 'Do you need anything, Oscar? Grapes? Something to read?'

'No . . . But you could kiss me again if no one's looking!'

He looked at her with such terrible longing that tears sprang to her eyes. With a quick glance around she saw that all the other visitors were busily exchanging news with the patients so she leaned forward and kissed his hand again, blinking back the tears as she did so.

He said, 'Try and come again, won't you?'

She nodded, wondering how to introduce the troublesome will into the conversation without upsetting him. It would be impossible and so she decided to ignore Hermione Fairfax's wishes. She would say she had asked the Sister and had been warned against anything that might be considered business.

'And give Elena my love and say I will write to her when I am strong enough. And, Winifred, take care of yourself.'

Winifred regarded him through a mist of threatening tears. What she wanted to say was that she loved him. What she longed to ask was when, if ever, they might be together as man and wife. What she needed to know was whether or not the affair between Mrs Fairfax and Mr Hatton might somehow bring about an end to the misery of the present situation. But this was not the time, she told herself. There was no way she could ask Oscar, in his present stricken state, for even the smallest glimmer of hope.

'Get well soon,' she said briskly. 'We miss you.'

Afraid to say more and fearful of breaking down, Winifred made her way unsteadily through the swing doors and back along the corridor. Poor Oscar. He had loved two women but had unintentionally brought them both unhappiness. Worse still, and harder to bear, there was no way on earth he could undo the wrongs he had done them. At that dark moment, Winifred could not see any chance of happiness for any of them.

Elena was in the nursery just after seven o'clock that evening when she heard the front-door bell ring.

'Run downstairs, Elena,' her mother told her brusquely, 'and see who that is. If it's one of the tradesmen about the late Christmas orders, tell them Cook has gone home and I am unwell and they should call tomorrow at a more suitable time. I'm in no mood to see anyone.'

Hermione was wearing an old dressing gown over her nightdress, walking to and fro with a fretful James in her arms, trying to soothe him into sleep. Her hair was untidy, her face set in a frown, her expression one of deep gloom.

Elena tossed her book aside petulantly, to show how cross she was at not having been allowed to help bath the baby.

'And take that look off your face, child! If the wind changes . . .'

'I know. It will stay like this!'

As she hurried downstairs her face cleared. It was rather nice being sent down to deal with the tradesmen, whoever they were. It made her feel grown up and important and, forgetting her grievance, she skipped cheerfully along the hall, reached up to remove the security chain, and opened the front door.

'Oh, Mr Hatton!' Elena tried to remember the message but wondered if he was a friend or a tradesman.

He looked taken aback. 'Er . . . I've called to see your mother, Elena. That is to see Mrs Fairfax.' He gave her a cheery smile and then peered past her into the interior of the house. 'Is she in – your mother?'

Elena looked up at him and hesitated. This was the man

Mama called Douglas and he had got her into trouble the day before. She had been sent to bed early and Nanny had refused to brush her hair.

Cautiously she said, 'If you're a tradesman she is but I have to give you the message.'

'I'm hardly a tradesman, Elena, but if you tell your mother I'm here I'm sure she will want to talk to me.'

'She doesn't. She's not in a mood to talk to anyone and if you are a tradesman . . .'

His smile faded. 'Look, Elena, be a good girl and go and tell your mother that it's Douglas.'

Elena said innocently, 'If it's about the Christmas lists – I mean Christmas orders, you should come back tomorrow when it's suitable.'

'It's suitable now, Elena. Just do as I ask, please!' He glanced over his shoulder as though he was expecting someone else to appear.

'Mama said she's unwell and in no mood to talk to anyone.'

He called past her, 'Hermione! It's me!' then stepped back.

Elena was put out by his action. 'She can't hear you and anyway she won't come down because she's trying to settle James because he likes Nanny best and he won't go to sleep for Mama.'

'Where's your nanny?'

'Gone to see Papa in the hospital. He's had a heart attack, but he'll soon be better.' Relenting slightly, Elena smiled. It was rather pleasant to stand here talking to Mama's friend. 'I sent him a letter from me and James and Toby. He's our dog. He's sad because Papa takes him for long walks and now he's in the hospital.'

'So when will your nanny be back from the hospital? Do you know? Did she say?'

'No.' She added, 'I'm so sorry.' That sounded very grown up, she thought, pleased.

Suddenly he leaned down to her and said in a whisper, 'If you go and tell your mother I'm here, I might find you a sixpence! You'd like that, wouldn't you? You could buy some sweeties, Elena. You needn't tell anyone.'

'I'd have to tell James. I tell him everything.'

'Telling James would be all right. I'm sure he can keep a secret. Here!' He fished in his trouser pocket and handed her a sixpence.

She accepted it and then stepped back and closed the door. She put the chain on again and went upstairs. Her mother had put the baby down in his cot and was dabbing at some curdled milk which he had brought up over the shoulder of her dressing gown.

'Who was it?' she asked irritably.

'Mr Hatton. He wants to see you.'

'What? Now?' She stared at Elena, mortified. 'I can't see anyone like this! What did I tell you, Elena? I'm in no mood to . . . Look at me! All in a mess and my hair's not done.'

Elena watched, her face impassive, the sixpence curled comfortingly into her right hand.

Her mother stared round distractedly, then rushed to the mirror above the fireplace. 'Oh Lord! Tell him . . .' She thought rapidly. 'Say I've gone back to bed with a bad headache and I'll get in touch tomorrow if I can.'

Obediently Elena retraced her steps to the front door but decided not to open it. Instead she lifted the inside flap of the letterbox. 'Mr Hatton!'

Part of his face appeared on the other side of the letterbox and Elena saw that he had rather nice eyes.

'Mama says she's all in a mess and . . . her hair's not done and she has a headache so she's gone back to bed . . . and she'll get in touch tomorrow if she can.'

'Wait, Elena!' he hissed desperately.

She didn't wait. She moved instead to stand at the front-room window to watch, from behind the safety of the heavy net curtains, Mr Hatton's eventual retreat.

Next morning, while Elena played in the garden with Toby, and James slept in his pram nearby, Winifred approached Hermione with a determined expression on her face.

'We have to talk, Mrs Fairfax,' she announced, standing in the doorway to Hermione's bedroom.

'We do, Miss Franks. I want to know why you didn't give my husband the will to sign.'

'I've told you already – the Sister wouldn't allow anything but a few moments gentle conversation. There was no way I was to bother him with matters of business. Oscar really is extremely weak, Mrs Fairfax. You either don't understand, or you do but you don't care!' She returned Hermione Fairfax's hostile stare with one of her own. 'I know what we agreed all those years ago, but now we seem to have come to a parting of the ways.'

Hermione sat at her dressing table, drying her newly washed hair on a towel. 'You're so predictable,' she said. 'As soon as something out of the ordinary occurs, you panic.' She combed her still damp hair, created a parting, then turned to look at Winifred. 'Sit on the end of the bed,' she told her, 'and let's get this over with.'

Winifred sat and folded her hands in her lap. She had told herself that whatever happened and no matter how Hermione provoked her, she would not lose her temper. 'I need to know what you plan to do,' she said. 'And don't say it's none of my business, Mrs Fairfax, because you know it is. You and Douglas Hatton – this changes everything. We agreed to live in this weird and wonderful way – and Lord knows, it hasn't been easy for any of us – but now you are likely to move on and that leaves me where, exactly?'

'That is hardly my business.'

Hermione removed her rings and placed them carefully on the dressing-table tray and reached for a bottle of hand lotion. She poured a little into her cupped hand, replaced the bottle and began to smooth the lotion over her hands and wrists.

Winifred said, 'If you are leaving Oscar I need to know. And I have to make it clear that I can't let you take Elena.'

'I don't intend to. The child has no feelings for me. You have seen to that. You and Oscar.'

'That's not fair. We have never suggested that you didn't love her. You made that clear yourself.'

'I was never unkind to her.'

'You showed her no affection. Children understand these things intuitively.'

'How would you have felt? Did you ever – either of you – put yourself in my shoes?'

Winifred was silent. She had tried more than once to imagine how Mrs Fairfax had felt, seeing her husband's ex-mistress around the house day in, day out. She had sometimes marvelled at her forbearance.

She said, 'It was your idea. It was your way of keeping Oscar. It was your way of preventing us from having a life without you. It wasn't easy for us.'

'Why did you agree to it, then?'

'Because you were in no state to be left alone and Oscar worried that you might kill yourself.'

'I wanted to do just that!'

Winifred resisted the chance to enquire further. With an effort she brought her thoughts back from the past. 'That's all over now. I need to know what you will do next.'

'If I go, I shall take James.'

'If?'

'We naturally have to talk things over. If I go I shall take James with me.'

'You think Oscar will allow it?'

'Oh, yes!' There was a triumphant gleam in her eyes. 'Once he knows the truth – which is that he is not the boy's father!' She smiled faintly. 'Odd, isn't it, that we have come full circle?'

Winifred hid her consternation. She was appalled for Oscar. He was fond of the boy and very proud. 'You cannot know that for certain!'

'Oh, but I do! The doctor will confirm it. The dates are quite definite. James is Douglas's child. He came very early, if you remember. That's why I shall never leave without him. Douglas would never allow it.'

Winifred breathed deeply and with effort. She was trying to appear calm in the face of confirmation of her worst fears. 'I hope you don't intend to tell Oscar just yet. The news could kill him!'

'That's my problem. I intended to break the news under certain conditions which I won't explain – but then this wretched heart attack happened! It has complicated matters and now I need time to think.'

'But you are definitely leaving Elena with us?' Winifred crossed her fingers. There would be no argument. It seemed too good to be true.

'If I leave Oscar for Douglas, then yes, I shall leave Elena.'

'She'll hate being separated from her brother. She adores him.'

'You forget that he is not her brother. Elena simply believes that he is.'

'He might be Oscar's child.' How would he take the news if what his wife had said were true? Winifred wondered fearfully. And could they ever really know for sure? Nobody but the mother could be really sure of a baby's parentage.

'James is our child – mine and Douglas's. Just as Elena is yours and Oscar's.'

The words seemed to linger in the air; words that Winifred had never expected to hear uttered again. The three of them had pledged silence on the matter and now the unexpected had happened and the silence had been broken.

Hermione said, 'I know how betrayed Oscar will feel because that is how I felt when I found out about the two of you. Oh, yes, Miss Franks! Oscar is going to suffer and I pity him. I do. I wouldn't wish it on my worst enemy. But Oscar will never be my enemy. I loved him for years and he returned my feelings – until you came along.'

Winifred realized that she was trembling. Doubts filled her mind and she began to wish she had been slower to force this confrontation, though it had appeared so necessary at the time. Far from clearing the air, however, it had proved very unsettling on an emotional level. It seemed she was still faced with a deep uncertainty with no discernible end in sight. It would all depend on Oscar's recovery, but even then there would be more questions to be asked and answered.

'I don't envy you either, Miss Franks,' Hermione went on coldly, sliding her various rings back on to her fingers with care. 'When you explain all this to Elena later it will shatter all her illusions. Poor Elena. I don't envy her. Or you. When she learns the truth, she might despise you and Oscar. Have you thought of that?'

Shocked by the unexpected direction in which the conversation was going, Winifred found herself full of guilt and, deeply agitated, forced herself quickly to her feet. 'We shall have to speak again when Oscar recovers.'

'We will indeed. In the meantime I shall talk to Douglas. Poor lamb! I imagine he is having a difficult time and may need some support. I shall invite him to join us for a meal some time during the Christmas period. I shan't feel up to visiting Oscar in the hospital again so feel free to go in my place. Oh . . .' She put a hand to her head distractedly. 'The will! He will have to sign it some time.'

'I shouldn't be too sure, Mrs Fairfax. Oscar is gravely ill. You do realize that, don't you?'

Hermione tossed her head scornfully. 'You can't frighten me. I've known him longer and know him much better than you do. Oscar is a born survivor. Trust me!'

The cottage in which Douglas sat was called Sunnyside and the thought of the name made his lip curl. There was nothing sunny about the house, he reflected unhappily. In fact nowhere looked sunny because beyond the front door a gusty wind was blowing a few drops of rain on to the arid square that the estate agent referred to as a front garden. Douglas, sitting on the stairs, gazed stonily at the front door and sighed heavily. Outside it was bitterly cold but that was to be expected in December. He shivered inside his overcoat. Maybe once they had all moved in it would prove to be an apt name. If only he could get hold of Hermione and bring her to see it. It was poky, he admitted, and now felt smaller than he remembered. But that was not the point of the exercise. The point was that he and Hermione and James should live in it together and be blissfully happy. That was all he asked.

He moved stiffly on the uncarpeted stairs and stared at the front door. He thought about the row on the telephone and was angry with his parents who cared so little about his happiness. Well, he had left them now and he hoped they were sorry. He had packed a few clothes and rushed out of the house.

'I live here now!' he declared to an invisible audience. Perhaps he would buy a pet. Not a cat or dog – they needed looking after. Maybe a bird in a cage. Surely budgerigars were easy to keep. Water and a few seeds . . . or a small fish tank. He tried not to remember the look on his mother's face when she clung to his sleeve, urging him to stay at home. To think it over. To see sense.

Tired of willing Hermione to turn up on the doorstep, he abandoned his vigil from the stairs, struggled to his feet and made his way to the kitchen. He had bought a few necessities earlier and now he surveyed them. A small kettle that whistled, a frying pan, two mugs, two plates, two knives, forks and spoons. He had covered the small rectangular table with a tablecloth – a circular one that he had bought by mistake while too depressed to concentrate on what he was doing. There were four eggs, a loaf of bread but no butter, and half a pound of lard. He planned to have an egg sandwich. Filling and nourishing, he told himself, and simple to cook.

The man had come round to fix the electricity and check the meter and the gasman had been to look over the stove Douglas had inherited. It was a far cry from his parents' comfortable home and he was trying not to regret his rash gesture.

He looked at his watch and wondered what Hermione was doing, what his parents were saying to each other about him and what decisions John Granger was making.

'Stop feeling sorry for yourself, old boy,' he said aloud, with an unsuccessful attempt at humour. 'Hermione's worth a few miserable hours. She's not having such a happy time either, bless her!'

Was it very unchristian, he wondered, to hope that Oscar died? Because that's what he did hope, and the sooner the better. Oscar was a very selfish person and he'd broken Hermione's heart. Damn him. What sort of man would start an affair a few months after their son died? Poor little Edward. Hermione would never recover from losing him. Damn Oscar! Who would miss him? – except the nanny. Douglas now saw her as 'the other woman'. Which made him, Douglas, 'the

other man'. Well, serve the blighter right! Oscar was getting
a taste of his own medicine.

He put a knob of lard into the new frying pan, struck a
match, lit the gas and watched with a small flicker of pride
as the lard began to melt. While the egg spluttered cosily
in the lard, he cut two slices of bread with difficulty and
made a note to buy a bread knife. He found something to
splash the fat over the top of the egg because that's the way
he liked his eggs. Couldn't bear the top to be runny.

At least he had a bed to sleep in although he had no
sheets or blankets. It was very different from his bedroom
at home.

'Make a list!' he said, and found a scrap of paper.

Minutes later he sat down to his frugal meal. He added
pepper and salt to the list and pretended to enjoy his meal
– a fried egg between two slices of dry bread.

A knock at the front door gave him sudden hope.
'Hermione!' He rushed to answer it.

His father's car was parked at the kerb and his mother
stood on the step. She had been crying, her face was blotched
and she looked ten years older.

She said, 'We know you've moved out, but I thought you
might like your bedding. We don't need these sheets any
more. Unless you've bought some new things.'

She had obviously practised this little speech.

He said, 'Do you want to come in?'

'No. That is, no, thank you.' She took a breath to steady
herself. 'You want privacy, Douglas. We understand. You want
a life of your own and this is what you've chosen.'

'Come in.' He held open the door.

Reluctantly she stepped inside and stared round at the
hall. 'It's cold in here. Have you any heating? A fire?'

'I haven't lit it yet. I've been busy.' He was lying. In fact
he had forgotten to buy coal and kindling.

The blankets, sheets and pillows were tempting. Could he
say yes?

'Why is Father sitting in the car?' he asked.

'He's got nothing to say to you. He won't even . . . talk
about you.' She swallowed hard.

'He always was stubborn!'

'That's a mean thing to say, Douglas. Don't punish us for what you've done. You've knocked your poor father for six, Douglas. You can't imagine the shame and disappointment.' Choked, she brushed a hand over her eyes. 'It's not too late, you know, dear. We could get over all this nonsense if you would just—'

'What exactly do you mean by nonsense?' His hackles rose. No one was going to speak disrespectfully of Hermione. Not within his hearing, anyway.

'You know what I mean, Douglas. You can change your mind. Apologize to John Granger. Douglas, it must have been her fault. This isn't like you!'

'I don't have to apologize to anyone. I'm one of the partners.' His stomach lurched coldly. 'He can't fire me!'

'Well, I hope you're right.'

His father sounded the car's horn and they both jumped. She said quickly, 'The bedding is on the back seat. You might . . .'

Suddenly Douglas couldn't bear it another moment. 'I don't need the bedding,' he lied. 'I don't need anything from either of you – except a little understanding and I'm certainly not getting that! I just want the woman I love. I don't expect you to—'

'To understand? No, we don't. You're right about that.' Her face twisted unhappily. 'We can't understand you at all. We've tried to bring you up properly to lead a decent life and not . . . not trample on decent human values. You've disgraced us, Douglas, and that's the simple truth. And as for Hermione Fairfax . . . the less said the better.'

'And you're also turning your back on your grandson!' he said through gritted teeth. 'How could you, Mother? Doesn't he deserve some consideration? He's not to blame.'

Her face crumpled into sudden despair and he regretted his words but it was too late. His mother, choking back tears, turned to go back to the car.

At the bottom of the tiny garden, clutching the small rusty gate as if for support, she said, 'If you've nowhere to go for your Christmas dinner, come to us.'

Douglas shook his head. 'I hope to spend it with Hermione and our son,' he told her. Most unlikely, he reflected. It was nothing more than a pipe dream and even to him it sounded unconvincing. 'It's a kind offer but I have everything under control!' He had a sudden vision of his parents' Christmas table – turkey and all the trimmings. But could he bear the silent gaze of his disapproving father and the sight of his tearful mother? 'Maybe I'll pop round. I'll see what Hermione is doing. If she's not free . . .'

Marion hesitated. 'Please take the bedding.'

Relieved to be persuaded, Douglas told himself he would agree for his mother's peace of mind. They walked to the rear of the car while his father stared straight ahead. Minutes later, Douglas stood on the pavement, his arms full of bedding, and watched through blurred eyes as the car drove away. For the benefit of any neighbours who might be watching, he shouted, 'Goodbye! Thanks for coming!'

Once inside he dropped the bedding and closed the door. 'Christmas!' God! He'd forgotten all about it. Back in the kitchen he sat down at the table, laid his head on his folded arms and wished he could cry.

Burton Ward, despite its full quota of sick people, was a cheerful place and, as he lay against the pillows, Oscar considered he might have ended up somewhere worse. He was grateful to be comfortable and looked after by caring staff.

The staff nurse had told him that he could expect a visit from the consultant. 'Mr Temple usually comes in on Thursdays,' she had told him. 'He'll be keeping an eye on you. He'll decide when you can go home again.'

Oscar hoped it wouldn't be too soon. He was dreading returning home to face Hermione and whatever new disasters were waiting in the wings. Here, in spite of his weakness and anxiety about his heart, he felt comparatively safe. Safe, but with time to think about what might happen next and, unfortunately, to remember the mistakes that had inevitably brought him to where he was today.

The swing doors opened but it was Matron who appeared and not Mr Temple. She spoke quietly to the Sister and the staff nurse, glancing sharply at various patients as she did so. While she was talking, the nurses and the ward orderlies scurried about nervously, trying not to be noticed, hoping not to be singled out for any minor infringement of the hospital's rules. Matron was to be feared at all times, thought Oscar, smiling inwardly.

She began her tour of the ward and when she reached Oscar she said briskly, 'Good morning, Mr Fairfax. Is there anything you wish to say about your stay so far?'

'No, Matron, but I shall have a better idea after I've seen the consultant.'

'Mr Temple?

He nodded.

'But you're comfortable?'

'Yes, thank you. I would like to write a letter. Am I allowed that much exercise?' He tried to speak humorously, but Matron's mouth did not even twitch.

She said, 'As long as it is not going to involve you in anything worrying. You have had a heart attack and you need to stay calm, firstly to allow the heart muscles to recover and secondly to prevent a second attack which is not uncommon.'

Without further ado, she swept on to the next patient – an elderly man who had confided in Oscar that he suffered from pains in his gut.

'Course they give it this highfalutin name,' he had told Oscar. '"Abominable pains". That's what they put on me notes. On that thingummy hooked on the end of the bed, like. My missus read it for me. Abominable pains and "in for exploratory". That's me.'

Now he shrank from Matron's stern gaze.

'I hear you don't like our food, Mr Ebdon!' Matron said accusingly. 'What exactly is your criticism?'

'Oh, it's nice enough, Matron, just not enough of it, is there? I mean a bit of steamed fish and mashed potatoes! Doesn't exactly fill me up.'

'You are on a restricted diet, Mr Ebdon. That is why we are not overfeeding you. You must trust us to know what we are doing!'

As she strode on to the next patient, Mr Ebdon slid beneath the sheets as if to make himself less visible, and less vulnerable to further attack.

Oscar closed his eyes, blaming himself yet again for the weakness that had made him give in to Hermione's frantic pleas so many years ago. If only little Edward had lived, life would have continued normally, the marriage would have remained intact and no one would have been hurt, but fate had been against them. Against all three of them. He recalled the countless times, after the baby's funeral, when he had approached Hermione. He was eager to make love to her and to make her pregnant again. But she had had two miscarriages before conceiving Edward and did not want to try again. The doctor had agreed that perhaps they could come to terms with the fact that Hermione might never raise a child. For one thing, her mental state, always slightly delicate, had deteriorated in the face of so much distress and failure.

Mr Ebdon's head appeared from beneath the bedclothes. 'Has she gone?'

'Just leaving. Give it five seconds.'

When he finally sat up, the old man glanced round with relief then smiled. 'That your missus, was it, that come yesterday? Nice-looking lass.'

'My wife is unwell. That was our daughter's nanny.'

The words slipped easily from his tongue and that gave him another jolt of remorse. Winifred was Elena's mother, not Hermione. He had turned to Winifred for solace after his wife's rejection, and Elena had been the result. He had promised a terrified Winifred that he loved her and would leave Hermione, but the latter had become hysterical when the facts were laid before her. So hysterical, in fact, that the doctor had become anxious for her sanity and feared a possible breakdown. It seemed that a 'delicate mental balance' ran in Hermione's family and Hermione's youngest and favourite aunt had suffered serious depression all her life and had finally been committed to an asylum.

'Unwell, is she? That's a shame, that is.' Mr Ebdon propped himself on one elbow and regarded Oscar with pity. 'I'm lucky that way. See, my missus has never had a day's illness in her life. Tough as old boots, she is. Me – now that's another matter, that is. Never well, me. I've had just about everything! Flu, impetigo, bronchitis, even broke my leg once, falling off a bus that was slowing down, but it wasn't and wham! Down I went in the gutter and an ice-cream man on his bike ran right over me. Snap! Broken leg! Ice creams and wafers all over the blooming road!'

Oscar murmured something vaguely sympathetic. Part of him longed to be distracted by his chirpy neighbour, but he had so much on his mind and desperately needed to think the situation through while he was alone. He wanted to look back and see where, if anywhere, he might have dealt with the problems more sensibly and, more to the point, try to discover a way forward for all of them.

'So . . .' Mr Ebdon leaned across the gap that separated the two beds. 'You're one of those people, then . . . people who have a nanny for the kids! Plenty of readies?' He rubbed a finger and thumb together and winked.

Plenty of readies? Yes, Oscar supposed that he did have, because obviously they had a nanny – but then he had two ironmonger's shops, one in Hawkhurst and one, newer and larger, in Rye. Yes, he supposed he would have to class himself as comfortably off. But what would happen if Hermione carried out her threat to leave him for young Hatton? Where would he stand in law? Where would Hermione stand? Would she be entitled to any of his money? Divorce was something he knew little about but he had heard, and read, that they could prove troublesome and sometimes costly. And – the ghastly thought would not leave him – what if James were not his son but had been fathered by Hatton? He closed his eyes, appalled.

'Mr Fairfax?'

Oscar opened his eyes to find a tall, pleasant-looking man standing beside him.

'I'm Mr Temple, your consultant.'

# Seven

Elena sat at the small table in the nursery and copied the date exactly as her nanny had written it. She wanted the letter to Father Christmas to look as grown up as possible so that he would take her request seriously.

She glanced across the room to where Nanny was bathing James in a small wooden bath.

'I'm going to send him one from James,' Elena announced, 'because James can't write yet, but I know what he wants and he has been good.'

'So what does he want?'

'A new rattle, a storybook made of rag all about the alphabet, and a train set.'

'A train set? Does he know what a train is, Elena?'

'No, but when he gets the train set he will, and I'll help him to play with it. And he wants a pig money box to keep his money in.'

'And what do you want, Elena?' She lifted the baby out on to her lap and wrapped him in a towel which had been warming by the nursery fire.

'A puppy to keep Toby company and a rabbit in a hutch and a doll with eyes that open and shut, and . . .' Suddenly she stopped and fixed her nanny with an anxious look. 'Did you tell Father Christmas that I'd been naughty, sitting under the table? Because if he isn't going to bring me anything I won't bother to write to him.'

'I didn't tell him, Elena.'

Elena let out a sigh of relief. Suddenly she said, 'Do you love James more than me?'

'Of course not! What put that idea into your head?'

'Mama loves him more than me, but I don't mind.'

Nanny let out a long groan. 'Mama loves you both the

same and so do I. Stop worrying, Elena. It's nearly Christmas and it's a time for lots of fun. And when you see your papa, don't ask him that question. Do you hear me, Elena? Everybody loves you and everybody loves James. Now get on with your lists while I take James to your mama to have his bottle.'

'Cook's going to let me help her with the mince pies because everything's so late and she's only got one pair of hands.'

'That's nice.' She made her way to the door. 'When James has settled down to sleep and you've finished your lists, I'll read you a story.'

'And then will you go to the hospital to see Papa?'

'I expect so.'

Elena watched her leave the room and then bent over her writing. She had to work carefully because Nanny said that Father Christmas couldn't read some children's lists because they scribbled so and Elena wasn't going to make that mistake.

Later that morning Hermione finally plucked up the courage to read her husband's letter.

> Dear Hermione,
>
> I don't want to add your present confusion but feel that the time has come to once again examine the problem we have. I know you are acutely disturbed by recent events and have no one to turn to for guidance so I feel that a first step would be for the three of us to look clearly at where we are today – especially in view of your feelings for Douglas Hatton . . .

Hermione crumpled the letter, her mind freezing with fear as she tried to anticipate what might follow. Winifred had brought the letter back from her hospital visit at Oscar's request and she found herself wondering whether or not the nanny knew anything of the contents. Had the two of them composed it between them? The thought made her feel nauseous and for a moment her head swam. Eventually she forced herself to read on.

> I want you to know that I deeply regret what happened and feel that our pledge never to mention it was a mistake that has put an unfair strain on all of us, but particularly you. I doubt you will ever be able to forgive me but I do feel sincere and deep regret for my part in the triangle.

Hermione stared at the words, mesmerized. Sincere and deep regret! For her it had been long years of misery and all he felt was sincere and deep regret? Her eyes narrowed angrily. Years of pure hell. That was no exaggeration, she thought bitterly, seeing him and his precious Winifred, day after day, with their beloved child . . . but as for having no one to turn to for guidance, he was quite wrong. Had he forgotten Douglas, who had given her another child and was a tower of strength?

> The reason for this letter is that I know my days may be numbered as the consultant does not rule out another attack and I would like to make what amends I can to both you and Winifred. Poor Elena is another matter entirely for how can I make amends to her without shattering her young life and what little security she has?

Tears pricked at Hermione's eyes. Elena was a nice if somewhat precocious child, but how do you love your husband's illegitimate daughter while her mother watches like a hawk? Hermione longed for the chance to live as a normal family with James and his father, but she wanted her son to have a share of the money Oscar would leave when he died. Why should Winifred's child have it all? She wanted a written guarantee that James would share in the legacy.

'Give me your written promise,' she whispered, 'and I will move out and you can live here with Elena and her wretched mother. Just let me go! Give me a chance of happiness, Oscar, for pity's sake!'

> Before I decide how to amend my will I need to have your word on the subject of James's parentage because you must realize that I now wonder if he is my son or not. If you will swear on the Bible that he is mine, I will leave equal provision for him and Elena. If, however, he is Hatton's child we will divorce and I will leave James nothing but will make a small provision for you in case your relationship with Hatton does not last. You may then decide to put the money in trust for James. That will be for you to decide.

Hermione gasped. Then, filled with suspicion, she reread the last three sentences. What was her husband up to? Was this a trap of some kind? It sounded too good to be true but there must surely be a sting in the tail.

> When I see you again you can tell me what decision you have made and my new solicitor will draw up the papers. I cannot see any other way through this dreadful maze but hope you will find it reasonable and fair. If not you must put forward your own idea and I will consider it.
>   Yours, in good faith,
>   Oscar

After reading the letter several times, Hermione's confusion deepened into apprehension. Her husband surely meant her some harm. This letter, which seemed so generous on the surface, must be deceptive. Somehow he was threatening her security. She was sure of it. He was relying on her confusion to miss the hidden intention that would almost certainly be to her disadvantage.

'But I'm too clever for you, Oscar,' she murmured. 'I've seen through you!'

Sliding from the bed, she donned a dressing gown and made her way slowly downstairs to the telephone. With trembling fingers she dialled Douglas's office. Miss Terry's voice was cold as she delivered the message she had been given.

'I'm afraid Mr Hatton is not in the office today and we don't know when he will return.'

Hermione's heart rate speeded up. This was a setback. She needed to speak to Douglas face to face. Taking a deep breath to steady her resolve, she dialled his home. 'Please, Douglas, be in!'

Douglas's mother answered and was obviously taken aback when she learned who it was. 'Oh, Mrs Fairfax!' she said, panic in her voice. 'I can't speak to you. I, that is, my husband says—'

'I have to speak to your son – about your grandson.'

'He's not here. He's moved out.' She was gathering momentum. 'I hope you understand just what you are doing. You are ruining his life! If my husband knew I was even talking to you he'd . . . He's resting at the moment. My . . . my grandson, did you say? Is that true? How can you know that for sure?'

Hermione hesitated. Desperate to talk to Douglas she was prepared to say almost anything. 'When the doctor confirmed that I was with child, I had not slept with my husband for years. The dates are quite conclusive.'

'So your husband knows?'

'No. That is, not yet. Not definitely. I made a point of a . . . a temporary reconciliation, but by then I was already six weeks pregnant.'

There was another gasp. This time of outrage. 'What a . . . What a wicked, devious woman you are!'

Hermione was terrified the woman would hang up on her. 'Mrs Hatton, James is still your grandson. Nothing will change that. I must speak to Douglas. He must be feeling quite alone and may be desperate.'

'Because of you!'

'Yes. Because we fell in love. Because we have a dear little boy. I'm astonished you don't care about little James.'

There was a long silence and then what sounded like muffled sobs.

'Mrs Hatton, please tell me where I can find Douglas.

He is probably feeling extremely depressed. I don't want him to do anything foolish.'

'Foolish?' Her voice rose querulously.

Hermione waited. Now that she had mentioned it, the idea suddenly frightened her. 'Tell me where I can find him,' she repeated.

'He's in that cottage on Highgate Hill.'

'Does it have a name or number?'

'Number Twenty-three but it also has a sign which says Sunnyside. It's halfway down on the right as you go down.'

'Thank you.' Hermione had a moment's compassion for this woman whose life was also being torn apart. She began to understand her agony of mind and said, 'Don't worry. I'll go to him and see that he's all right. I'll go right now.' She was thinking aloud. 'I'll get dressed and take a taxi.'

'Get dressed?'

'I've been unwell. The baby's birth and then my husband's heart attack.'

Unable to go on, she hung up the receiver. She had intended to go back to bed after speaking to Douglas but that was now out of the question. The spectre of his desperation had now been raised and she could not ignore it. She must reassure herself that Douglas was coping with all his problems. Hermione rang for a taxi and went upstairs to inform Winifred that she was going out and would return in time to release her for the evening's hospital visit.

Unaware that Hermione was on her way, Douglas stood in the back garden and tried to concentrate on the business in hand. He wanted to invite Hermione to come over and see their new home but at present he had to admit that it looked uninviting. This, he had decided, was because of the outlook at the rear of the cottage. From the kitchen window the garden was small, but looked even smaller because of two unsightly sheds that had once presumably housed gardening tools and other odds and ends. Perhaps he could pull them down and replace them with one small well-designed shed. And he could buy some shears and lop off a few of the branches that overlapped what had once been a flower bed along the right-hand side of the garden but was now a tangled mass of dead and twisted stalks. They would need a space to put the pram and later a small area of grass for the boy to crawl over. He tried to visualize his son as a toddler and smiled at the prospect.

He hoped Oscar would stay in hospital for weeks, or even months, so that he could visit Hermione on a regular basis. He wanted James to know him, to recognize him when he visited. He wanted poor Hermione to be happy around the boy and to bond with him in the normal way. How, he wondered, had anyone ever expected her to love Elena? She must have been desperate to agree to the pretence of an adoption. She should have insisted that her husband's mistress played no part in the arrangement.

Walking to the end of the garden he paced it out, calling each stride a yard. So roughly it was fifteen yards long and six yards wide. They would need a swing. Since there was no suitable tree they would have to buy a swing with a supporting framework . . . and maybe James would like a slide. Most would be too big and too expensive but what about a small sandpit?

'See you've got yourself a car!'

He looked up. The tenant of the house to the right of his garden was peering over the fence.

Douglas said, 'What's that?'

'Your car?'

Douglas laughed. 'Thought it was time I got myself a motor.' He moved closer to the fence and offered his hand. 'Douglas Hatton.' Immediately he regretted giving his surname. Would this man recognize the name from the rumours that were flying round the village?

'George Goff. Nice to meet you.'

Not even a glimmer of recognition. Douglas breathed again as they shook hands.

George said, 'Can't beat a Ford so I'm told. Keep meaning to take some lessons, but you know how it is. Always some-thing else to spend the money on.'

'I learned to drive in my father's car. That was useful.' Changing the subject, he went on, 'Your garden's very neat.'

'That's the way my wife likes it. Proper taskmaster, she is.'

'This one needs some attention.'

'Needs a lot of attention! Poor old Meg just abandoned it years ago. Rheumatism. Crippled with it, she was. Dead now, poor old soul.'

'I think I'll get rid of the old sheds. Buy a new one. Fresh start.'

'Can't see the landlord objecting to that.'

At that moment a woman Douglas assumed was his neighbour's wife, came to the back door, wiping her hands on her apron, and called to Douglas. 'You've got someone at the front door. Came in a taxi!'

Douglas's mind did a whirlwind muster of possible visitors – his mother, father, John Granger – or Hermione. Suddenly panicking in case it was the latter and she went away again, he mumbled an excuse and rushed back through the kitchen, into the hall and snatched open the door.

'Hermione! Come in! Oh, my dearest girl!' Pushing the door to behind him, and dizzy with excitement, he pulled her into his arms and for a long, long minute they clung together in their desperation. Douglas was breathless with relief, and Hermione was crying.

When he tried to hold her at arm's length she said, 'Don't look at me, I'm a total mess. I've only just got up from my bed. I had to see you. I've had this letter from Oscar and I don't know what to do. You have to help me, Douglas.' Her voice rose. 'He's up to something. Something bad!'

'How did you find out where I – where we live?' He was leading her gently towards the sitting room which now boasted two second-hand easy chairs upholstered in faded stripes of brown and gold. They had only been delivered an hour before.

'Sit here,' he told her, helping her into the chair. 'I'll just be a minute fetching some bits for the fire.'

When he returned with paper, kindling wood and a small coal scuttle, Hermione was huddled in the chair, clutching her coat around her and looking somewhat disenchanted. He fussed with the fire, coaxing a few flames, then pulled the second chair a little closer to her, so that he could reach forward and hold her hand.

She said, 'I can't stay long. The taxi is waiting.'

'Taxi? Oh, there's no need. I've bought myself a car. Bit of an old banger, but it will get me around. I'll run you home.' He hurried out, paid the taxi driver and came back inside. It gave him a wonderful feeling to be looking after Hermione's needs.

'I came to see you,' he told her, 'but Elena said you were unwell and you were not to be disturbed. I was so disappointed. I knew Oscar was in the hospital, but Elena was adamant and, of course, the nanny was at the hospital. I couldn't just barge in.'

'Never mind. I'm here now and from now on you can call in whenever you like – until they discharge Oscar from the hospital. The secret's well and truly out – apart from Elena, naturally.' She shivered. 'Could you make me a hot drink, darling? I really shouldn't be out of bed but I was desperate to see you.'

'Tea or hot milk?' he asked, proud to be able to offer a choice.

'Hot milk with sugar and a splash of brandy would be nice.'

'Ah! Sorry, but there's no brandy – but I'll get some in before you come again. And you will receive a proper invitation and there'll be a roaring fire and lots of nice things to eat!' He beamed at her. 'It's so wonderful to be here with you. I've been longing for you to see it.

'Douglas, you must look at this letter from Oscar. I don't know . . .'

'I will, but first let me warm you up.' His eyes lit up. 'We could go up to bed. You'd be warm then. It was going to be a surprise when it was fully furnished but it doesn't matter.' He jumped to his feet and held out his hands.

Hermione was shaking her head. 'I haven't got the strength, Douglas. You don't seem to realize that with the shock of the heart attack on top of James's birth and all this worry I feel totally exhausted.'

'Of course! What an idiot I am. But –' his smile returned

– 'my mother brought round some sheets and things but I've bought some sheets and pillowcases and two blankets and a beautiful silk eiderdown! They're so pretty. And I've ordered a rug for each side of the bed. They'll be delivered in a day or two. There are no curtains yet, but . . .' He faltered at the expression on her face. 'What have I said, Hermione?' Bewildered, he stared at her, amazed that she showed so little interest in the home he was preparing for them.

'Please, Douglas,' she begged. 'Could you bring me the hot milk? My teeth will soon be chattering.'

'Oh! Sorry!' He rushed back into the small scullery and fussed with a mug, milk and sugar. And he had biscuits. He smiled again as he put four rich tea biscuits on to a plate and added them to the tray. He was trying not to show that he felt crushed by her attitude.

Returning with the tray, he set it down on the floor beside her and handed her the hot milk. 'And biscuits!' he told her. 'You must be hungry. Is the nanny looking after you properly? Is she looking after James?'

'I suppose so. She's doing her best, but she has a lot on her plate. She has to look after both the children as well as me. I'm not quite up and about yet and the doctor tells me I must rest.'

With her hands clasped round the comforting mug, Hermione seemed to relax a little and Douglas added some coal to the fire.

Sitting on the floor beside her, Douglas found it hard to believe that this was happening. The two of them in their own home. Everything would work out, he assured himself. It might take a few weeks but the outcome was assured. This moment together was just the beginning.

Hermione asked, 'What has John Granger said about us?'

His doubts rushed back. 'Forget about John!' he cried with false heartiness. 'I don't even want to think about him. I want to talk about the three of us and when you can move in. It's really quite convenient – shops at the top of the hill, the milkman calls and there's a local man with a horse and cart who sells eggs and cheese and bread and a few tins of this and that. Oh, and the neighbours are very friendly.

Mr and Mrs Goff.' He rattled on in a vain attempt to delay the moment when he would have to read Hermione's letter from Oscar.

Interrupting him again she asked about his parents, telling him about her conversation with his mother.

'Oh, they'll come round,' he replied airily. 'My mother's always teased me about producing a grandson. She won't be able to resist James when she sees him.'

He watched Hermione sipping the milk and felt a warm feeling of satisfaction at the sight. He insisted that she ate three biscuits 'to keep up her strength' and then told her his plans for the garden. He tried to imagine James upstairs in his cot while Hermione, in a frilly apron, pottered about in the kitchen, frying egg and bacon for Sunday breakfast while he pulled up a few weeds from the flower bed and chatted over the fence to George. It all seemed very feasible, but the image was immediately shattered when Hermione handed him the letter and brought him back to reality with a bang.

The next day was Christmas Eve and should have been a time of bustle and excitement, but instead Downsview was unusually quiet and Cook found that very depressing. Winifred had taken Elena and James for a walk, Oscar was in hospital and Hermione was upstairs doing goodness knows what. In the kitchen, Millie was ironing the tablecloth ready for the big day – a white damask which had been in the family for years. Cook was decorating a steaming ham, spreading it with a sticky orange sauce and preparing to stud it with cloves. She was full of resentment because she had had no cosy conferences with Mrs Fairfax about the Christmas menus and had been told to 'do what you usually do' which she found insulting. Proud of her cooking skills, she looked forward to special occasions like Christmas, Easter and birthdays, when she could produce a meal that was marvelled over and was followed by little speeches of appreciation. This year she suspected that her efforts would be largely disregarded in the climate of uncertainty which prevailed.

Approaches to Winifred had been equally unsatisfactory.

'I'm truly sorry, Cook,' the nanny had said a few days earlier, 'but I'm so busy. I don't think I should interfere. You'll have to insist on speaking with Mrs Fairfax.'

'Fat chance of that! She's not interested in Christmas. Other things on her mind!' She'd rolled her eyes suggestively.

Winifred shrugged. When pressed she had relented far enough to suggest a big baked ham.

The kitchen door opened at ten thirty-five on Christmas Eve to admit Hermione. Cook and Millie stared. She had actually given up the familiar nightwear for a smart day dress in blue crêpe with matching shoes. She had rouged her cheeks a little to hide her pallor and her lipstick was a defiant crimson. Her hair, too, had been carefully brushed into a sleek cap. For a moment no one spoke and Millie tried to look as inconspicuous as possible in case anyone found fault with her.

'Oh, Cook!' Hermione said brightly. 'Did I mention that we shall have a visitor at lunchtime? Mr Hatton will be calling in to discuss some family matters so I suggested he stay for a bite to eat, so lay an extra place, please. I take it we can feed one extra?' She gave Cook a challenging look which dared her to query the arrangement.

Millie, however, said, 'Working on Christmas Eve! Crikey!'

Too late she heard Cook gasp.

Hermione swung round. 'What have I told you, Millie? I was speaking to Cook, not you, so please keep your impertinent comments to yourself!' Her eyes flashed and Millie cowered back, throwing a beseeching glance in Cook's direction as she mumbled an apology.

Cook stammered, 'I'm sure she didn't mean any harm, Mrs Fairfax. We're all at sixes and sevens, I'm afraid. Hardly know what we're doing, to tell you the truth. I haven't had a chance—'

'Don't make excuses for her, Cook. I know her as well as you do. She was questioning Mr Hatton's presence and also my judgement!' Hermione was breathing quickly, her face white as she glared at Millie. 'One more outburst like that and you can leave this house and never come back. Do you understand me? I've had just about enough of this insubordination, Millie!'

She turned to Cook. 'And I'm sick of your sulks. Don't think I haven't noticed.'

Cook could take no more. 'All I wanted was to talk to you about the preparations and such like in any normal household—'

'You're a cook, aren't you? All you had to do was your job!' She laid a hand on her heart, breathless and distressed. Gasping she snapped, 'So you can also take warning. If I don't get some cheerful support from you, you can also think seriously about finding another position!' Her voice had edged up a notch and suddenly her face was suffused with angry colour. 'I'm the mistress of this house and I can do what I like without having to ask your permission. If I want to invite Douglas to – I mean, Mr Hatton – to lunch on Christmas Eve it is no concern of yours and I'll thank you to keep your mouths shut and get on with your work! Is that clear?'

She clutched at the back of a chair and swayed.

Cook and Millie watched her for a long moment. Cook finally said, 'Are you all right?'

'Of course, I'm not all right, you stupid woman!' She gulped in air. 'I'm . . . I'm totally surrounded by . . .' Her voice cracked ominously and Millie and Cook watched her uneasily. 'I can't rely on a soul in this house! Not a soul! Oh God!'

As she staggered, Cook rushed forward to help her, but Hermione pushed her away with surprising violence and stumbled to the door with tears in her eyes.

'Now look what you've done!' she said pitifully. 'I shall have to go. What's the time? Oh! He'll be here in an hour!' She looked round wildly and then her gaze settled on Cook. 'I'm going back to my room. Send me up a small glass of brandy.'

Hoping to repair her reputation, Millie exclaimed, 'I'll bring it!'

'You certainly won't!' Hermione glared at her. 'You won't come near me if you have any sense.'

They heard her making her way unsteadily along the passage and regarded each other soberly. Cook sat down heavily and dabbed at her forehead with a nearby tea towel. She, too, was breathing noisily, saying nothing, while Millie leaned against the sink for support, both hands flat against her chest.

Millie said, 'She's gone mad!' and looked desperately at Cook for reassurance.

There was no such answer forthcoming. Cook continued to breathe heavily, her mind racing. Inviting Hatton to lunch on Christmas Eve seemed much more of a betrayal than on a normal working day and she wondered whether Oscar would be told. Miss Franks might spill the beans, though Mrs Fairfax might forbid her to tell him. Would she, Cook, come in for any of the blame? She gave an anxious sniff. She had taken it upon herself to order plenty of food – that was no problem – but could she object on principle?

'What can we do?' she asked aloud. 'If we refuse we'll get the sack from her . . . and if Mr Fairfax finds out . . .' She stabbed a fierce finger in Millie's direction and said, 'Don't you dare cry! Not one tear! You've been very silly and you bring trouble down on your own head.'

For once Millie was lost for words.

Cook said, 'We'd best go ahead and hope Mr Fairfax never finds out.' She frowned. 'I wonder if Miss Franks will be at the table – and Elena. They usually are on Christmas Eve, but they might be told to eat in the nursery so the other two can be cosy together.'

They looked at each other in dismay. It was an anxious moment.

Cook said, 'Just our luck. Christmas is supposed to be a time of goodwill but not in this house! Here it's tears and tantrums, and all sorts of goings-on! All our hard work counts for nothing. Thank the Lord we've got the ham ready.'

Millie narrowed her eyes thoughtfully and then opened them wide. 'Wouldn't it be a shame,' she said with exaggerated innocence, 'if the lunch was . . . awful.'

Cook stared at her without understanding. 'Awful? How?'

'I mean . . .' She pursed her lips. 'Suppose things went a bit wrong with the food. If it got a bit burnt or was too peppery.'

'Would he even notice? He'd be too busy staring into her eyes!'

'No, but she would notice and she would know!'

Light dawned at last and a slow smile spread across Cook's face. 'And we'd be really, really offended if she accused us of any such thing!' Cook's imagination took flight. There were several things they could do to ruin the meal, but it must not be too obvious. They must be able to deny any intention to spoil the romantic occasion.

Millie said, 'What d'you think? Dare we? She's probably going to sack us anyway!'

Slowly Cook nodded. The angry altercation with her employer had been the last straw and a small revenge would be sweet. 'But we have to be bombproof and we mustn't go too far. She has to suspect but have no proof. We have to play innocent, whatever she says. Let's put our thinking caps on, Millie!'

When Marion Hatton returned home from her walk, her husband was in his usual chair, reading *The Times*.

He glanced up. 'They're talking about banning the use of gas in wartime.'

'About time, too! It's a barbaric thing, gas. Pity they can't ban war altogether!' She took off her coat and went into the hall to hang it up. When she came back she sat down opposite him.

'Aren't you going to make a pot of tea?' he asked, surprised. Normally they had a comfortable routine breakfast, then he would potter in the garden if the weather was fine while his wife tidied the house and then walked to the shops. By the time she came back from her walk, he'd be reading the paper and waiting for what he jokingly referred to as 'the workers' tea break'. Eleven o'clock was time for tea and one of Marion's home-made cakes.

'Not just yet,' she replied, and something in her voice alerted him. He was about to hear something unpleasant.

'What is it?' Not Douglas, he hoped, immediately afraid. He would never admit it, but he had liked it better when his son lived at home and they knew where he was. 'Not an accident?' He crumpled the newspaper in his lap so that he could give his wife his undivided attention.

Marion was sitting up very straight and now that he actually looked at her he could see that she looked different in some indefinable way. Ivor didn't like the way Douglas's behaviour had divided him and his wife, and he didn't like the fact that he had no one to talk to about the Government and foreign affairs. Marion was a good wife and always had been, but the Douglas business had unsettled them and created a certain coolness between them. He no longer entirely trusted her which was terribly worrying to him.

'I didn't go shopping, Ivor,' she told him. 'I went for a walk and I saw the little Fairfax girl out with her nanny and the baby. Our grandson. Douglas's baby.'

His insides somersaulted and he found himself unable to answer her astonishing assertion. Instead he stared helplessly at his wife.

She went on calmly. 'I spoke to them, but they didn't know me, of course. The girl's called Elena . . .'

He recovered slightly from his shock. 'Hang on a minute, dear! How did you recognize them?'

'I waited near their house on the off chance, Ivor. I was determined to see the baby if I could . . . and I did. They were very pleasant, the nanny and the girl. Elena adores the boy, that's plain to see, and the nanny was very polite.'

Now that he could see where the conversation was leading, Ivor was aware of an unexpected leap of the heart. But he struggled to remain calm.

Marion smiled. 'James is a wonderful little chap, Ivor. And he's the image of Douglas! The absolute image! That photograph we had taken when Douglas was tiny. Same broad forehead, the same shaped head. Douglas to a T!' Her smile broadened. 'I thought you'd like to know.'

'I thought we already knew. That's the trouble. When Douglas told us—'

'But that was before we were certain. Now I've seen him I know that he's our grandson. James is Douglas's son. No room in my mind for the smallest doubt. And the thing is,

Ivor, I've decided to end this ridiculous situation. Regardless of the rights and wrongs . . .'

Ivor didn't like the way his wife was behaving. She seemed too much in control and it unnerved him. 'I don't want to hear any more!' he said half-heartedly, and held up his hand. But the truth was that he did want to hear more. He wanted to know about his grandson and he wanted everything to be happy again and it never would. Never could. He felt a deep longing to take control and make good things happen for everyone concerned and he hated the feeling of power-lessness. The truth was that he couldn't help the ones he loved and that meant he was weak; not at all the person he wanted to be. He crumpled *The Times* into a ball and tossed it to the floor.

Relentlessly, Marion went on. 'We have to do something and the first step is to insist that Douglas spends Christmas with us. Christmas and Boxing Day – if he'll come, that is. Then we can talk.'

'Never!' It sounded very unconvincing, but Ivor was trying to hold on to a few shreds of his self-respect. 'We can't meddle, Marion. We'll make things worse.'

'I thought you'd say that, dear, so if you won't agree then I'll cook the meal and take two helpings down to the cottage. I'll have Christmas at Sunnyside with our son. You'll be fine on your own.'

'It's . . . That's . . . That's the most preposterous thing I've . . . Have you taken leave of your senses, Marion?'

'No, Ivor. I've just come to my senses. No one is going to keep me away from my grandson and that woman's baby is my grandson. Not exactly the situation I would have wished for, but we can't have everything we want in this life. So when Christmas is over I shall write to Mrs Fairfax and ask if I can visit James.'

He looked at her wildly, shaken to the core by her un-expected strength. Or was it defiance? He felt the ground shift beneath him as he tried to come to terms with this new Marion. What on earth should he do now? He could either go along with her scheming or he could resist, chal-lenge her and put an end to this nonsense. The problem was that if he gave in gracefully and supported his wife, he would have lost the initiative. Throughout their married life he had been aware of the fact that she was older than him and infinitely wiser, but he had never actually spoken of it. Marion, bless her, had always allowed him to be the decision maker. The protector. Did he want to relinquish all that?

On the other hand if he fought her on this crucial matter, the gulf between him and Douglas would deepen over the coming months and years and he, Ivor, would, to all intents and purposes, have lost both his son and his grandson. It wasn't that simple, he reflected. Being reconciled to his son meant a climb down and it also meant accepting Hermione Fairfax for whom he had no respect at all.

As if aware of his continuing dilemma, Marion stood up and said briskly, 'Now then – a pot of tea seems a good idea, Ivor, and I made some almond cakes – the ones you like. Shan't be a moment.'

With a bright smile she whisked out of the door and left him alone with his thoughts.

# Eight

At five minutes to two everyone gathered in the dining room and took their seats. Hermione, recovered and positively glowing, sat at the table end where Oscar normally sat. Douglas was on her right-hand side and Elena on her left. Winifred was further down, on the same side as Elena.

'Well,' Hermione said cheerfully, 'Christmas has crept up on us again.'

She looked reassuringly at Douglas, who was looking ill at ease but trying to appear relaxed. 'Christmas Eve and here we all are – safely gathered in, as they say in the Bible.'

Elena smiled at Douglas. 'All except Papa. He isn't safely gathered in, is he?'

'Er . . . No, I suppose not.'

'But he will be tomorrow because he is going to have some Christmas pudding in the hospital. The nurse told you, didn't she, Nanny?'

'That's right, Elena. Your papa will be well looked after.'

'Will he have crackers to pull?'

'Probably.'

Elena turned back to Douglas. 'I've written two lists for Father Christmas and Nanny told him I've been good so tonight we'll burn them in the fire and if the elves don't collect them they'll turn into smoke and float to Father Christmas's house in the middle of the snowy wastes. Then he'll know what to bring us.'

'That sounds exciting, Elena!'

'Oh, yes, it is – and James wants a rattle and a book made of rag. He's my new brother and I'm teaching him to read.'

Hermione said, 'That's enough, Elena. You talk too much.'

'But he wants to know all about James, don't you, Mr Hatton?'

'Er . . . I do, yes. Of course.' He looked warily at Hermione and then down at his plate.

Quickly Hermione changed the subject. 'When the wine arrives we'll have a toast to . . .' She turned to Douglas. 'To loved ones!'

Winifred said firmly, 'To absent friends!'

'And Papa!'

Winifred said, 'Your papa is an absent friend. Absent means that—'

'That's enough, Nanny. Don't encourage her!' Hermione exclaimed.

Elena laughed. 'Children should be seen and not heard! That's what Millie says because Millie's—'

'Stop, Elena!' Hermione gave her a fierce look. 'I don't want to hear a word about that dreadful girl. Millie talks too much for my liking. Now, where on earth is the wine? Elena, run to the kitchen and remind Cook. Say we are waiting for the wine.'

As Elena hurried away, brimming with importance, Hermione rolled her eyes. 'Staff!' she said. 'They're more trouble than they're worth sometimes.'

Douglas said, 'I'm sure they've made us a good dinner, Mrs Fairfax.'

'Of course. The cooking is not the problem. It's the attitude. Mind you, since the war satisfactory staff have been hard to find. I blame the war work. Helping out in hospitals, working on the land, even driving trams. Young women now seem to think those jobs were more exciting than being in service. Lord knows why!'

'Perhaps they felt more valued during the war,' Douglas suggested cautiously.

Hermione shrugged. 'Young women have become more demanding and want more interesting work. There was a time when going into service was considered a very good career. Not now, I'm afraid.'

Winifred said, 'Many women don't want servants. They have a few labour saving devices and prefer to do the work themselves.'

Douglas went on earnestly: 'I know of a woman, a widow, who is a wonderful cook. She makes her living from it. She cooks private lunches for business clients who wish to entertain friends in private rather than eating out at a restaurant.'

'Really? How enterprising!' Winifred looked at him with interest, but just then Elena returned, followed by Millie who carried a bottle of red wine.

'Cook says she's sorry but it might be on the cold side,' Millie announced. 'What with all the upheaval this morning and you being so cross and upset, we got off to a late start.'

Winifred knew Hermione would not like that treasonous little speech.

'Give it to me!'

Hermione tried to take it from Millie's grasp, but she seemed reluctant to give it up and for a moment they almost wrestled with it.

Millie raised her voice. 'We've been at sixes and sevens ever since . . .'

Her face flushed, Hermione finally wrenched the bottle from her. 'Go back to the kitchen at once!' she hissed. 'We'll manage!'

The wine bottle, which had already been opened, now allowed a small dribble of red wine to fall on to the clean tablecloth and, before anyone could stop her, Millie sprang forward and rubbed at it with a corner of her apron. Hermione mouthed something in a low voice which sounded like 'Get out of here!' but no one was quite sure.

Disgruntled, Millie retreated as slowly as she could.

Hermione forced a smile. 'I'm afraid I'm no good at pouring.' She looked imploringly at Douglas who rose to his feet somewhat nervously.

'I'd be honoured to help, Mrs Fairfax.'

Elena said, 'I have a little wine but mostly water, Mr Hatton. Papa says I should get used to alcohol very slowly from a young age. If I don't I might get drunk and be sick and fall down in the gutter.'

Hermione wagged a trembling finger at her. 'I won't warn you again, Elena.'

'But Papa saw a man . . .'

Winifred put a finger to Elena's lips and reluctantly the girl fell silent.

Carefully Douglas made his way round the table with the wine, terrified of spilling any more. He finally sat down slightly pink cheeked but satisfied that he had succeeded. Hermione patted his hand by way of thanks, then reached for her glass, caught the nanny's eye and said, 'Oh! Of course! I nearly forgot. Absent friends!'

They raised their glasses in the toast. The wine was stone cold but no one mentioned the fact. They chatted for a while – and then a while longer and eventually Hermione became tired of waiting and sent Elena out to the kitchen, for a second time, to tell them to hurry up with the first course.

Cook eventually arrived with a tureen of vegetable soup which she ladled carefully into their bowls while maintaining a respectful silence. Millie handed round a basket of home-made bread rolls. As soon as they were on their own they discovered that there was no butter for the rolls and this time it was Hermione who, with an exasperated sigh, left the room. She reappeared with a dish of butter and the meal started and the now tepid soup was consumed in a self-conscious silence.

Nobody commented on the fact that it was slightly salty and none of it was left in the bowls so Hermione's smile returned. As the meal wore on, however, she almost regretted that she had invited Douglas to lunch. It seemed that fate was being very unkind. The platter of warm ham slices had been carelessly arranged and was without the usual parsley garnish. The boiled potatoes were ever-so-slightly mushy, the buttered parsnips were underdone and there was grit in the creamed leeks.

Suddenly Hermione noticed Winifred's puzzled glance and an unpleasant suspicion entered her mind. The truth began to dawn on her . . . But no, Hermione argued inwardly, not Cook and Millie. They wouldn't dare! Would they? Recalling the row they had had earlier it seemed possible, but . . . Was she being paranoid? They wouldn't be so unkind, would they? Did they hate her? Deeply hurt by the idea she struggled to convince herself that she deserved their loyalty. Hadn't she been good to them over the years? Hadn't she given Millie a second chance and then a third chance when she deserved the sack?

She looked at Douglas to see if he thought anything untoward was happening, but he was talking animatedly to Elena, asking her riddles, and she was giggling at something he had said.

Hermione might have managed to convince herself that she was imagining things, but Cook chose that very moment to reappear and place a rather unappetizing trifle in the middle of the table.

The awful truth came to her like a physical blow. They had deliberately sabotaged her luncheon with Douglas! Her throat tightened. Hermione was so upset that she could no longer breathe. Fury and a kind of grief filled her and added to that was the bitter realization that she was helpless. There was no way on earth she could prove her suspicions and if she tried she would sound hysterical and would almost certainly make a fool of herself.

Leaning forward, she held her napkin to her face as she gulped for air and fought hard to regain control of her emotions. Her heart began to race uncomfortably and she thought immediately of Oscar and his heart attack and then fear became part of the equation. She must not faint, she told herself despairingly. Last time that had happened she had come round to find herself in a dishevelled heap on the floor and had been deeply mortified. No. Please! Not now, she begged. Not with Douglas beside her. Whatever would he think? Slowly her eyes closed. Somewhere in the distant recesses of the room, she could still hear voices but the words were meaningless. A weakness seized her, a great heat rose up suddenly through her body and she felt a heavy perspiration break out on her skin.

Terrified that she might be dying, she cried, 'Miss Franks! Help me!' but her voice was nothing but a croak. Her eyes rolled up as the room faded into darkness and, with agonizing slowness, she felt herself topple from the chair.

'It was ghastly, Oscar!' Winifred told him that evening. 'She just slipped from the chair. I felt so guilty that I had been finding the situation rather amusing. Poor Hermione was obviously taking it very seriously and wanting the lunch to be a success and it all went horribly wrong. Really, Cook and Millie were so unkind.'

'Did you tackle them about it? Did you ask them? Are you sure it was deliberate?'

'Yes, they admitted it. They, too, were shocked by what happened and they are full of remorse. It seems that Hermione had hauled them over the coals earlier and had been really unpleasant and they felt very hard done by because Cook felt that your wife's obsession with Hatton had caused her to neglect them. It seems she had scarcely bothered about Christmas and had left Cook to get on with it. I have to admit that they do have a point.'

'You're making excuses for them.'

'It was partly out of loyalty to you. Misguided, maybe . . .'

He stared ahead, trying to visualize the scene, shaking his head. 'Wait until I get back!' he said angrily. 'They'll regret it, I can promise you that.'

So far Winifred had only told him of the disastrous meal, but now, somehow, she had to break it to him that Hermione's faint had proved to be more of a collapse. 'Hatton wanted to stay and help, but I sent him off immediately so that if necessary we could call in the doctor. I thought his presence might start some gossip so I insisted.'

'The doctor? But surely it was just nerves. You know how she is.'

The occupant of the next bed suddenly leaned across and tapped her arm. 'He's looking a lot better, isn't he, miss? Mr Fairfax, I mean. Bit more colour in his face.'

'Er, yes, I suppose so.' She turned back to Oscar.

He lowered his voice. 'The nerve of the woman! Inviting him to lunch while I'm stuck here! God! How could she?'

'She said it was a meeting about a financial matter but . . .'

He was shaking his head, his interest in her well-being already fading, she noticed. Did he really care so little about Hermione?

'Did you check up on my businesses?' he demanded. 'I should be supervising them – especially now. If the managers mess things up over the Christmas period . . . Well, I don't need to remind you how important the Christmas sales are.'

'I popped into the Hawkhurst one, as you asked, and Mr Ellis seemed to be coping very well with the rush. No problems, he said. But I had to telephone Rye because—'

Oscar tutted, annoyed. 'I asked you to visit! Let them see they can't get away with anything just because I'm stuck here.'

She bridled at his tone. 'I do have a lot to do, looking after both the children—'

'Sorry! Yes, I know you're doing your best. So there are no problems – no late deliveries, no dissatisfied customers. Nothing like that?'

'Not as far as I could see, no.'

Mr Ebdon was at her elbow again. 'I've got to have an operation.' He shook his head anxiously. 'They say it's standard, whatever that means.'

Irritated by the second interruption, Winifred turned to him sharply. 'We're having a private conversation, Mr Ebdon. There may be time later for you to tell me about your problem.'

'Oh, right,' he said, only slightly taken aback. 'If not he'll tell you. He knows what's in store for me. A standard operation. That's what! God help me!' He retreated, and, to Winifred's relief, began a similar conversation with the man on the opposite side of his bed.

Winifred took a deep breath. 'The thing is, Oscar . . .' She paused. His Christian name had slipped out. Perhaps he hadn't noticed. 'The thing is that Hermione is in a very poor state of mind. We did have to call the doctor. When she came round – and she was unconscious for some time – she was extremely confused.'

Oscar frowned. 'What do you mean "some time"? How long?'

'Nobody timed it but we were becoming rather alarmed. She just wasn't responding. Maybe two or three minutes. People usually come round quite quickly from a faint. As soon as Hatton had driven away – he has bought himself a motor car – I telephoned the doctor who came as soon as he could.' She stopped to allow those facts to sink in before going on to what might well be a more serious problem.

Oscar put a hand to his head. 'As if I haven't got enough to worry about! Why does she do this to me?'

Startled, Winifred snapped, 'I don't think she was doing it just to upset you! I think she has had — at least the doctor thinks she has — a sort of minor breakdown.' Disappointed by his reaction, she could not look at him but stared down at her clasped hands. She had hoped for a little support from Oscar — or at least some appreciation of her attempt to hold the family together. 'I can't stay long but I thought you would want to know. I had to ask Cook to stay on so she will need to be paid for a few extra hours.'

'Why couldn't Hermione look after the children? She usually does when you come here.'

'Because she is so unwell! I don't think you understand. She was extremely confused and has been sedated.'

At once his expression changed. His eyes darkened and when he spoke, Winifred sensed the apprehension in his voice.

'You don't mean . . . I hope this isn't a recurrence of . . .' He faltered to a stop.

Winifred hedged. 'The doctor wouldn't say too much. He wanted to speak to you but obviously that is out of the question at the moment. I do think he fears a recurrence. Hermione's memory was very disturbed. It took her a few moments to grasp who I was and when she heard James crying she thought it was . . .'

'Edward!' He groaned.

'I'm afraid so. But that may be a temporary thing. In a day or two she may recover her memory. The past few weeks and months must have put a strain on her mind.'

'Her own fault entirely! No one asked her to have an affair with that wretched man.' He looked at her, waiting for her to agree.

Instead she said, 'Please don't get excited. You know you have to remain calm.'

'Then why bring me this dreadful news?'

Winifred closed her eyes so that he wouldn't read the hurt she felt. She told herself that it was natural in the circumstances for him to be a little unreasonable, and she must make allowances.

'I'm just the messenger,' she reminded him. 'I'm the innocent party in this mess.'

'None of us are innocent parties!' he snapped.

She noticed that he was becoming agitated. His breathing was more rapid and he was fumbling with the bedclothes.

'I'm sorry. I'd better go,' she said.

'No, wait!' He held out his hand to restrain her. 'Forgive me. I'm an ungrateful brute. The thing is . . . I think I must come home. At least then I shall know what's going on in my own home. If I'm going to be confined to bed for a time, I'd rather be at home, away from the Mr Ebdons of this world. At least then Hermione won't dare to bring Hatton in to the house. God! She's changed. At least she used to have a modicum of common sense and decency.'

She's in no state at the moment to bring anyone to the house, Winifred thought desperately. Dare she tell him her suspicions about the woman they had met on their walk? Winifred felt strongly that the woman's interest in the baby was not as impartial as she pretended. She had made such a fuss of James and something about her enthusiasm seemed excessive in the circumstances.

She was also unsure whether Oscar's return home would be a good thing. Instead of stabilizing the situation, it might make things worse. She would end up looking after two invalids as well as both children.

She saw the staff nurse approaching and said quickly, 'I'd better go before I get my knuckles rapped!' She held his hand for a moment, then hurried out before he could utter a protest.

Previously she had believed that matters could not get any worse. Now she was not so sure.

Christmas morning arrived at last and despite the lateness of the sunrise, Elena woke up just after six and was filled with the most wonderful excitement. Christmas Day.

Had Father Christmas been and, if so, had he left the required toys? She crept out of bed, glanced at Nanny who was still asleep and at James who was awake, waving chubby arms but making no fuss.

'I'll go and have a look,' she told him in a whisper, and, still dressed only in her nightdress, ran quickly down the stairs holding carefully on to the banisters which were decorated with ivy and red ribbons. In the sitting room the tree now sparkled with glittering decorations and white candles.

Elena glanced first at the ashes of yesterday's fire and at the dusty hearth, and was relieved to see that Father Christmas had been – the mince pie they had left for him had been eaten, the glass of milk drained and the neat bundle of long grass eaten by the reindeers. Sighing with relief, she looked underneath the Christmas tree and gave a small gasp of delight. A pile of brightly wrapped presents waited to be discovered and Elena clasped her hands, turned her gaze upwards and said, 'Thank you! Thank you!' and blew Father Christmas a kiss. However, kneeling beside the tree, and carefully feeling the shape of each gift, she began to wonder if he had forgotten anything. There was nothing that looked or sounded like a rabbit in a hutch. No squeaking or snuffling. And no sign of a puppy to keep Toby company. There was a largish box wrapped in red tissue paper which might be a doll, but Elena was careful not to shake it because she had asked for a doll with eyes that opened and shut and she was afraid the eyes might come loose.

She found a small present that felt the right shape for a piggy bank and another that was definitely a rattle. Her eyes gleamed. Nanny had warned her that if Father Christmas did not have a certain toy, he would make a note and bring it the next year. So maybe there had been a shortage of rabbits and puppies. Probably lots of children wanted one. Never mind, she would explain it all to James.

'And this must be the rag book!' she decided, and to make sure, she tore a very small hole in the paper to take a look. Satisfied that she had guessed correctly, she carefully rearranged the coloured ribbon and ran back upstairs.

The presents would be opened after breakfast but in the

meantime there was the stocking which hung from the end of her bed. Clambering back into bed she settled down to examine it and a wealth of tiny surprises greeted her eyes. Chocolate pennies, a clementine, a small tortoiseshell comb, some mixed nuts, a pencil with a tassel on the end, a handkerchief with her initial in the corner and a new ribbon for her hair. She spread the treasures over the eiderdown and reached for the first chocolate penny with a feeling of deep joy.

The long-awaited Christmas Day had finally arrived.

Hermione was awake but her eyes were closed. She was frightened to open them and see exactly where she was. Her sedated night had been filled with weird dreams that felt threatening although now she could not pin down why. No harm had come to her but they were eerie and unsettling, and each time she woke she had found herself sweating but chilled. She longed for morning but now it had come she didn't want to discover reality.

She had forgotten it was Christmas but vague memories troubled her concerning Douglas Hatton. What exactly had happened, she wondered, as slivers of memory slipped through her mind and out again before she could grasp them? Something about the maid, Rosie . . . No, Rosie was no longer with them. Now it was Millie. Or was it the nanny? She remembered Nanny lifting her up so she must have fallen over. Maybe that was it. Perhaps she had tripped over and banged her head.

Opening her eyes, Hermione reached out, picked up the small bell from the bedside table, and rang it. Oscar would come and he would comfort her – unless he had gone to work.

Elena appeared in the doorway. 'Happy Christmas, Mama!' She rushed into the room, her small face alight with excitement. 'Father Christmas came and the reindeers ate all the grass and I don't think he had enough rabbits, but there's a rattle for James and I've eaten all the pennies except two – this one's for you and the other is for Nanny.'

Hermione put a hand to her head. This girl was . . . Yes!

Of course. This was Elena. The bang on the head must have made her a bit hazy. 'Is it Christmas?' she asked.

'Yes, Mama, and this chocolate penny is for you!' She placed it firmly in Hermione's limp hand.

'Thank you, Elena.' Hermione frowned. 'Please ask your papa to come here. I need to talk to him.'

'He's still in the hospital, Mama.'

'In the hospital? What happened to him?' She struggled to sit up. Her mouth was dry and her voice sounded different. But she was who she thought she was. She was Hermione Fairfax.

'Nanny will be along in a minute and Cook said to ask if you want a cup of tea brought up.'

A vague image of Cook produced an odd sense of anger which Hermione failed to understand, but she nodded. 'A cup of tea. Yes. That's a good idea.'

Elena paused at the door. 'I think he brought the train set.'

'Who did?'

'Father Christmas. For James.'

'His name's Edward, not James. Third time lucky! That's what Oscar said!' She smiled at the memory, struggling meanwhile to sit up straighter, and looking forward to the promised tea. That would help clear her head, she told herself. She wanted to be properly awake when Oscar came to her.

'Not Uncle Edward.' Elena looked puzzled. 'He's mouldering bones. Millie told me.'

In spite of her efforts to stay alert, Hermione was overtaken by weariness and closed her eyes. Uncle Edward? What on earth was the girl talking about? she wondered irritably.

'Mama? Have you gone back to sleep?'

'My tea! I want my cup of tea!'

Hermione didn't open her eyes, but she heard Elena leave the room, intent on her errand. She wriggled back under the bedclothes, exhausted by the brief encounter and the strain of making sense of the world around her. She breathed deeply, allowing her mind to drift and at once sleep seized her and the dark dreams claimed her once more. By the time Cook arrived with the tea tray, Hermione was fast asleep.

★　　★　　★

Although it was Christmas Day, the doctor called in briefly to examine his patient; five minutes after he left, Cook sat down in the kitchen and burst into tears. For a moment Millie watched her aghast, but then she moved closer and put an arm round the shaking shoulders.

'Don't cry, Cook,' she begged, 'or you'll have me at it. Things aren't so bad.'

Cook paused long enough to give her a withering look which made her withdraw her arm. 'Aren't so bad? They're bad enough. The mistress in bed half out of her mind and on a light diet! Mr Fairfax in the hospital. What are we going to do with all this food? You work your guts out and for what? Nobody here to eat and nobody blooming well cares! Nobody. A turkey in the oven, potatoes waiting to go in, sprouts and parsnips and bacon rolls! Everything.'

She tossed her apron over her face and sobbed into it while Millie watched helplessly.

'And yesterday!' Cook went on. 'What a mess that was with her fainting away and Miss Franks fetching the doctor and him frightening everyone and—'

'He didn't frighten me!'

Cook lowered her apron and fumbled for a handkerchief. 'Well, he should have done. A breakdown. Don't you know what a breakdown is?' She tapped her head meaningfully. 'Seems she had one years ago when her first child died. My sister remembers hearing about it. Took her away in the end and she was gone for weeks. Never been quite the same since.' She sighed. 'Course, it was before our time. I came here when Elena was three months old and you arrived six years after that.'

Millie put the kettle on and found teacups. 'D'you think the baby is his? That's what they're saying. My pa heard it in the pub.'

'I wouldn't be surprised.' Cook dabbed her eyes and sniffed hard. 'Christmas isn't supposed to be like this!' She watched Millie's preparation with the teacups and said, 'Put an extra sugar in mine. I think I'm going to need it.'

They turned as footsteps sounded in the hall and Winifred came in. 'Something smells good!' She smiled but looked tired and anxious. 'Mrs Fairfax is still asleep, but I shall wake her around one and then she is to have a thin slice of turkey, a little potato mashed with gravy and three or four sprouts. The doctor says she's has to eat little and often to keep her strength up.' She hesitated. 'Please don't get upset, Cook. I know it's difficult, but we have to live with it. A day at a time. That's the only way.'

Cook pulled herself together with an effort. 'So who's going to eat in the dining room? Anybody?'

'Well, there's only going to be me and Elena but I suggest we have a change of plan. Just for this one occasion because this particular Christmas is a bit . . . troubled. Let's all eat together in the dining room. What do you think? It would be more cheerful, wouldn't it, to all be together? You and Millie and me and Elena.'

Millie said, 'Eat in the dining room? Crikey!' and looked at Cook.

Cook hid her surprise. 'Would it be all right with Mr and Mrs Fairfax?'

'We can't ask them because one of them is asleep and the other is in hospital, but I shall tell them and I'm sure they won't mind. It's the sensible thing to do.'

Millie said, 'Elena will be sure to tell them. She won't mean to, but she will!'

Winifred laughed. 'Well, that's true, but she's only young so we have to make allowances. Anyway, it won't matter because it won't be a secret and I'll take all the blame.'

Cook nodded. 'Let's do it, then, but –' anxiety made her bold – 'suppose he calls round – Mr Hatton, I mean. He might be worried about Mrs Fairfax and I don't think I could stand another scene.'

'Oh! D'you think he would?' Millie looked startled.

Winifred pursed her lips. 'Good point, Cook. Perhaps I'll telephone him. He's probably having Christmas with his parents. I'll tell him about the doctor's visit and warn him not to come round.'

She left them looking a lot happier. She hoped she had salvaged all that she could from the special day, for Elena's sake as well as the staff. And Cook had been very helpful.

Whatever the rights and wrongs of the affair between Hermione Fairfax and Douglas Hatton, she found it hard to condemn them. In a way she felt that Mrs Fairfax deserved the excitement of her not-so-secret love affair for the way she had borne the situation for the past years. Remembering how she herself had felt about Oscar she almost envied Mrs Fairfax – until now, that is, when disaster had overtaken them. Being in love and being loved in return was a rare but fragile gift but it was fraught with dangers and poor Mrs Fairfax was cracking under the strain.

Ivor took a mouthful of crispy roast potato and chewed appreciatively.

Winking at his son he said, 'Your mother makes the best roast potatoes in all of England!' He chuckled and glanced at her.

'Honestly, Ivor, you say that every Christmas!' Marion smiled, but she was hiding her triumph, holding it close to her heart. Here they were, all together at the dinner table on Christmas Day and she had made it happen. Against all the odds, she had succeeded. And she had seen her grandson and intended to see him again.

She took a surreptitious glance at her son and a little of her joy faded. He had confided in her about the previous day's lunch at Downsview and the way it had ended and she knew he was desperate to know how Hermione was. There! She had used the woman's name again. Hermione. She would have to get used to it. Now that she had seen little James, she wanted her son to be with Hermione so they could be a real family, but how was that going to happen?

Ivor raised his glass and said, 'To absent friends.'

'To loved ones,' Marion amended.

Last to raise his glass, Douglas said, 'To Hermione and James!'

They drank and resumed the meal.

Ivor and Marion had bought their son a framed painting by a local artist – a view of the Strand at Rye with boats on the river and unloaded timber stacked alongside.

'I think I shall hang it in the front room,' said Douglas, helping himself to another potato.

Marion said, 'See what Hermione thinks.' She didn't look at her husband, but she registered his nervousness. She didn't want to push him too far too fast, but she had made up her mind that Douglas and Hermione would end up together and was resigned to it. All she had to do now was help her husband to surrender gracefully.

When the phone rang Ivor jumped visibly and Marion stood up. 'I'll get it. You two eat before it gets cold.'

She picked up the phone and gave the number.

A voice said, 'This is Winifred Franks.'

'I think you have the wrong number.'

'No, please wait. I think we met a day or two ago when I was out with the children – Elena and James. We met—'

'Oh! The nanny. I didn't know your name. I'm so sorry.'

'I need to get in touch with your son and wondered if he was with you.'

'Yes, he is. I'll call him to the phone.'

When Douglas left the dining room he closed the door carefully behind him.

'Was it her?' Ivor hissed, a forkful of turkey poised halfway to his mouth.

'No. The nanny.'

They regarded each other like two conspirators. Ivor chewed thoughtfully. He lowered his voice. 'We don't want this Fairfax woman coming round here.'

'It was the nanny, I told you.'

'But . . .'

'Eat your dinner, Ivor. More bacon rolls? Stuffing?' By way of encouragement, Marion began to eat again.

'We'd better not ask – I mean about the call. I mean, what it was about.' He looked at her anxiously.

He'd rather not get involved, thought Marion.

'I shall ask,' she said. 'We have to know what's going on or we can't help him. Pass the gravy, dear, will you?'

Douglas returned and one look at his face told them it was bad news.

'That was the nanny, Winifred. She said the doctor's been

again and has sedated her. Hermione. She's . . . Her memory is rather erratic.' He stood behind his chair, his eyes dark with misery. 'I said I'd like to see her, but Winifred didn't advise it just yet. She described Hermione as fragile. Whatever that means.'

Marion said, 'It means she needs a good rest before she's fit to have visitors. That's all, Douglas, so sit down and get on with your dinner.' He did as he was told. 'So the nanny is looking after James?'

He nodded. 'I suppose so. James and Elena and Hermione. Quite a handful.'

He put a single sprout into his mouth, crushed it and swallowed it whole. 'She said she'd keep me informed, but on this number. I have no telephone at the cottage.'

Ivor said, 'That was very decent of her to let you know.'

'Yes . . . Poor Hermione.'

Marion laid a hand on his arm. 'Women are very resilient, Douglas. I always say if you can survive childbirth, you can survive anything. And she survived James's birth so that's promising. I have a feeling everything will turn out well. Stop worrying. Even if you and Hermione can't be together, I'm sure she would want you to enjoy your Christmas.'

Marion's words obviously brought him some cheer and, while he toyed with the food on his plate, he made a visible effort to think positively. 'Who knows, with a kind fate we might be together this time next year.'

Marion beamed at Ivor and then at Douglas. 'Well, there you are then,' she said.

# Nine

There seemed to be fewer visitors than usual, Winifred thought as she made her way past the beds on the way to see Oscar. She was trying to appear calm, but in fact she was disturbed by her chat with the specialist. Mr Temple had not been very hopeful that Oscar would be back at work in the near future although he did say he might be able to return home. 'But only to bed rest,' he had warned her. 'I'm afraid he is not out of the woods yet and needs time to recuperate.'

She wished Oscar a happy new year and pulled up a chair. She was repeating the specialist's words to Oscar when he grasped her hand tightly.

'Never mind me. What is happening at home? How is Elena? How is James?' He hesitated. 'Is he . . . changing in any way? His eyes? Has he any hair?'

Winifred had been dreading these questions, knowing that to lie would serve no useful purpose, but reluctant to tell him her own take on the child. She drew a sharp breath. 'You'll have to know sometime, Oscar,' she told him. 'James now has a fine layer of red-gold down on his head . . . and I think his eyes are going to be blue.' She sighed. 'I know you are going to ask my honest opinion.'

Oscar was visibly shocked. 'He's Hatton's child! That's what you're telling me.'

'I'm afraid so.'

'Perhaps . . . Does he look at all like me?'

She shook her head wordlessly. 'And nothing like Hermione either. He has Hatton's broad forehead and from certain angles . . .' Her voice trailed off. He had to know and now he did.

'What does Hermione say?'

'She has rather lost interest in him for the moment. She never asks after either of the children. She is very depressed most of the time, but then on occasion is very volatile – laughing and pretending that everything is fine. It's rather unnerving, actually.' She resisted the urge to tell him how tired she was herself, but knew that sharing her problems would only add to Oscar's. There was one matter, however, she knew they must discuss.

Tentatively she said, 'Oscar, we are going to have to think about Elena. I think we have to agree to let her know somehow in a roundabout way, that she is not Hermione's child.' He groaned out loud, but she forced herself to continue. 'You know my feelings on this matter. The younger she is, the less she will understand the ramifications – and the easier it should be for her to accept it. What worries me is Hermione's condition. If we ever faced a time when she needed to go away . . . for special care.' She did not mention the clinic Hermione had previously attended. 'Or if she died or left you . . .' Unhappily she fell silent. A quick glance showed her that the last few words had left no impression on him. After a moment she said, 'I don't want it to destroy Elena. Deep down she is a very sensitive child.'

A nurse stopped at the end of the bed and greeted Winifred. 'Would you like a cup of tea, Miss Franks?'

'No, thank you.'

Oscar said, 'I would, please, nurse.'

'You've just had one!' she argued with mock severity and smiled at Winifred. 'You could float a battleship on all the tea this man drinks!'

'It's the air in this ward,' he protested. 'It's too dry!'

She bustled away obediently and while they were waiting for her, Winifred noticed that Mr Ebdon was no longer in the next bed.

Oscar shrugged. 'Didn't survive the operation,' he said in a low voice. 'Poor chap. He went off as cheerful as anything. Just didn't come back. Cast rather a gloom over the ward, I can tell you!'

'I can imagine.'

Once the nurse had delivered the tea, Winifred tried again to engage Oscar's attention. 'I'd hate it all to come out while she's at the boarding school – and I know I was against the school idea but things have changed.'

He sipped his tea thoughtfully. 'You look peaky, Win. Rather pale.'

Exasperated, she said, 'Are you listening to me?' Peaky? Pale? Were these criticisms? She felt vaguely slighted.

'Your face is thinner.'

'I told you, I'm very tired.'

He looked worried and she was touched by his concern, but she persevered.

'Oscar, please try to understand. I'm run off my feet and when you come home you will spend most of your time in bed. If, as you suggested, I am to keep a watchful eye on both your shops . . . How am I going to cope? I shall be exhausted. That's why I've changed my mind about Elena.'

'Wouldn't you miss her?'

'Of course I'll miss her!' She swallowed hard. 'I'd much sooner keep her with us where I can see that she's happy, but it would be selfish to keep her at home for my peace of mind. She has so much to deal with in the future – at least her childhood should be secure and happy.'

'It's all such a mess!' he exclaimed. 'I think the greatest hell on earth is hurting those you love, making mistakes, not being able to put things right again.' He closed his eyes.

Winifred watched him for a moment. There was so much she wanted to say but this was not the time. Here in the ward . . . She sighed. It never was the right time to tell Oscar how much she loved him. Perhaps, if Hermione left him, it would be easier.

She forced her attention back to the present. 'Elena might be better off at school where she will miss all the family upheavals. And if Hatton tries to take James there will be an almighty upheaval! I don't want Elena to go through that. She's so bright. She wouldn't miss much and it might be devastating for her.'

'Hermione wouldn't allow him to take the baby!'

'No, Oscar, but she might very well go with him.' He looked startled. He's in denial, she thought unhappily. He's refusing to see the wider picture. 'When you see your wife you will understand how . . . how volatile the situation is. Lord knows what might happen over the next few weeks and months. We seem to be teetering on a knife-edge!'

After he finished his tea she took the cup and put it on the bedside cupboard and for a few minutes they sat without speaking.

Oscar broke the silence. 'But would you want to tell Elena that you are her mother?'

'I can't make up my mind. What do you think?'

'I think that once she knows she is "adopted" she will have to know it all, as gently and as simply as possible. Could you do it, Win?'

'I suppose so. I think if I choose the right moment . . . but maybe it would be better coming from you because she already accepts that you are her father. You'd have to re-assure her in case she starts to think you aren't and that would be too much for her to bear. She adores you. You know that, of course.'

A nurse appeared at the end of the ward and rang the bell. Visiting time was over.

Oscar looked fretful. 'Temple says I'm not to worry about anything. Little does he know. I do nothing but worry!'

She stood up and said softly, 'Our sins have found us out, Oscar.'

'With a vengeance,' he said, as she patted his hand by way of farewell. 'With a vengeance!'

That same night Elena awoke. As usual she climbed out of bed, put on her slippers and immediately trotted over to James's cot and checked to see if she could do anything for him. Sometimes one of his bootees had come off and she could put it on again. Sometimes his blanket had come untucked and she could replace it. She was always careful not to disturb Nanny, but she did not mind at all if James woke because then she could coax him back to sleep with a very quiet version of 'Rock-a-bye Baby', which she assured herself was his favourite nursery rhyme. There was some-thing about singing to him in the middle of the night that soothed her often troubled mind. Tonight, however, he did not need any help and she was preparing to return to her bed when she heard footsteps on the landing and hurried to see what was happening.

It had to be her mother because Nanny was asleep in the nursery. Hermione was halfway down the stairs, wearing only her flannel nightdress. She paused uncertainly when Elena spoke to her through the banisters.

'Mama! You should go back to bed,' she said. 'You'll catch cold.'

'It's your father, Elena. I can't find him.'

'He's not here, Mama. He's in the hospital. He was ill and the doctors are making him better.' She moved down the stairs to take hold of her mother's hand. 'Come back to bed.' She considered waking Nanny, but preferred to think she could deal with it on her own.

'He might be in the garden.' Hermione withdrew her hand. 'You go back to bed. I'll find your father.' She continued down the stairs and Elena was forced to follow.

'He's not in the garden, Mama,' she insisted. 'He doesn't go in the garden in the dark. Please come back to bed.'

But by now Hermione had reached the kitchen and was soon struggling to unbolt the back door. She turned angrily. 'How many times do I have to tell you, Elena? Go back to the nursery at once.'

'But, Mama, it's raining. Look!'

Her mother had managed to open the door and now stood peering out at what little she could see of the rain-swept yard. Without pulling on a coat and with nothing on her feet, she stepped out into the darkness, splashed across the paving stones and was soon out of sight.

Elena hesitated – should she run after her mother or go back and fetch Nanny? She was a little alarmed by Mama's behaviour, but Nanny had warned her that her mother was getting forgetful. Elena was also in her nightdress but at least she was wearing her slippers. She would go after her mother, she decided, and persuade her to come back into the house. Plunging off the step into the rain she was quickly soaked so that her nightdress clung to her uncomfortably.

'Mama! Where are you?' It was too late now to go back

and find a torch. There was no moonlight to help visibility either so Elena had to rely solely on the sounds of her mother's progress. Was she still on the path or was she stumbling among the bushes or halfway across the lawn? 'Mama! Please stand still and let me find you!'

She stared into the gloom and was suddenly aware that Toby was beside her. His ears were back and he looked thoroughly miserable. 'Good boy!' She patted him, grateful for his presence.

From somewhere to her left, near the old potting shed, a faint cry gave Elena the first hint of her mother's whereabouts. Toby rushed in the direction of the sound and Elena also left the path and fought her way through the dripping azaleas. Suddenly she heard sobs and abruptly came upon Hermione who appeared to be trapped by various small branches of surrounding shrubs.

'Oh, there you are!' said Hermione, catching sight of Elena. 'I can't find your father anywhere.'

Thankfully, Elena grabbed her by the hand. Ignoring her protests, she tugged her free. 'We're going back to the house,' she said firmly. Inspired, she added, 'I think that's where Papa is – in the house. We'll go and see, shall we?'

Without protest her mother allowed herself to be guided back towards the kitchen where the light from the window gave them a sense of direction. They were nearly at the back door when Nanny appeared in the doorway. She had put on shoes and wore a macintosh over her nightwear.

'What on earth is going on?' she demanded. 'Look at you both! Elena, you should be in bed – and look at you, Mrs Fairfax! What were you thinking of?'

She bundled them both into the kitchen and paused only to pour some milk into a saucepan. Grumbling at the bedraggled dog, she sent him into his basket and Elena rubbed him down with a towel and found him a garibaldi biscuit to cheer him up.

To Elena, Winifred said, 'Go up to the nursery and take off that nightdress, rub yourself down with a towel and put on a clean nightdress. Then hop into bed and I'll bring you some hot milk.' As Elena began her explanation, Winifred raised her voice. 'You can tell me later. Now go. I have to see to your mother before she catches her death!'

Elena went with bad grace. She felt unappreciated and paused at James's cot as she passed. She wanted to tell him what had happened but was afraid to wake him. When he was older, however, it would be different. She would tell him everything and he would sympathize. He would tell her his own troubles and she would try to help. They would be close. Brother and sister. She smiled at the picture this inspired. It would be the two of them against the grown-ups!

Following the instructions, she was soon in bed and before long her nanny appeared as promised.

'Here we are. Hot milk with a spoonful of honey!'

She was trying to sound cheerful, thought Elena. Poor Nanny.

'What's wrong with Mama?' she asked. 'She can't remember things. She thought Papa was having a walk in the garden.' She sipped the milk, watching her nanny's expression.

'Your mother is not at all well,' Nanny said carefully. 'She's been upset and that has made her memory go a bit funny. The doctor thinks she might like to go away for a rest – to a nice place called a clinic. She can have a long rest there and kind people to look after her and help her get better.'

Elena said, 'It's because of Mr Hatton, isn't it? Because when he came to lunch Mama fell down on to the floor and everyone was worried – and Cook says it's all Mr Hatton's fault.'

For once Nanny seemed to have nothing to say. Elena didn't know whether to be pleased or worried. She continued to sip her drink, peering hopefully at her. When the silence lengthened she said, 'Is Toby all right? He was very brave and clever.'

'He's fine. He's gone back to sleep.' Nanny pulled up a chair and sat down. 'You need to understand, Elena, that families sometimes get into a muddle. It's nobody's fault, really, but they do. We're a family – the Fairfax family – and . . . and things keep going wrong and we have to try and sort it out.'

'Am I in the muddle? Is James?' She felt vaguely alarmed.

'Not exactly but – well, yes, I suppose you are, but you have nothing to worry about.'

'Will I have to go to a clinic? Can James come with me?'

'No! Of course not – because only your mother is worried and upset . . . and forgetful. You and James will stay here with me – and with your papa when he comes home from the hospital.'

'When is he coming home?' Elena knew she would feel much safer when he left the hospital and returned to Downsview. 'Is Toby in the muddle?'

'No. Dogs and cats are pets and they don't get muddled.'

'Is Mr Hatton in the muddle, because his name isn't Fairfax?'

Nanny shook her head but said nothing.

Elena asked, 'When Papa comes home, will Mr Hatton still come to our house?'

Nanny stared at her, shocked. 'Why . . .? Why do you ask?'

'Because I think he likes Mama too much and Papa might be jealous.'

Standing up slowly, Nanny replaced her chair. She leaned down to kiss Elena goodnight. 'It's all part of the muddle, Elena, but you mustn't worry. You're not grown up so no one expects you to sort things out. We're the grown-ups and we can sort out all sorts of muddles. Do you understand?'

Elena nodded even though she did not understand. She said, 'I won't tell James then.'

'No. He's too young.' For some reason she took out a handkerchief and pressed it to her eyes. Did that mean she was crying? Elena wondered uneasily.

'Good girl! Now go to sleep. I'll go back to your mama.'

Obediently Elena snuggled further down under the bedclothes.

'I'm glad I'm not a grown-up!' she whispered when she was alone once more. She wondered for a moment about muddled families and whether being Toby was better than being a little girl, but she fell asleep before she had reached any firm conclusions.

The following morning Winifred set off for the Hawkhurst shop after a worried phone call from one of the assistants. Elena pushed the pram in which a sunny baby gurgled happily and almost knocked himself in the eye with his new ivory rattle. Winfred leaned over and took it gently from his small clutched fingers.

'He likes it!' Elena protested. 'It's his new rattle! Father Christmas—'

'It's a bit too heavy for him just yet. He'll grow into it.'

Elena scowled. 'But Father Christmas must know the right size. He chose it.' Her scowl deepened as she tried to manoeuvre the pram up on to the pavement after crossing the road. 'Don't help me! I can do it by myself!'

'You can't, Elena.' Winifred steadied the wobbling pram. 'Now we're nearly there and I'm hoping the pram will go through the shop door because if not I shall have to ask you to stay outside and guard James until I come out again. Hopefully I won't be too long.'

Fortunately the pram did go through the door – just – and Elena was put in charge of it while Winifred talked to the shop staff.

Mr Ellis, the manager, was a small fussy man who worked well under supervision and knew everything there was to know about ironmongery, but Oscar felt he was inclined to flounder when left alone to make decisions.

'The rep called in yesterday from Fosters,' he explained breathlessly, 'wanting to know why he hadn't received an order for the garden supplies and I said to him, "Don't ask me! Ask the boss!" but then . . .' He gulped for air. 'I realized he couldn't because Mr Fairfax is in hospital, and he said why couldn't I give it to him, and I said because I don't know what we need and can't leave the shop to go ferreting round in the store shed!' He looked at her indignantly. 'I've only got one pair of hands!'

Winifred bit back a sharp reply. Had she really had to make a long walk in a cold wind with two young children to discuss this trivial problem? 'You could have spoken to me on the telephone,' she began, but he rushed on.

'And the window cleaner hasn't turned up for two weeks and his wife came in to say he's down with bronchitis.'

'Oh, dear!'

'And we're getting low on paraffin oil and a chap brought back a hammer saying the first time he used it the handle split and I said, "How were you holding it?" – a perfectly reasonable question, I thought, but he was quite unpleasant. "There's only one way to hold a hammer!" he said, and said I'd been rude to him and he was going to tell Mr Fairfax!' His voice trembled.

Winifred now realized that this was the main reason for the call for help. Poor Mr Ellis was under a lot of pressure and needed reassurance. Well, she could sympathize with him! She said, 'What a silly man! I'd ignore that idle threat. I'll explain to Mr Fairfax when I go to the hospital this evening.'

'You will?'

'Certainly. Don't give it another thought.' He seemed to relax a little.

Elena materialized beside them holding a rubber plunger. 'James wants to know what this is.'

Mr Ellis managed a smile. 'It's for unblocking drains,' he told her. 'We stock two sizes. Never had any complaints.' He turned to Winifred. 'So this is Elena? How she's grown! And the baby?'

Elena beamed. 'His name's James and he's my brother.'

Winifred held her breath. Please don't speak out of turn, Elena! she prayed silently. There was probably plenty of talk in the village without Elena offering any more interesting snippets. Fortunately a woman came into the shop needing candles and began a conversation about her mother's rheumatics so Elena wandered back to the pram.

When the woman left, Winifred did her best to give advice on the problems relating to the shop and was about to leave when another woman came into the shop.

'Elena!' she exclaimed, then caught sight of Winifred.

It was Mrs Hatton, the woman who had stopped to speak to them when they were on their walk.

Marion Hatton said eagerly, 'I've been meaning to tele-phone you.'

Hastily Winifred suggested that they chat on the pave-ment and hustled Elena and the pram through the doorway again. She was tempted to hurry away while the woman made her purchases but common sense prevailed.

'It's that nice lady,' Elena said. 'I expect she wants to see James again. I think she likes babies.'

Winifred nodded, distracted.

'I must introduce myself properly,' said Mrs Hatton as soon as she rejoined them.

Elena said, 'We had to leave Toby behind because he's afraid of motor cars and he always barks at the baker's horse.'

'I'm Marion Hatton, Douglas Hatton's mother.' Smiling, she looked into the pram approvingly. 'He looks bonny. And so happy. A really lovely child. Who's looking after him?' she asked. 'I heard that Mrs Fairfax is ill.'

'The doctor's very hopeful,' Winifred lied. 'I'm managing for now.'

'I wondered if I could help in any way. If you have to keep an eye on the ironmonger's shops and do the hospital visiting and everything else. Douglas has told me so much about you all. It can't be easy. My husband suggested I offered to come round and sit with the children from time to time. I'd enjoy being useful. Ivor teases me about being a lady of leisure, and I must admit . . .'

'We do have a cook and a maid,' Winifred told her quickly. Whatever happened she knew she must never confirm this woman's suspicions about James's parentage. Even if Marion Hatton knew or suspected the truth it must never be admitted – at least not by Winifred. Mrs Hatton also appeared to be watching what she said and how she said it. The word grandson had not been uttered, which was a relief. How much did she know? Winifred wondered. 'I would have to discuss it with Mr Fairfax, naturally, and I'm not sure if he would approve.'

'Oh, I wish you would talk to him, Miss Franks. He knows my husband from the golf club, of course, so we are not exactly strangers. I do love children and I was a children's nurse in my youth before I married Ivor. I wanted a brood of children of my own.' She laughed. 'But fate decreed otherwise and Douglas is my only child.'

Elena said, 'James is my only brother. I'm his only sister.'

'Ah, yes.' She tried to catch Winifred's gaze, but she avoided eye contact. 'Well, I've made the offer, Miss Franks. I know the decision will not be yours to make and I shan't be offended if the answer is no – but I shall keep my fingers crossed. I do hope we can come to some kind of arrangement. It would be a pleasure to spend time with Elena and little James. They are charming children.'

Elena said, 'Except me. I'm not a child.'

'Dear me. Then I should say a bonny baby and a charming young lady!'

Elena beamed at the compliment. They made their goodbyes and Winifred watched Mrs Hatton walk away.

Elena peered up over the pram's handle. 'What a nice lady. I like her. Shall I ask Mama if she can—?'

'No, Elena! Leave that to me.' She turned the pram in the direction of home, already wishing that she could leave the children in Mrs Hatton's care while she made a trip to the Rye shop. It was unlikely, she knew, because Oscar would almost certainly refuse the offer and, in the circumstances, who could blame him? But stranger things had happened, she thought with resignation. She was now no longer surprised by anything or anyone.

Later that evening at the hospital Mr Temple listened carefully to what Winifred had to say, but then reluctantly shook his head.

'I hear what you're saying, Miss Franks,' he said, 'and I agree that your current home situation will not help Mr Fairfax one bit. The trouble is that we need the bed for the next patient and it would be wrong to deprive him or her of the bed. My only suggestion is that the home situation is changed in some way. Perhaps your doctor is right and a stay in a suitable environment would be helpful to Mr Fairfax's wife. That way they might both benefit – Mrs Fairfax by being removed from the worries of home and Mr Fairfax by being able to leave hospital and return to comparative calm.'

Winifred hesitated. 'I'm not terribly hopeful on either account,' she admitted. 'Mr Fairfax doesn't yet know how serious his wife's condition is. It will be a great shock when he sees her . . .'

Mr Temple held up his hand by way of an apology for interrupting her. 'There's another solution, Miss Franks. Suppose you take on extra help at home. Either a private nurse for Mrs Fairfax or a girl who will look after the children for a few hours each day. That might solve your problems.' He glanced somewhat impatiently at his watch, but Winifred had covered her face with her hands and missed the gesture.

Raising her head she said helplessly, 'There are other difficulties which I don't feel able to share with you, Mr Temple, but I do appreciate your time. We shall have to talk it over. The family did toy with the idea of sending Elena to boarding school, but I'm not sure. Nine seems terribly young.'

He brightened. 'Oh, no. Plenty of children go away to school as early as nine, Miss Franks. In most cases the children love it. Plenty of company, interesting things to do and a careful, caring trained staff to watch over them. I myself was sent away at nine and loved every minute of it. It would relieve the burdens at home for you and the child would be removed from what we can only call a very difficult, albeit temporary, background. I think the family should give it some thought, Miss Franks.'

Seeing by her expression that she was not convinced he went on. 'It can be a short-term solution, you know. Most schools will take a child for perhaps a term or two until the tensions have eased at home. Elena would probably enjoy herself more than you expect.'

Winifred thanked him and made her way to the ward to pass on most of what the specialist had suggested. Oscar listened, scowling.

'It seems to me that no one wants me to return home,' he said. 'Hardly encouraging, is it?'

Winifred bristled. 'You know that's not how it is, Oscar.

You're just feeling sorry for yourself and I understand why but there are other people to be considered.' Even as she spoke she regretted her response, but something told her that Oscar was going to be a very difficult patient and she was not looking forward to it. A shameful thing to admit but illness seemed to have brought out the worst in him and, much as she loved him, she was now seeing him in a rather unfavourable light.

She counted to ten slowly and told him about Mrs Hatton's offer of help.

His eyes widened and she braced herself. 'I'm only the messenger!' she reminded him, holding up her hands defensively.

'I don't know how she has the temerity,' he began angrily. 'She seems to have taken it for granted that James is Hatton's son. No one can ever know the truth and that being so—'

'Oscar, she and I have talked on the telephone and, well, I'm sorry to say, she is quite adamant about it. Perhaps you should consider when you and Hermione resumed . . .' She hesitated to say 'marital relations' because it sounded so impersonal.

'I know! No need to spell it out! But the child came early.'

'According to your wife,' she reminded him cautiously. 'To me, James looked like a full-term baby.' She avoided his gaze.

Oscar caught his breath and then released it in a hiss of suppressed pain. When at last he met her eyes his expression was bleak and her heart ached for him, but she knew she was helpless to prevent this unravelling of his life. He needed to face the fact that his longed-for son would be snatched away from him.

She said, 'Maybe at some time in the future – when all this is over – you and I could have another child.' If she could give him a son she might save him from his despair. Winifred wanted more than anything to give him hope.

Slowly he looked at her. 'Maybe.'

She took his hands in hers. 'We could make it happen,

Oscar. There's still time. Let your wife go to Hatton. Close the chapter. Start again.'

His gaze was rueful. 'I'll hold on to that idea,' he promised. After some reflection he sighed. 'And Hermione? What does she say?'

'She's not in a fit enough state to say anything convincing, Oscar.' She told him about Hermione's midnight walk and saw how shocked he was. She asked carefully, 'If you have proof that James is Hatton's child . . . what then? Will you give him up?'

'It depends on Hermione. The child must be with her. If it's proved, and if she wants her freedom to start afresh with Hatton . . . God knows!' He closed his eyes, his face screwed up as if in pain. 'I'd let her go. We'd be alone then, you and I, with Elena.' He smiled faintly. 'That wouldn't be so bad, would it?'

Winifred took his hand. 'No, dearest,' she said. 'It would be very good. It could be wonderful.'

Early on Tuesday morning Albert Mills walked down Monastery Hill, turned left along Cinque Ports Street and was fumbling in his pocket for the shop keys when he came to an abrupt stop. Unable to believe his eyes he saw that a policeman stood outside Fairfax Ironmonger's arguing with two lads.

He heard the constable say, 'None of your business so hop it!'

'What? Was it robbed?'

'You heard. Hop it!'

Albert felt winded. *Robbed? The shop? Oh, no!* He rushed forward.

'What's happened?' he demanded. 'I'm Albert Mills, the key holder. I'm the manager.'

One of the boys grinned. 'Someone's broke into your shop!'

The other said, 'Bet they've pinched stuff an' all!'

The policeman shooed them away and they retired to a safe distance.

Albert said, 'A break-in? I don't see any signs of that.'

'It's at the back, sir. It was reported by the woman in the bakery.' He indicated the shop next door. 'If you like to let us in, Mr Mills . . .'

Albert produced the key and opened the door with hands that trembled, but even as he did so he was rehearsing what he would say to Mr Fairfax to ensure that there was no way anyone could blame him. Then he remembered that Mr Fairfax was in hospital and explained the situation to the policeman. 'But I'll telephone the house and maybe his wife will come instead,' he suggested.

He saw nothing untoward in the shop itself, but in the rear of the premises it was evident that the stockroom, inhabited by various tea chests and cardboard boxes and sacks, had been disturbed. The rear door had been forced and would need immediate repair and a trail of muddy footprints led to an empty shop three doors along.

The constable told Albert that the plan had been a neat one. 'They stashed the goods in the empty shop then called in there earlier and loaded the stuff in to a van. The postman had passed them and thought little of it. They even exchanged "Good mornings!"'

Albert sat down for a moment to calm himself. 'Might have to close for the day,' he said. 'And I shall have to telephone Mrs Fairfax. I suppose she should come along and see for herself.'

'Might be best, sir.'

'Just give me a minute.'

'We shall need a list of the stolen property as soon as possible, sir.'

Albert said, 'Certainly. I just need a moment. It's been a bit of a shock! Eleven years I've worked here without so much as . . . Ah!' He pointed. 'A box of secateurs! The expensive ones from Myderns. Should have been on the shelf above you. They've gone! Haven't even opened them yet . . .' He peered into a corner. 'And a reel of garden hose . . . and a boot-scraper.' He turned his head. 'Oh! And a box of china finger panels for bathroom doors. Pretty they were!' He pushed himself upright. 'I'll make that telephone call and then check the stock. If you like to put the kettle on –' he pointed to a small gas ring – 'I'll make us a cup of tea. We're going to be here some time.'

Mrs Hatton put down the telephone and clasped her hands together. Closing her eyes she said, 'Thank you! Oh, thank you!' and rushed out into the garden where she found her husband in the potting shed, cleaning the shears with an oily rag. He was not supposed to do anything strenuous but liked to sit in the potting shed 'pottering'.

'You'll never guess,' she told him, 'who I've just been talking to . . .! Who do you think?'

'Father Christmas?'

'Ivor! Grow up, dear! No. It was Miss Franks – the Fairfaxes' nanny. Ivor! You're not listening properly.' She snatched the rag from his hand. 'Stop what you're doing and listen to me. I've just been talking to Miss Franks and she's taken me up on my offer. She wants me to go over there and stay with the family while she goes into Rye because their shop's been burgled!'

Ivor surrendered the shears but regarded her anxiously. 'You mean you're going to be there alone with the children and . . . and Hermione?'

'Yes. That's the whole point. There's no one else.' She tossed the rag on to a sack of peat and urged him to his feet. 'You have to drive me round there, but you needn't change. No one will see you. We have to hurry. She's ordered a taxi to take her into Rye.' She smiled broadly. 'This is my chance to get to know Hermione and James.'

He followed her out of the shed and back into the house. 'I thought you didn't like her.'

'I'm going to like her, Ivor, for Douglas's sake. That baby is Douglas's son and Hermione is the child's mother. Like it or not, that's the situation and we have to live with it. Poor Hermione has had a lot to put up with all these years according to Douglas, and I want to be fair to her.'

'But nothing alters the fact that she and Douglas . . .' He trailed off, sensing her disapproval.

'I know what you mean, Ivor, and I know what I've said about them in the past, but she is the baby's mother and she is also the woman Douglas loves. The baby changes everything in my view.'

'But it's her fault he might lose his job. You said—'

'He hasn't lost it, Ivor, but he's probably going to resign. He feels justifiably that John has given him no support when he needed it most and he doesn't want to work with him again. The new solicitor will sort it out for him and he's already put out a few feelers. He'll probably start up on his own and then advertise for someone to join him.'

'It's still a major setback in my opinion.'

'All of life is a major setback if you ask me, dear. We'll talk about it some other time. Now, do please hurry yourself.'

Five minutes later they were on their way.

'When will you be back?' Ivor asked. 'I mean, what about lunch?'

'Lunch? Good Lord, is that all you can think about?' Her voice rose slightly. 'This is a heaven-sent opportunity to get to know little James and you're worrying about your stomach!'

Ivor raised his eyebrows but wisely said nothing.

# Ten

It was twenty to eleven when Hermione, somewhere between waking and sleeping, heard a knock on the door. Winifred entered with a woman she didn't recognize . . . Or did she? Should she know her?

Winifred said, 'Mrs Fairfax, this is Mrs Hatton, Douglas's mother.'

'Oh?' Something stirred within her hazy memory, but nothing definite. Nothing that she could latch on to. That was all she had left now – vague memories, some good, some bad. It was so exhausting trying to keep things clear in her mind.

'Mrs Hatton has kindly come to help look after the children while I go into Rye. She's a qualified children's nurse so they will be in good hands. There's a small problem in the Rye shop and—'

Alerted by the word 'problem', Hermione struggled to sit up. 'What sort of problem? Is someone ill?' she interrupted.

'No, no one is ill. There's been a break-in – some lads most likely but nothing much has been—'

'A problem? Does Oscar know?'

'I'll tell him tonight. Mrs Hatton will stay here and keep an eye on things until I get back.'

Mrs Hatton stepped forward, smiling. 'I'm Douglas's mother. I've been looking forward to seeing you, Mrs Fairfax.'

Hermione, feeling wary now, stared at her, but said nothing.

Winifred said, 'James is asleep in his pram in the garden and Elena is with him. She's reading him a story even though he's fast asleep. Millie is keeping an eye on them and I'll be back before long, Mrs Hatton.'

Hermione said, 'When will you come back?'

Winifred assured her that she would be back around one o'clock. 'But Cook is still here and Millie and Mrs Hatton. They will bring you some lunch and prepare something for the children. You don't have to worry about a thing. Now I must rush into Rye to deal with the police and help Mr Mills.'

Hermione watched her leave the room with some misgivings. She had belatedly remembered who Mrs Hatton was and did not know how to react or what to expect.

For a moment the two women regarded each other in silence and Hermione considered whether she could pretend to fall asleep so that they need not have a conversation, but before she could put this plan into action, Mrs Hatton pulled up a chair and sat down beside the bed.

'May I call you Hermione?'

Hermione nodded cautiously.

To her surprise Marion Hatton then leaned forward, picked up her right hand and kissed it.

'I do hope we're going to be friends, Hermione.'

Her homely face was kindly, thought Hermione.

'My son Douglas speaks so very highly of you, you know, and I have always maintained that if Douglas finds a woman he loves, then I shall love her also.'

'Douglas?' Hermione smiled. Ah, yes. Douglas. She nodded again, still feeling hazy.

'Douglas is my son. He tells me that the two of you are very much in love and that you have given him a lovely little baby boy. James.'

'Yes, James.' Hermione frowned. 'I keep getting mixed up, you know. I hear him cry sometimes and think it's Edward. My first child.' Her voice trembled. 'He died when he was very young. Not even one year old.' With a heavy sigh she closed her eyes, trying to recall him.

Mrs Hatton said, 'That must have been so terrible. Heartbreaking. You poor dear.' She patted Hermione's hand. 'No one can understand such a loss. They want to, and they imagine they can, but I'm sure the reality is so much worse. You've been very unlucky – until now. But now you have Douglas, a man who loves you, and James – your dear little boy.'

Hermione was surprised by the woman's kindness. It seemed to her that it was years since anyone had cared enough about her to spend time with her and show sympathy. Making a big effort she asked, 'So, you are Douglas's mother?'

'Yes.'

'I'm not at my best just now,' Hermione told her earnestly. 'I can be very cheerful. I know I can . . . I was very happy as a young woman, but at the moment I think I'm rather ill. Or so they say. I need rest.'

'And love. You need love, Hermione.'

'And love, yes.' Hermione closed her eyes again wondering if this was some kind of dream. A happy dream in which she was loved. A knock at the door startled her and she opened her eyes. Elena stood in the doorway.

'James is awake and he's smiling.'

Mrs Hatton looked at Hermione. 'Shall I bring him up to you?'

Hermione hesitated before agreeing. Her visitor and Elena disappeared and Hermione was left alone. 'Douglas.' She spoke his name aloud, determined suddenly to retain a grasp of what was happening around her. Douglas was James's father. Yes, of course. A faint smile lit her face as his image floated into her confused mind. Douglas loved her and she had given him a son. The nanny was nowhere to be seen – she had been called away somewhere but that didn't matter either. But Oscar . . . was he in hospital? Not that she cared. Oscar might be her husband, but she no longer loved him . . .

Perhaps later or tomorrow, she would ask for a paper and pencil and write all this down so she wouldn't keep forgetting . . . Then there was Elena. Poor child . . .

There were footsteps on the stairs and she sat up, straightening the bedclothes, determined to compose herself. When Mrs Hatton carried James into the room she held out her arms for him and tears of joy fell on to his small, shining face.

Days passed and Sunday morning blew in with a cold east wind. Despite Elena's protests, she was sent off to church with Millie and arrived home just before twelve thirty. Warmly dressed in a tweed coat with fur collars and cuffs, and with matching tweed leggings, her face still glowed from the effects of the rough wind and she was out of breath.

'We were nearly blown away, Nanny,' she said as she pulled off her gloves. 'When we reached the church Millie pretended she was blown down the path and waved her arms and screamed and everyone had to jump out of the way!' She giggled, struggling with the buttons on her coat. 'A lady said, "Really, what a way to behave!"'

Her nanny groaned but said nothing. Instead she turned away and hung the coat on its hanger and put it back in the wardrobe then knelt to deal with the buttons on the leggings.

Elena had the feeling that she wasn't really listening and changed the subject. 'Whose motor car is that outside?'

'That's Mr Hatton's car. He has come to talk to your mother, and before you ask the answer is no. You can't join them. It's a private matter.'

Elena frowned. 'But Mr Hatton likes me.'

'I'm sure he does, but they have important things to talk about. And we do, too.'

From the tone of her voice Elena immediately expected the worst. 'It was Millie,' she insisted. 'I didn't pretend to be blown away. Truly I didn't.'

To Elena's relief, Nanny smiled and patted the bed. 'Sit here with me, Elena. I've got something to tell you that is very, very exciting.' She paused before continuing cautiously. 'Do you recall me telling you about boarding school? All the fun you can have and all the friends you will make?'

Elena simply nodded, aware of a strange feeling inside her.

'Well, your papa has said that you can go to one of them. Isn't that kind of him? He wants you to be happy and he knows you will have lots of fun there.'

'I'm happy here,' she said doubtfully. Was this some kind of trick? Did she want to go to boarding school and be happy? She wasn't at all sure.

'But you don't have lots of friends here, Elena, and you don't have lots of exciting things to do. You don't have a special friend or—'

'I have James!'

'True, but he's very young. With a girl friend your own age you can tell each other secrets and have lots of fun and play games and wear a smart uniform. We'd have to buy you lots of new clothes. A navy blue drill-slip and white blouses. Your papa wants you to have an exciting time. He said you can learn to play the piano if you want to.'

Elena said nothing, trying desperately to consider all these wonderful things Papa had said she could have and weighing them against her present life. It was almost too good to be true, she thought cautiously, but she trusted Papa. He would know.

'James would miss me,' she said slowly. 'And so would Toby.'

'You could send James a little picture every week when you send your letter home. Everyone writes home. The youngest children copy it from the blackboard. You could draw James a picture and I will show it to him. He would love to get a picture or a little card from you every week. I could show it to Toby too.'

'Do dogs like pictures?'

'Of course they do. I could tell him you'll come home in the holidays and play with him and take him for walks.'

'Holidays?'

'Yes. You stay there for a few weeks and then come home again and then go back.'

'And then have another holiday?'

'Yes,' Nanny confirmed.

Elena began to feel a little more confident. If she didn't have to stay there for ever then it might be fun. 'Papa said I would have a governess.'

'He's changed his mind because the boarding school will be fun and you might not like the governess.'

Still uncertain, Elena asked, 'When I come home for the holidays will you be here and Mama and Papa and everybody?'

'Of course. Everyone will still be here.'

'But you said Mama might go into a nice place where they will make her better.'

'Oh, yes! But that will only be for a short time and then she will come home again.'

'Oh.' Elena drew a deep breath. The funny feeling inside her was still there.

Nanny smiled. 'When your mama has finished with it, I'll show you the brochure – that's a little book that tells you all about the school. It's called the Leighton School for Girls and there are pictures of the girls wearing their uniforms and playing rounders and walking together to church. It came this morning, but your mama wanted to read it first to make sure it was a very, very nice school.'

Elena brightened. If Nanny and Mama and Papa liked it then she would like it.

Nanny looked at her, and Elena knew what she wanted. She smiled obediently and nodded.

'It was worryingly easy,' Winifred told Oscar that evening. 'I was prepared for tears or even tantrums so I was very relieved. We've ordered the uniform and when that comes I suspect we shall be hard put to get her out of it. She was enthralled by the brochure, especially the picture of the children doing their drill in the playground.'

'Well, that's one worry out of the way,' he replied. 'Now, tell me the latest on Hermione.'

He was sitting up and looked much better to Winifred than when he was first admitted. He had more colour in his face and his eyes had lost the dullness which had been partly caused by the sedatives which had been reduced in volume over the last week. Oscar had been told he could return home a week next Friday. It happened to be the thirteenth but nobody else seemed to have noticed this unfortunate date and Winifred had decided not to draw attention to it.

'Mrs Fairfax,' she murmured. 'Well, she seems to vary from day to day but she has agreed to the doctor's request to go into the private clinic for two weeks, but she hasn't actually gone yet.'

'I meant Hermione and Hatton and his interfering parents. And the child. Do we know anything certain about him? About his conception? Have you spoken to the doctor?'

'I tried but he was adamant he couldn't disclose any particulars to me. But he did say he felt we should trust Mrs Fairfax's judgement on the matter. Whatever that is supposed to mean.' Winifred knew exactly what the doctor had meant but was hoping Oscar would reach the same conclusion without help from her. She added, 'I don't think it's fair to call his parents interfering. They obviously are convinced the child is their grandchild and they are prepared naturally to see that he is never separated from his father.'

'And what do you think, Win?'

She blinked rapidly as tears pressed against her eyelids. He so rarely called her Win. 'I have to say that James looks just like Douglas Hatton. You can't miss the likeness even though he is still so young. And . . .' She drew a sharp breath. 'I have to tell you something else. After Mrs Hatton came round to look after the family – when the Rye shop was robbed – I noticed that Hermione spoke very kindly of her after she left. She said Mrs Hatton was the first person for years who had been kind to her.' She hung her head. 'I really felt very unhappy about that, Oscar. I want to think it's not true, but I wonder. With you and me and Elena together under her roof . . .'

'It was her choice!' he cried. 'She wouldn't or couldn't let me go. It was her idea to claim she had adopted Elena. Her insistence that we could somehow make it work. I always doubted it.'

'Perhaps we should have refused.' She was longing for Oscar to say something that would help her feel better about the past, but he simply glared at her.

'She begged me to stay,' he went on, his expression full of anguish now. 'You begged me to leave her. How was I to know what would be best for all of us? I'm as human as anyone else. God knows how hard I've tried!'

Alarmed, Winifred saw tears in his eyes. He was becoming too emotional and would make himself ill. 'Darling, don't be so hard on yourself,' she begged. This was an Oscar she hadn't seen for years – a vulnerable man, aware of his frailties.

Her words failed to stop him. 'We are all fallible, Win.

We make terrible mistakes.' He closed his eyes. 'Don't think you're the only one with regrets.'

Winifred shrank back, physically hurt by his unsympathetic words. Tempted to run from the ward, she found herself unable to summon the energy to move from the chair and, instead, sat there in silence, crushed by the tension between them.

He opened his eyes. 'God only knows how we can sort this out. If James is not my child then Hermione must make a decision . . .'

With an effort Winifred answered, 'Hatton won't allow her to stay, Oscar. He wants her to be his wife and—'

'Does he understand quite how fragile her condition is?'

Winifred hid her disappointment at his obvious reluctance to let his wife go. She understood that Oscar's pride suffered from the knowledge that his wife might prefer an untested life with Douglas Hatton to the far from perfect life she now had with her husband.

'I imagine so,' she replied, 'but his mother says he's determined to marry her and to bring up their son. Mrs Hatton will help them. I think Mrs Fairfax will go to him, Oscar. Maybe it's her only chance of happiness.'

Oscar's shoulders seemed to sag and he was quiet for a while, thinking. At last he said, 'Then perhaps we should let her go and wish her well. Wish them all well.'

Winifred nodded, relieved by his acceptance of the situation. 'She won't take Elena. Even if she wanted to I would fight her tooth and nail – and so would you.'

He smiled wanly at the vision she had created. 'If Elena is to remain with us, which she is, she will have to be told something to explain what is happening.' He rubbed his face tiredly. 'How can we protect her? The truth could be devastating. She is so trusting.'

'I shall tell her the truth, in simple language, Oscar. I suspect she already understands much of what has been going on and I don't trust Millie to keep quiet. I wouldn't put it past her to drop a few hints.'

'But how much does Millie know?'

'She's got eyes and ears! The one thing she cannot know is that Mrs Fairfax is not Elena's real mother and I am.'

He shook his head despairingly. 'Why does life have to be so desperately complicated?'

He took her hand and for a moment Winifred thought, with a rush of longing, that he was going to lift it to his lips. Instead he seemed to scrutinize it and then release it.

She swallowed her disappointment. 'I think we are reaping what we have sown, Oscar,' she said hoarsely. 'No one to blame but ourselves.'

He looked at her for a long time and then seemed suddenly to recognize the extent of her need for reassurance. He took hold of both her hands and drew her closer.

'In that case we can forgive ourselves, Win. We can let Hermione go to whatever the future holds for her . . . and we can give ourselves another chance. We have our sweet Elena and we have each other.'

'But first you must get well again, Oscar!' She spoke lightly but as he put up a hand to stroke her hair, she felt some of the tension lift and a spark of warmth touched and comforted her.

Hermione opened her eyes and blinked hard to clear her vision. She felt heavy and dazed as she looked round at the small white room in which she found herself. The door, also white, stood ajar, propped open by a chair on which a young woman in a white uniform sat reading a book. Hermione closed her eyes again and tried to remember what had brought her to this place. She had a vague memory of darkness and the loud horns of motor cars and then nothing.

Determined to make sense of the situation she sat up and noticed a rail round the sides of the bed. Sensing that her patient was awake, the nurse stood up, put her book on the chair and moved towards her.

'You're awake, Mrs Fairfax. Did you sleep well?'

Hermione tried to put a few words together but her throat was dry and she doubted she could speak clearly so gave up the attempt.

'I'll tell the doctor you're awake. Don't try to get out of bed. She'll be with you in a moment.'

While she waited, Hermione's mind cleared a little – enough

for her to realize that she was probably in a clinic. Suddenly everything came back with a rush – Oscar and Winifred and Elena and Douglas and . . .

'Ah! Mrs Fairfax. You're looking so much better today. I'm Dr Prentiss.' The woman smiled cheerfully as she held out her hand.

Hermione ignored it. The doctor poured some orange juice into a glass and said, 'Drink a little of this, Mrs Fairfax. You must be thirsty.'

'How long have I been in here?'

'You came in two days ago on the second of January. You were very confused and agitated so we let you sleep. Today is Wednesday the fourth. You haven't missed much.' She laughed, revealing nice teeth. She might be in her late thirties, Hermione thought.

'You mean I was given something to make me sleep?'

'Yes. Sleep is a great healer, Mrs Fairfax.'

'Why am I here? I don't remember agreeing to—'

'You were in no state to agree anything, Mrs Fairfax. You wandered into the street after dark and were almost knocked down by a motor car. No one was hurt, thank the Lord, but the car swerved to avoid you, ran up on to the pavement and hit a pillar box! Made a bit of dent, apparently. Do take a few sips, Mrs Fairfax. It's only orange juice.'

Reluctantly Hermione obeyed and found the drink refreshing. She glanced round. 'I don't see my clothes.'

'They are in the wardrobe – I'll show you. Your dressing gown and slippers. You seem to have been sleepwalking and were rushed here wrapped in a blanket.'

The doctor opened a cupboard door to reveal shelves and coat hangers and Hermione was relieved to recognize her own dressing gown as well as some of her own clothes. The doctor closed the bedroom door and carried the chair to the bedside and sat down.

She looked harmless enough to Hermione. Tall and slim with short wavy hair and nice eyes behind small round spectacles. She wore an open white coat but beneath it Hermione saw a tweed skirt and the woman was neatly shod in expensive-looking buttoned shoes. Hermione was thankful the doctor was a woman and not a man.

Hermione said, 'So I can go home now.'

'Not today, Mrs Fairfax. No,' she said soothingly. 'Your husband wants you to stay for a week or so until we are satisfied about your mental health. Sleepwalking can be a sign of something more serious and we wouldn't want to neglect any symptoms.'

'Serious? How do you mean?'

'Well, it might be a sign of inner anxiety or depression or—'

'Of course I'm depressed! My situation is intolerable.' The words came out more forcibly than she had intended and she at once recognized the words as Mrs Hatton's. 'You poor dear. Your situation is intolerable.' That is what Douglas's mother had said and she was right. His mother was the only person who understood what she had gone through over the past ten years.

'Oh dear! That was heartfelt, wasn't it?' Dr Prentiss was looking at her with renewed interest, the way someone might look at a new species of butterfly. 'Do you want to talk to me about your problems? It sometimes helps to share anxieties.'

Hermione shook her head. 'I talked to Mrs Hatton. She listened. She understood.'

'Did she now? That was helpful, then, wasn't it?' She was slowly pulling a notebook and pencil from the pocket of her white coat and she opened this and made a few notes.

Hermione said, 'Mrs Hatton is a very good friend of mine.' She reminded herself not to mention Douglas, as the doctor's pencil continued across the page. 'Miss Franks, the nanny, is quite the opposite. So is Oscar. They don't care about me.' Did she sound like a petulant child? Very probably. Hermione decided not to say anything else. Tomorrow she would go home whether Oscar liked it or not.

Dr Prentiss looked up from her note-taking. 'Can you think of anything that might have triggered your sleepwalking?'

'No.'

'You're sure? Nothing happened to upset you?'

Hermione hesitated. She recalled very clearly that Miss Franks had told her Oscar would soon be coming out of hospital, and she, Hermione, had burst into tears. It had been so easy to forget, with Oscar out of sight, that he and the nanny had once been in love with each other and probably still were. Day after day, pretending that he was the master and that wretched woman was simply the child's nanny. Unbearable for them, no doubt, but equally so for her. Elena made it impossible for her to forget or to pretend it had never happened.

Elena. Yes! Quite unexpectedly the name triggered something at the back of her mind and some of the confusion fell away. Suddenly her mind felt clearer than it had done for weeks. She regarded the doctor through narrowed eyes as pieces of the jigsaw tumbled relentlessly into place. 'Elena is being sent off to a boarding school and I have been edged out of my home and into this . . . this place – whatever it is.'

'It's a clinic, Mrs Fairfax. Nothing sinister.'

Ignoring the soothing words Hermione rushed on. 'Now my husband is coming home from hospital and they will be alone together. How I hate the pair of them!' She closed her eyes for a moment, gripping the rails of the bed. 'How very convenient for them!' Her eyes wide open she looked into the doctor's face. Dr Prentiss was no longer smiling but looked startled by the revelations. Hermione wondered what she had been told when they brought her in. None of the background, obviously.

Immediately the soothing expression returned to the doctor's face. 'I'm sure things are not quite as bad as you—'

'So very convenient, don't you think?' Hermione murmured, glaring at the doctor. 'The two of them together under my roof. So bloody convenient!'

As the startled doctor began to protest at her unacceptable language, Hermione closed her eyes, slid down into the bed and refused to say another word. The session had ended.

The afternoon meeting began promptly at five o'clock. Three staff members attended. Dr Prentiss was one of them, the clinic's director Hubert Willoughby was another, and the newest and youngest member of the team, Ronald Tegley was straight out of his training and comparatively inexperienced. The first two reports dealt with other patients but then they came to Hermione Fairfax.

Dr Prentiss gave them a quick appraisal. 'Hermione Fairfax, married with two children. Admitted on the second of this month, finally surfaced this morning. She was brought in as an emergency after being found wandering among the traffic in the High Street in Hawkhurst wearing only her nightwear. She was the unwitting cause of an accident. No one seriously hurt so no claim being made against her. No further police interest. Any questions so far? Dr Tegley? Dr Willoughby?'

Willoughby and Tegley shook their heads and she resumed the report.

'I interviewed her briefly this morning, but she soon withdrew her cooperation and ended the session.'

Willoughby said, 'So, presumably suffering from exhaustion and depression?'

Dr Prentiss confirmed this.

Tegley said, 'Have you done any tests yet?'

She gave him a cold look, annoyed by his presumption. 'Not yet. It's a little too early for tests. We naturally want her to settle a little before we start probing too deeply.' Her tone held a slight but apparent reproof at his eagerness. 'We don't yet have her full confidence. I needed to see the extent of her alleged memory loss and—'

'Alleged?' he challenged, mortified by his slip.

'We never take things for granted, Dr Tegley.'

'Is it true that she's the wife of Oscar Fairfax?' the director asked.

When she nodded, he turned to the younger man. 'Lives in Hawkhurst and owns a couple of ironmonger shops? Well known locally. Quite wealthy, I believe. My brother plays golf with him – or did once upon a time. Had a heart attack recently. Fairfax, not my brother.'

'That's the one, yes.' Dr Prentiss referred to her notes. 'Mrs Fairfax was willing to talk at first but only briefly and I sensed hidden anger and deep resentment. There seems to be a family secret – some kind of tragedy, maybe – that plays on her mind. For the moment, I shall simply encourage her to talk about it and allow her to express the repressed anger.'

Tegley leaned forward eagerly. 'Would you allow me to be present at one of the interviews with her? I think I'd find it interesting and hopefully might contribute something useful.'

She gave him a cool smile. She hadn't taken to the latest team member, and was finding him a sight too confident. 'It might be possible, Dr Tegley, but not yet. If it appears to be a good idea I shall let you know in good time – but only if the patient is willing. I must have her complete trust first. As you will know from your studies the patient's co-operation is of the utmost importance in these cases.' Turning the pages of her notebook, she refreshed her knowledge. 'There was some information from the family nanny who came in soon after she was admitted. She spoke of serious confusion in the patient's mind.'

Willoughby sat up straighter. 'But not dangerous? No signs of violence? No need for restraints?'

'No. There certainly is some confusion, but so far I would agree that it is no more than serious. Certainly not dangerous.'

Tegley said, 'But she did wander off into the street.'

'Here she is watched throughout the day, Dr Tegley, and the outer doors are always locked and—'

'Worrying, though.'

Dr Prentiss held her temper. Why did he have to interrupt when he had nothing useful to say? She finished her sentence. 'We take all necessary precautions.' She took a last glance at her notes. 'During our talk Mrs Fairfax had a few surprising moments of clarity and these were very encouraging. Hopefully the symptoms are not as deep rooted as I had been led to believe.' She closed the file.

Willoughby glanced at his watch. 'And visitors? Have you decided?'

'Yes. I shall only admit people she wants to see. At the moment that will probably be a Mrs Marion Hatton – a good friend of hers. From what little she has told me I assume she doesn't want to see the nanny or the husband – but the latter is anyway confined to bed after a heart attack so there need be no worries over that particular exclusion.' She looked from one to the other. 'It's very early days but at present I'm hopeful. If the patient can give vent to that pent-up anger we might gradually be able to bring about a change for the better. "Slowly, slowly, catchee monkee!" as they say. Very, very slowly!'

Thursday arrived at last – the day when Elena started her new school. They were on their way to the station and Winifred was becoming anxious in the extreme. Once the decision had been made it had all happened so quickly and she had been trying for days to talk to Elena, to break the news to her that Hermione was not her real mother and that she was. Now it was the second day of the term at the Leighton School for Girls and she and Elena were waiting on the station platform for the train to arrive. She was taking Elena to meet her new headmistress, and to leave her in the capable hands of the school's staff. Elena would be in Meadows House, a separate building specifically for the younger girls, in the care of their housemistress, Miss Dalton, who had ten years' experience at the school and was highly thought of.

Winifred's main worry was that, by the time Elena returned at half-term, Hermione might have left Oscar and be living with Douglas Hatton. In which case James would also be gone. She could imagine what a shock this would be to a nine-year-old and had promised herself that she would tell Elena the truth before she went away to school. Each day she had tried to broach the awkward subject and each time she had found it too difficult or had been interrupted. Now time was running out and she was going to have to tell Elena the facts as they travelled to the school which was on the far side of Canterbury in a pleasant rural area.

When the train hissed to a stop at the platform, they climbed up into a carriage which was almost empty. Elena, impeccable in her new school uniform, sat proudly gazing across at an elderly lady who paid them no attention as she busied herself with her knitting. Winifred said, 'Good morning,' but when the woman appeared not to hear, she comforted herself with the thought that she might be a little deaf.

In a low voice she said, 'Elena, I have something to tell you. Something very exciting, but . . .'

Elena pointed. 'Oh, look, Nanny! Look at those matching cows! They're all exactly the same colour. I expect they're sisters, don't you?'

'Probably . . . Look, Elena, I have a secret to . . .' She fell silent as the old woman glanced up at her. Had she heard the word secret, Winifred wondered uneasily, and waited impatiently until the knitting was resumed.

Elena cheerfully swung her feet, admiring her sturdy new shoes with the brown laces. 'I like Miss Dalton,' she said firmly. 'She's smiley.'

'You haven't met her yet, but I'm sure you will like her.'

'I have seen her in the little book. There's a photograph of her and I like her.'

'Oh. Yes, there is.' In fact the teacher featured in the school's brochure was not named, but Winifred didn't want to disillusion her. 'I'm glad you like her. If you have any worries you must go to her and—'

'What sort of worries? Oh!' As another train passed them Elena gave a little shriek and covered her ears.

'Elena, you do know that you are adopted, don't you? That your mama – that is Hermione – is not your real mother.'

'I think so. I heard when I was under the table.' She nodded vaguely. 'Where's my tuck box, Nanny?' Suddenly anxious she glanced around.

'It's up in the rack, Elena, above your head.' She lowered her voice. 'Well, don't you want to know who your real mother is?'

Elena looked up at the rack. 'Cook has made me some biscuits with currants in and there's a jar of lemon curd which I have to share with the other girls at teatime.' She caught the old lady's eye and beamed. 'I'm going to boarding school,' she told her. 'That's my tuck box up there. Millie says that going away to school is very posh, but I don't mind.'

'Mmm?' The old woman smiled, only momentarily distracted, and then concentrated once more on her knitting.

'Elena, don't you want to know who your real mother is?' Winifred took hold of her hands. 'The fact is—'

'Is it you?'

Shocked, Winifred was lost for words. Suddenly she felt the train compartment was too public. Delaying, she tried another tack. 'Did you know that your mama is . . . is in a clinic? Because . . .' She felt her face grow hot.

Elena leaned forward and addressed the old lady. 'I've got a special uniform. It's a navy blue drill-slip and you wear it over a white blouse. Millie says I shall look a right little madam.' The perceived compliment obviously pleased her. 'And I have four pairs of navy blue bloomers and four bloomer linings, whatever they are and . . .' Distracted, she glanced up as the train pulled into a station and a middle-aged couple entered the carriage. The man had a military look about him and the woman carried a small basket as well as her purse. At the same time a ticket inspector appeared and Winifred fumbled in her purse for the tickets.

He took them and glanced at her. 'One single and one return?'

'That's right.'

He grinned at Elena. 'Off to school, are you?'

'Yes.'

'Leighton's, is it?'

'Yes.'

He punched the tickets and returned them to Winifred.

'Lots of little girls go there,' he told Elena. 'We had dozens yesterday. First day back. You must be new. New girls arrive a day later, see. That's how they work it.'

Please move on, thought Winifred desperately, begrudging the time he was wasting, although she realized he was simply taking a kindly interest.

Glancing out at the station clock she saw that only ten minutes remained before the end of the journey. Was there time to get a few main facts into Elena's head without frightening her? She felt perspiration break out on her forehead as her anxiety grew.

She said quietly, 'If – I mean when – your mama goes to live with Mr Hatton they won't be far away and you can still visit them and see James and tell him all about school and your friends.'

Now Winifred had her whole attention.

'Will he still be my brother?'

'Of course he . . .' No, he wouldn't. Fatally she hesitated, not wanting to tell any lies, but wondering how Elena would deal with the news that she no longer had a baby brother. Was that one fact too many for her to bear today or should she continue? She was anxious to prepare her for her uncertain future but afraid of saying too much or too little. The decision was taken for her, however, as the couple settled themselves on the opposite seat and a small meow came from the basket she carried.

Elena's head swung round sharply and the woman laughed. 'It's a kitten, dear,' she told her. 'I'm taking him to my granddaughter for her birthday. Would you like to see him?'

As Elena nodded, already sliding from the seat in happy anticipation, Winifred knew she was beaten. There was no way she could compete with a kitten. She had failed, she thought wearily, as a weight of guilt settled across her slim shoulders. Elena was now unprepared for the events that threatened to totally disrupt her life. Winifred knew that due to her tardiness she had left her daughter vulnerable to future revelations.

Oscar, waiting at home for news, would not be pleased when he heard what had happened.

# Eleven

Winifred panicked as soon as she walked out of the school gates even though Elena, in the care of an older girl named Pearl, had waved her 'nanny' off very casually and without the slightest hint of nerves. Winifred had called her back for a second farewell kiss but too late. The door had closed behind the two girls and her chance had gone. It was Winifred who suffered. Just as it seemed that her daughter might be returned to her by way of Oscar's probable divorce, she felt she was abandoning her to the uncertain care of others.

What sort of mother did that make her? she wondered dolefully as twenty minutes later she waited on the station platform for a train to take her back to Hawkhurst. What awaited her at home did not excite her in any way. The man who might once have become her husband had somehow turned into a rather taciturn, unhappy creature, who seemed more interested in his shops than in the people who shared his home. Being brutally honest, Winifred admitted that the last nine years had come very close to killing whatever affection they had once had for one another. Could it be rekindled? Would his eyes ever brighten at the sight of her? Would she ever again be thrilled by the sound of his footsteps?

The train arrived and she found a seat and her thoughts reverted to Elena. Was she really as confident as she had appeared when they parted? She was only nine years old. Nothing had prepared her for finding herself alone among strangers. How would the girl feel when bedtime arrived and she found herself in a small dormitory with no nanny? Suppose she was frightened or unhappy – who would be on hand to comfort her? Would Elena feel that she had been abandoned; that nobody cared? If so, would she ever forgive Winifred for not preparing her properly for the stress of a major parting?

As the train rattled on, Winifred's distress grew until at last a possible solution offered itself. She would telephone the headmistress and explain the situation. She would ask for a progress report. If she were not satisfied she would insist on speaking to Elena.

It was nearly six o'clock when the school's secretary hurried into the headmistress's office.

'I'm afraid I have a distraught person on the line, Miss Randall. The nanny of Elena Fairfax. She says she must speak to you.' She rolled her eyes. 'She insists it's urgent.'

Miss Randall glanced at the clock. 'Could you say I've just left the room?'

'I'm sorry – I said you were still here. The truth is she sounds quite tearful and keeps saying there's something you must understand. She should have told Elena something about a family problem. She's not making much sense.'

The headmistress sat down again. 'Very well, you'd better transfer her. Then you can go. It's been a long day for all of us.'

The secretary said, 'It always is on the second day of term.'

Once the door had closed between them Bridget Randall glanced at a nearby file to refresh her memory then lifted the receiver. 'How can I help you, Miss Franks?' she asked, keeping her voice neutral.

'Oh, Miss Randall.' The words seemed to burst from her. 'I know you'll think I'm overreacting, but I'm in such a state and I have to speak to you about Elena's background. It really is rather . . . Oh, that is, I think I should have told you that back here we are in rather . . . Excuse me!'

Miss Randall heard her blowing her nose, but when the woman came back on the line it was obvious that she was crying. The headmistress shook her head and waited hopefully for the storm to blow over and while she did so she wondered what was happening that merited so much angst.

Hearing nothing but hysterical sobs she said loudly but calmly, 'Do pull yourself together, Miss Franks. I can't be of help if you don't tell me what is wrong.'

'I know . . . I'm sorry . . . Please, it's just been . . .'

When the tears resumed the headmistress began to feel rather anxious. The poor woman sounded close to the point of collapse. She waited, doodling on the edge of her blotter and trying to remain sympathetic; trying not to feel superior. It was a long time since Bridget Randall had found herself in such emotional turmoil.

'It's awful, Miss Randall, but at the time . . . I mean with hindsight we were very wrong and we're to blame. Entirely. Elena is my daughter by Oscar Fairfax . . . at least, she was but he couldn't leave his wife – Hermione – so she suggested that they adopted Elena instead, but of course I couldn't bear to lose her so we . . . we all pretended . . . Oh! It was a nightmare!'

The headmistress blinked. What an extraordinary story – if it were true. It crossed her mind that the Franks woman might be drunk . . . but surely not. She had seemed eminently respectable earlier in the day. 'I'm sure this is not as bad as you think, Miss Franks—' she began, but was interrupted.

'But you see Elena doesn't know the true story and it's worse. Much worse. The woman she calls Mama is – that is, Mrs Fairfax – has recently had a baby by another man and now she is planning to leave Mr Fairfax and take the baby, Elena's brother . . . Oh, it's such a muddle and I should have told Elena the facts calmly and sensibly when I had time, but I put it off and put it off and then today I tried to tell her on the train, but people kept interrupting. I know that makes me a bad mother, but . . . Oh God! This is all my fault!'

More tears followed. Bridget put a hand to her head. She tried to think how best to bring this sad outburst to a sane conclusion. Patience, Bridget, she told herself silently. Give the poor soul time. She waited until it sounded as though the woman had her emotions under some control and then spoke firmly.

'Just listen to me, Miss Franks. Please don't interrupt, just listen. You seem to suggest that all these changes are imminent and you are understandably anxious. That's perfectly natural. In your situation I'm sure I would feel the same. No! Please don't cry. I want you to take deep breaths while

I talk to you. It's perfectly natural to feel this way when you part with your daughter in these circumstances. All the other mothers—'

'But the other mothers haven't behaved as I did. They haven't betrayed their daughter's trust.'

'How do you know that? Do you imagine that you are the only mother at fault? I can assure you that this is not the case at all. We all make mistakes and we all have regrets.' Not for the first time Bridget Randall was reminded how different her own life would have been if she had accepted her marriage proposal instead of refusing it in favour of her teaching career.

'But will she ever understand?' cried Miss Franks. 'Or forgive me? I feel that—'

'Now stop and think, Miss Franks, please. Would you forgive your mother if she made a mistake?'

'I–I think so. Yes, I would. Of course I would.'

'Then give your own daughter the benefit of the doubt.'

There was silence at the end of the line and Bridget Randall was hopeful. Was this the winning argument? she wondered. After a few moments she spoke into the silence. 'I suggest you write a letter to Elena, Miss Franks, explaining the facts as simply as you can and enclose it in a letter to me. If you wish it, I can then read it to Elena quite calmly and making it all sound very matter-of-fact.'

'You think that would . . . Yes, you're right, I dare say.'

'It is not my problem and so I will not be at all emotional. You understand? You must realize, Miss Franks, that children here come from all kinds of complicated backgrounds and for reasons you can only guess at. Deaths, divorce, un-married parents . . . one girl had a father in prison and another had been abducted by her father and taken to India!'

'Good heavens!'

'The list is endless. I hope it reassures you to learn that most of the children, in this very secure and stable environment, are happy and well adjusted whatever their backgrounds. They are so resilient, Miss Franks. Until you have known as many children as I have, you can have no idea.' She sat back in her chair, pleased with the way her arguments were being accepted. This was an important part of her job and it was always satisfying to know she was helping someone.

'Really?' Miss Frank's voice had steadied. 'I had thought our situation was . . . rather extreme . . .' She trailed off.

'Not at all. Life can be very complicated, Miss Franks, and it's often the case that our best intentions somehow turn sour. Blaming yourself is quite pointless, you know. So dry your tears and take comfort from what I have told you. Elena's life is not going to be blighted by whatever happens at home.' She hoped this was true. 'When she is older she will know that, whatever happened, initially you all wanted what was best for her.'

'Oh, I do hope so!'

'Trust me, Miss Franks. Here at Leighton's she will be given every support, and rest assured we will keep a wary eye on her. Your daughter will be happy and well cared for until the crisis is over. I recall that she is only booked in for the remainder of the term but you may change your mind and allow her to stay on with us.'

There was a long silence. Miss Franks said, 'I'm so grateful . . . I feel so much better. Truly, I don't know how to thank you.'

'Telephone me tomorrow and I will see that you speak to Miss Dalton who is in charge of Meadows House. She will reassure you. I'll be in touch with her as soon as I put down the telephone.'

The conversation ended and Bridget Randall sat back in her chair. It had been a long exhausting day, but she was buoyed up by her conversation with Miss Franks. 'What a tangled web!' she murmured.

Poor Miss Franks. How did people get themselves into such nightmare situations? she wondered. Thank heavens her own life was secure and well planned – and entirely free of such sordid entanglements.

And yet she was aware of a sneaking envy for Miss Franks. The woman had known love; she had experienced passion; she had a daughter. Whatever the ramifications of the affair and regardless of the unhappy outcome, she had lived in the outside world. Bridget Randall knew what it was to be cushioned from most of life's problems. When she retired in six years' time she would have her comfortable cottage and enough money to live on. But parts of life had somehow passed her by and she would be quite alone.

Ivor Hatton dipped one of his toasted soldiers into his boiled egg and smiled at his wife across the breakfast table. 'Perfect, dear,' he told her and took a first bite. This was always the perfect start to his day.

She spoiled the moment by saying, 'I've been thinking, dear.'

His heart sank a little. 'What's that then, Marion?' He knew it would be about Hermione Fairfax, but he would let her tell it in her own time. That way he could put off the evil hour when he would have to consider something unpalatable.

Slowly and meticulously his wife spread butter on her toast and then added honey. Ivor finished the first soldier and started on a second, but he was no longer enjoying it. Over the past weeks and months his well-ordered life had crumbled so that now every day seemed to bring fresh problems, most of them inspired by his wife. Not that she wasn't doing what she did for the best – he knew she had their son's best interests at heart – but Ivor's life was being disrupted as well and he was unable to see where it would end.

'Hermione has been in that place now for more than a week,' Marion told him, 'and I am not satisfied.' She looked at him, defying him to argue.

'Aren't you, Marion?' He concentrated on his egg.

'No, I'm not. I've spoken to Douglas about it and he agrees with me. It seems that Hermione is willing to see us so we must take the initiative and visit her. He is her husband in all but name and I am her mother-in-law by the same token.'

But not legally, Ivor thought, not daring to interrupt her. He had a suspicion that she had concocted a certain plan and would put it into action despite any doubts he might have. All he needed to know now was the extent of the plan. With a sigh he stabbed the empty eggshell with the spoon – to prevent it being used by a witch as a boat – and pushed his plate away. 'So-o?'

'So tomorrow I am going to this clinic to visit Hermione and see for myself if any progress is being made. I don't believe in long incarcerations. They tend to drain the spirit.'

'But I do believe the doctor recommended the stay, even before she wandered off. And it's hardly an incarceration, Marion. You make it sound like a prison sentence.'

His wife gave him one of her withering glances. 'Don't be flippant, dear – and certainly not at my expense! I suggest we persuade Hermione to . . . to move in with us and bring James with her. We have a spare room. Look at me, dear. I want your opinion. What do you think?'

Forced to look at her, he saw with a shock that her lips trembled but her eyes blazed. He knew the expression. She had already made up her mind and was nervous in case he tried to block her.

'It's a possibility,' he began diplomatically. 'But she might not want to come here. She has a husband. He might object. Marion, think of the scandal! He might go to the police and say we have . . . have forced her into the decision.' He fussed with his egg. 'Her husband might pretend we've abducted her!'

That stopped her. 'Oh, Ivor, surely not!'

'I don't know, Marion, do I? I'm just saying we should be prepared for some resistance.'

'But Oscar will be filing for divorce, won't he? Why should she be forced to go back and live with him and Miss Franks?'

'I thought you liked Miss Franks.'

'That was before I knew the whole truth. Look, Ivor, if Hermione comes to live with us – just for a few weeks – then she and Douglas will be together and she will be happy and we'll have our grandson under our roof. All happy together. You'll see. Hermione will blossom.'

Or not, he thought. It would be a crush and his peaceful retirement would be at an end. 'For ever?' he said weakly.

'Of course not, Ivor! Think about it. As soon as Hermione is fit, she and Douglas and the baby can move into the cottage he has rented.'

'Ah. I see.' There was light at the end of the tunnel. He allowed himself a small smile. 'I've always said I didn't marry you for your looks alone!'

Marion beamed and he could see that the compliment pleased her.

'Thank you, dear. So that's settled.'

Ivor nodded. 'So Douglas agrees, does he?'

'Well, not exactly, but you know how he is. He has the problem of a job to think about and he's always been rather single-minded. He's not having much luck in this area and he says he might have to move further afield. The business with Hermione has rather poisoned his chances. I do rather wonder whether he needs a fresh start somewhere else.'

Now Ivor's shoulders sagged. He should have known it was never going to be easy. 'Move away from us?'

'Of course not. We would move with him. Do you remember that holiday in Devon, when we stayed some-where near Honiton?' She stared at him. 'Now, what's the matter? You look as though you've seen a ghost!'

'Move away? Oh, no, Marion. You know I hate moving and how much we love this place!'

'We love our son more, dear.'

Desperately he fought off the sensation that his world was falling apart and would never be the same again. 'Douglas may not want us all to move. He might want to have Hermione and James all to himself. He might prefer us to stay here.'

'Of course he won't. He'll need us nearby to help out if Hermione is unwell or . . . or if there is any kind of emergency.'

'I suppose you're right, Marion. We shall have to talk to him – and Hermione. We shall see.'

'We certainly shall!'

Ivor swallowed the last mouthful of toast but it seemed to have lost its flavour.

By the time Sunday arrived, Elena had settled into the Leighton School for Girls and was enjoying herself. The routine suited her and she found her days full and interesting and the other girls were ideal playmates. With a few exceptions, of course. She didn't much care for Celeste Hackett who showed off a lot about having a French mother nor did she like Amelia Chinn who had three brothers whose names all began with 'D' – Donald, Derek and Dennis – and who were all older than her and apparently called her their 'little princess'.

She found the dormitory exciting because after the prefect fell asleep they could whisper and giggle to each other from their beds. She enjoyed the morning assemblies and the hymns and prayers and important announcements, and relished the fact that she was one of dozens of girls in identical uniforms – she felt she belonged. The lessons were much better than the lessons Nanny had given her and she was looking forward to her first piano lesson. Elena was quite sure she would learn very quickly (faster than the other girls) and would astonish her parents and Nanny with a party piece when she went home for half-term.

So when, in the middle of an arithmetic lesson on Wednesday morning, a senior girl by the name of Frederica arrived to take her to see the headmistress, Elena jumped to her feet willingly and hurried out into the corridor.

'What's it about?' she asked.

'I don't know. I'm just this week's monitor so I run errands for Miss Randall.'

'Am I an errand?'

'Sort of.' She laughed as they went upstairs.

Elena recognized the room when they went in. She had been here with Nanny when she first arrived. It seemed ages ago.

When Frederica went out Elena was told to sit down.

Miss Randall smiled, holding up a sheet of paper. 'I've had a letter from your nanny,' she began. 'A very interesting and exciting letter. She has asked me to explain it because she thinks you are now old enough and clever enough.'

Elena nodded. 'I expect it's about my brother James. Nanny said she would tell me.'

'It is about James, in a way, Elena, but it's also about you and your mother – the one you call Mama. You know, of course, that you are adopted but that Oscar Fairfax is your father.'

Elena was suddenly stilled.

Miss Randall continued. 'But your real mother, before you were adopted, was Nanny.' Before Elena could react she went straight on. 'So you have been extra lucky. Your nanny loves you, your father loves you and your mama—'

'Mama hates me.'

The headmistress hesitated. 'She doesn't hate you, Elena, but she is sad about you. Because she wanted you to be her little girl. She wanted to be your real mother.'

Elena's thoughts tumbled for a moment. 'But James is my real baby brother. I know he is – because . . . because I'm his sister.' She watched the headmistress's face carefully.

'Well, no, Elena. I won't pretend he is your brother because he isn't, but that's the other exciting thing. When you are both grown up James will be your best friend. Your very best friend – and that is sometimes better than a brother.'

Elena considered this suggestion. Miss Randall held out a small bowl of toffees and Elena took one but made no effort to unwrap it. Before she could think of something to say the headmistress turned over the page and read a few more lines of the letter.

'You see, Elena, if your mama goes away you still have your nanny, who is your real mother and loves you such a lot.'

'Is she going away with Mr Hatton?'

'Maybe. Maybe not. But even if she does . . .'

'Will she take James?' Elena wondered what was happening to her voice which seemed to be getting smaller.

'Yes, she will, because she is his real mother and Mr Hatton—'

'Is his real father?'

The headmistress smiled again. 'How clever you are, Elena. Your nanny said you would understand.'

After a long moment Elena asked, 'But who am I?'

'You're Elena Fairfax, exactly the same as you were before except that you don't need a nanny now because you are so grown up. That means that your nanny can now go back to being your real mother.'

Elena unwrapped the toffee, stared at it then rewrapped it carefully.

'I feel a bit different,' she said shakily.

Miss Randall stood up, pulled a chair up in front of the desk and patted Elena's knee. 'That's because you have had such a big surprise. Such exciting news. It's a lot to think about, isn't it?'

Elena could only nod. She was aware of an uncomfortable feeling in her tummy, rather like a hard lump. Then she frowned. 'But I do like having a brother.'

'You could have an honorary brother.' Miss Randall looked very excited by the idea. 'That's fun, too, Elena. An honorary brother is someone who isn't really a brother, but you pretend he is and he pretends you are his sister.'

She brightened. 'So am I his honorary sister?'

'Exactly. Now that would be very nice, wouldn't it?'

'And I can still send him pictures?'

'Oh, yes – and letters when he is bigger. And you could send a photograph and he could send you one!'

Elena decided that she liked Miss Randall's smile. It seemed to make her whole face shine.

'Now, Elena, I'll give you the letter to keep in your locker next to your bed where it will be safe. Then you can read it again sometimes. Your real mama is going to telephone me later this evening to know how excited you are by all the wonderful surprises. If you think of any other questions you want to ask me just tell Miss Dalton and she will let you come along and talk to me again.' She stood up. 'Now, where are you supposed to be?'

'Arithmetic.' Elena slid from the chair. 'We're doing subtraction. I call it "taking away" and I can do it.'

'I'm pleased to hear it.'

'Two hundred and twenty-six take away sixteen . . . is two hundred and ten!'

'Excellent.'

The headmistress went to the door, opened it and rang a small bell. Moments later Frederica appeared and Elena, still clutching the toffee, was escorted back to the classroom, her thoughts whirling.

Nearly six weeks passed. Life at Downsview was very different. Oscar was at home, recovering slowly, but not yet back at work. Elena was still at school, and Cook and Millie, unsure about the future of the Fairfax family, were more subdued than usual. One afternoon Winifred went up to Oscar's room with her mind made up. Her head throbbed and her whole body ached with the tension she always felt when approaching a possible confrontation. Today she was going to tackle the problem head-on, she told herself, as she reached the top of the stairs and made her way along the landing. Oscar wouldn't be pleased, but she thought she would scream if they didn't face facts. Time was passing and there seemed to be no progress.

'Where we sleep matters to me even if it doesn't matter to you!' she muttered, rehearsing the lines of her coming argument. Determined she went into his bedroom and without giving him time to put down his newspaper she said, 'I think we should sleep together, Oscar, now that Hermione has moved out. She is not going to be—'

'Moved out?' He moved the paper so that he could look at her. 'That's the first I've heard of it.'

His tone seemed slightly truculent to Winifred – the way he always was when she needed to discuss something important.

He had returned to bed as usual after a morning downstairs and a light lunch. She waited until he had folded the paper and laid it aside with just a hint of impatience.

'She's moved in with the Hattons, Oscar. You know she has. You just won't admit it. She's happier with them. It's understandable. Why should she stay here where nobody loves her?'

'Because she's still my wife and she has no right to leave me without a word. I understood that she had gone to stay with them for a week since she and Mrs Hatton seem to be such good friends.'

'But you must have guessed that this was the thin end of the wedge.'

'It was supposed to be a short stay.'

'Well, it doesn't look that way, Oscar, and I don't understand why it troubles you. Don't you enjoy being alone with me for the first time ever? Aren't we allowed to enjoy her absence? This way you and I can be together. Isn't that worth something?' Still standing beside the bed, she realized she was clasping her hands together – a clear sign of anxiety – and made an effort to relax.

Oscar sighed heavily. 'You know very well that there is only one double bed and that is the one I share with Hermione.'

'For heaven's sake, Oscar! You haven't slept in that bed with her for years. She slept alone in it and you slept here. For the moment Hermione sleeps at the Hattons. She may well be sleeping with Douglas Hatton for all we know! I don't see why you and I – after all those years of . . . of repressing our feelings—'

'Please, Winifred! Can't you see this is not the time or the place for these wild imaginings? You can't pretend we are a normal couple – not until—'

'There's no way I could suggest that!' she cried bitterly. 'We are a most abnormal couple and have been for years except that we were never a couple at all! And even now I wonder what exactly I am supposed to be doing here. The Hattons are caring for Hermione and James, Elena is at boarding school and you and I rattle around with only Cook and Millie for company.'

'You have me, for God's sake!'

'You?' Desperation made her throw caution to the winds. 'All you think about, Oscar, are your two shops and I am your errand girl, running backwards and forwards to keep an eye on them for you!' She turned her back on him, unwilling to let him see the tears welling in her eyes.

He said, 'But you know I love you.'

'That's just it, Oscar, I don't. I need some reassurance.'

Oscar frowned. 'How could I cope without you, Win? I depend on you, don't I? You oversee the housekeeping and . . . and walk the dog.'

She spun on her heel to face him. 'I am not employed

as your housekeeper nor am I a dog walker.' She swallowed
back her frustration and tried to speak in a reasonable tone.
'I was here to help with Hermione when Edward died and
then I came back to be with my daughter – and now I am
nothing.' She put a hand to her heart and tried to calm
herself. 'I'm not exactly happy, Oscar. I thought you might
have noticed. You would if you cared for me at all!'

Turning from him, her throat tight, she crossed to the
windows and stared out into the garden. The sun still shone
but the garden was sodden from the very recent rain and
the rainbow looked thin and dispirited.

After a long pause he said, 'I know what is troubling you,
Win. It's the divorce. You're right. We must make a move
on it. I'll send for John Granger and we'll start proceedings.
Will that help?' Suddenly he reached out for her. 'Win.
Come here. Tell me that if I start the proceedings you will
feel happier – and in the holidays Elena will be home with
us for three weeks and—'

'Only for two weeks.' Feeling slightly relieved by his change
of attitude, she crossed back to the bed. 'The Hattons have
invited Elena to spend a week with them, so she can still
see James. Her honorary brother!' She smiled. 'I told you,
but I don't think you were listening. But, yes, do send for
a decent solicitor, somebody you trust. A divorce might help
us. It might even save us. If this situation goes on any longer
I don't think there will be anything left of us to save!'

For a moment he stared at her and then his expression
changed. It was as though light was suddenly dawning.

'What is it?' she demanded shakily.

Oscar pointed to the wardrobe. 'Bottom drawer, left-hand
corner!'

Puzzled, she obeyed and found a large box of chocolates.
It had a picture of overblown roses on the lid and was tied
with curling red ribbons. 'Oh, Oscar!' she gasped. 'You did
remember!'

'Happy Valentine's Day, Win,' he said with feeling. 'I asked
Cook to buy them for me last week, but then I forgot it
was today. I didn't like to ask her to choose a card. Winifred
Franks, will you be my valentine?'

'Of course I will!'

'So am I forgiven for being such a churlish devil? If you promise to go on loving me, I'll promise to be extra thoughtful and considerate!'

By way of an answer Winifred tossed the box on to the bed and threw her arms round his neck. 'Thank you, thank you, Oscar.'

Kissing him hard she felt her despair fade. For so many years she had watched Hermione Fairfax receive the flowers from Oscar on Valentine's Day, because chocolates gave her a sick headache. Naturally he had never sent anything to Winifred but this year she had hoped it would be different. Hermione had absented herself, and Winifred had prayed that Oscar would remember the date. Foolish of her to care, she knew, but she had cared.

And he had remembered. A bright smile lit her face and she drew in a long breath. Oscar had remembered. He still loved her. She would take it as a long awaited sign that, despite the many setbacks, everything was going to be fine.

By the middle of June the divorce proceedings had been started by a man by the name of Joshua Ollins who had plenty of experience with such cases.

Winifred, with time on her hands, still spent a lot of her day with Oscar in connection with his shops and was surprised to find that she had something of a flair for business. Oscar was up and about but could only put in half a day's work and Winifred frequently found herself dealing with problems in either Rye or Hawkhurst, and on some occasions she stood in when one of the staff absented themselves for health reasons or family difficulties. Baby James and Hermione had not so far returned from the Hattons and neither Oscar nor Winifred made any further complaint about this state of affairs. Although Winifred missed the baby she was relieved to be free of Hermione's presence and was, in many ways, happier than she had been for years.

Elena, in the middle of her second term at the Leighton School for Girls, was making steady progress and was now best friends with a girl named Charlotte – a dumpy, cheerful child with ginger hair that reminded Elena of James's hair. Charlotte lived mostly with her grandparents while both her parents worked as medical staff on a mission station described by Charlotte as being 'in the wilds of Africa'.

On Friday the sixteenth, when the post was handed out, Elena received a letter from Mrs Hatton which she had promised to share with Charlotte. That same evening, after tea, both girls were sitting towards the rear of the room where the children in their class were engrossed with the prep which had been set for them by the geography teacher and were being supervised by Miss Bridger who was marking a pile of exercise books.

The girls' geography homework consisted of tracing a simplified map of England from the geography textbooks, colouring it brown or green (depending on the position of low and high ground), shading in the blue sea and writing in all the names of the major rivers. Elena had finished, having added a few fish and a starfish to the wiggly lines that represented waves. She had also included an odd–looking cow which appeared to be grazing somewhere between Kent and Sussex. Charlotte's map, also nearing completion, was similar but without the adornments.

Leaning towards Charlotte, Elena drew Mrs Hatton's letter from her pocket and handed it to her. While Elena stared innocently in the teacher's direction, Charlotte held the letter in her lap and struggled to decipher Mrs Hatton's hand-writing – an elaborate script on expensive notepaper.

> Dear Elena,
>
>     James says thank you for your last picture. I have given it to him and he waves it about a lot and says, 'Goo!' I think he means 'Good'.
>
>     We enjoyed your visit and missed you very much when you left. Hermione missed you, too, and is making you a lovely rag doll with yellow wool hair and a big smile. You will have to think of a name for her . . .

Charlotte leaned across towards Elena and told her, 'I had a rag doll once, but Grandma's dog chewed it up!'

Elena put a hand over her mouth to cover her giggles. Charlotte read on.

> James's father is very happy because Hermione is much better now, thank goodness. Be a good girl at school. We all send our love.
> Auntie Marion
> XXXXX

Enviously Charlotte folded and returned the letter. 'Who is Auntie Marion?' she whispered, eyeing the teacher warily.

'She's James's grandmother, but she says I can call her auntie and her husband is Uncle Ivor. They're both very old.'

'Old enough to die?' Charlotte's blue eyes widened.

'No, silly! Not that old. And look. You see there? Five kisses. One from each of them. Uncle Ivor, Auntie Marion, Mama – I mean Hermione – Mr Hatton and my honorary brother, James.' She gave her friend a triumphant look.

Charlotte said wistfully, 'I wish I had a family like that.'

'They're not my real family. My real—'

The teacher glanced their way. 'Are you talking, Elena?' she asked crisply.

'No, Miss Bridger.' She tried to sound indignant.

'Have you finished your prep?'

'Yes, Miss Bridger.'

'Bring it here, please, Elena.'

Stuffing the letter back into the pocket of her drill-slip, Elena carried over the homework.

Miss Bridger considered the map while Elena held her breath. Would she be made to do it again? She now regretted the fish, the cow and the starfish, but it was too late to undo them.

'Are you supposed to add these creatures?' Miss Bridger asked.

'I don't know, Miss Bridger. I think so.'

'Let us hope so, Elena!' She glanced at the small watch which hung on a chain round her neck, and referred to a list of names on the desk beside her. 'I see you have a piano lesson now, Elena?'

'No, Miss Bridger, it's tomorrow. It's been changed because Mrs Cartwright has to take her cat to the vet.'

'Her cat?'

'Natalie says it has to have an operation.'

Miss Bridger looked confused. 'What has this to do with Natalie?'

'Because Natalie had her piano lesson yesterday and the cat was in a cat basket with Mrs Cartwright because she was worried about it and she said to Natalie to tell me my lesson is changed and . . .'

'Yes. Thank you, Elena. I understand now. That will do.'

'Natalie says it's called Tabitha because it's a tabby cat so—'

'That's quite enough about Natalie.'

Charlotte's hand shot up.

'Yes, Charlotte?'

'Please Miss Bridger, I've finished too.'

'Then bring it over, please.'

Minutes later the two girls had been released from prep and were skipping gleefully in the direction of the common room where they were free to amuse themselves for twenty-five minutes until seven thirty. Then the bell would be rung signalling bedtime and the girls would troop off to their respective dormitories.

*Early to bed and early to rise, makes a man healthy, wealthy and wise.* The well-known saying, slightly adapted, might easily have been written specifically for the pupils of the Leighton School for Girls.

# Twelve

James, nearly eighteen, still bore a marked resemblance to his father with bright sandy hair, an abundance of freckles and the same bright blue eyes. Aware of the family traumas surrounding his birth, he found it interesting but of little real importance and had grown up surrounded by love and security. He was sturdy, an only child, but his outgoing nature made him popular.

As soon as he opened his eyes he remembered it was Monday and a special day and leaped out of bed. Elena was coming to spend a week with them and the family had been looking forward to the visit.

'But we must be tactful,' his grandmother was saying after he rushed into the big farmhouse and joined his grandparents for breakfast. Still in delicate health, his mother had opted for a breakfast tray and would be down later.

As soon as the divorce had been finalized Douglas and Hermione had married and the entire Hatton family had moved to the small town of Ottery St Mary, in south Devon. Failing to find a suitable partnership as a solicitor, Douglas had found work on a neighbouring estate and discovered that he had a talent for the day-to-day work of farm management, particularly the legal side. Now he had worked his way up to a senior managerial position.

Ivor, now as thin as a reed with thin grey wisps of hair, regarded his wife over his boiled egg with toasted soldiers. 'Of course we'll be tactful, Marion.'

'Poor Elena has had a very unhappy few months,' Marion reminded them, while she filled her grandson's teacup and topped up her own. 'I know what you men are like,' she went on earnestly. 'You don't understand love and you certainly don't understand women!'

James rolled his eyes. 'She's only been jilted, Mother! It's not the end of the world.'

'There!' exclaimed Marion. 'That's what I mean. You don't understand and I don't want you to say anything that might upset her.'

James refused to be impressed. 'Women get jilted all the time! Men get jilted too. What's so important about being jilted? At least she wasn't standing at the altar in her wedding dress. I'm glad for her sake. '

He reached for the marmalade, but Marion automatically slapped his hand. 'Ask, James. Don't reach!' She sighed but handed him the jar.

Ivor said, 'I don't know why she thought so much of that man. Max whatever-his-name was. I didn't care for him. Rather an inflated opinion of himself. That's how I saw it. Mind you, we only met him once. I wish we saw her more often. She's becoming a bit of a stranger.'

'Of course she's not a stranger, Grandfather. She never will be.'

Marion said, 'Elena has her own life to lead and she obviously spent most of her spare time with her young man. It's not as if she's deserted us.'

'He wasn't good enough for her,' James declared. 'Not much to choose between him and the previous one. If you ask me, he's done her a favour by breaking off the engagement. Mother said he was too big for his boots.'

Marion nodded. 'I admit none of us took to him but it was a fleeting visit. The point is that Elena cared for him and him going off like that must have hurt her pride.'

Ivor stabbed the empty eggshell. 'Dented her confidence, I expect.'

They both stared at him in astonishment.

'Grandfather! You've been reading mother's magazines again!' James said, laughing.

Ivor tapped the side of his nose. 'I know what I know,' he told them. 'I know more about women than you think. I've been married for donkey's years to your grandmother and that's been quite an experience!' He winked at James, who grinned.

'Only because I put up with all your silly notions!' she replied good-humouredly, inclined to take her husband's remark as a compliment. 'Anyway, don't go saying to Elena that he was no good. Just let her tell it her way – if she decides to tell us anything. She's not a child any more.'

'She'll tell me,' James declared. 'She always did in the old days.'

'Confided in you?' Marion exclaimed. 'What do you know about love or affairs of the heart? You haven't even bothered to find yourself a girlfriend!' She cut three more slices of bread from the loaf.

'I don't need one. I'm going to marry Elena.'

Ivor said, 'She'll be wed long before you are old enough to marry anyone.'

He grinned. 'Doesn't look much like it at the moment!'

'You wait,' said Marion. 'Elena will find the right man eventually and she'll make the lucky man a splendid wife.' To James she said, 'Pop upstairs, will you, and see if your mother wants anything else?'

While he was gone she said, 'I did think, dear, that we might have invited Oscar and Winifred, but . . .' She looked at him for reassurance.

'Very wise not to, Marion, in my opinion,' he said, shaking his head. 'We tried it once and it wasn't a success. We did our best, but we know better now. Oil and water, as they say. Too many old wounds. Better as it is, in my opinion.'

Marion nodded reluctantly, agreeing in principle, but always wanting everybody to be happy though knowing that they never could be. It wasn't that kind of world. To cheer herself up she ran over in her mind the food she had planned for their regular summer picnic. This year it had been arranged as a surprise for Elena's visit.

Every year Marion determined to vary the menu and scoured the recipe books, but each year she reverted to the old favourites and this year was no exception. She had made a large apple cake the previous day, also the individual potted crabmeats which Ivor insisted upon. In his opinion no picnic was complete without them. As soon as breakfast was over she would set to in the kitchen to pop a chicken into oven, and make a large cheese and tomato pasty. Hermione would put a salad together, prepare the fruit salad and wrap the cheeses in greaseproof paper.

Douglas would come home at midday because it was Saturday and they would set off for the river around one thirty.

James came back with his mother's tray. 'Mother's getting up. She seems very cheerful today.'

Marion said, 'Be grateful for small mercies, James. Hermione will always have her good and bad days and will be depressed sometimes – that's the nature of the illness – but she is so much better than she was when your father first met her. Even the doctor has commented on it. Having you and marrying Douglas were the best things that ever happened to her.'

James leaned against the sink. 'I don't know why Elena is in such a hurry to get married. She's only twenty-six.'

'That's not too young if you want to start a family.'

'Perhaps she doesn't.' He grinned at her. 'She grew up in a very odd family. Maybe it's put her off the idea.'

'Really, James! What a thing to say!'

Ivor wandered from the kitchen into the garden for his daily inspection of his small vegetable garden which had slowly become almost a passion, much to Marion's delight.

'She thinks families are tricky.'

'Well, hers certainly was. I always thought it was badly handled – all those revelations at such a tender age, and letting the headmistress break the news. I know Winifred claims that Elena took it very well but children are good at hiding their feelings. Even after all these years it's probably left her feeling a bit wary, poor girl.'

'I don't think she trusts men – or else she doesn't trust her own judgement – or else she knows from her family just how easy it is to get it all wrong.'

Marion raised her eyes humorously as she filled the

sink with the breakfast dishes. 'And you're the expert, are you?'

'I proposed to her once when I was about twelve and she didn't laugh. She said she didn't know if she could wait until I grew up.' Changing the subject, he asked, 'Could I meet her at the station? I could cycle down and take your bike for Elena. You hate me being around when you're cooking anyway. I'd be out of your way.'

'She sometimes gets a taxi, but, yes, meet her if you like. Her train's due in at ten past eleven – but first get the hamper down, please, from the attic.'

'No sooner said than done.' James pushed himself away from the sink and headed for the passage. He met his mother coming down and dodged as she tried to ruffle his hair. He could tell she had made an effort to look good for Elena and was pleased that over time the tensions between her and Elena had given way to a guarded affection.

Hermione said, 'Picnic day! And perfect weather. I hope Elena's remembered her bathing suit. It will be just right for a swim.'

Elena glanced out of the train window as it slowed down. Filled with mixed emotions she had felt nervous about the visit and wondered if Hermione was also feeling doubtful. Over the years her erstwhile 'Mama' had written to her from time to time, but it was the Hattons who had tried hardest to keep the friendship alive – prompted no doubt by James.

'Hawkhurst!' yelled the stationmaster who stood, hands on his hips, watching the train's arrival.

Elena could hardly believe it was already August – it had been such an unsettling year. The threat of war hung over them as Hitler's power grew and Europe trembled. If the worst happened and England declared war, James and thousands of young men like him would soon rush to join up. They would be catapulted into a dangerous new life. Some of them would die. The thought preyed on her mind but she tried to forget it. It seemed ages since she had seen them and if war came and the worst happened, she might never see James again.

As the train ground to a halt with much clanking and squealing of brakes, the porter hurried towards the engine and the luggage van, and began unloading various baskets and packages on to the waiting trolley.

Catching sight of James, Elena smoothed her dark hair and smiled broadly as she swung open the carriage door and stepped down, almost into James' arms as he rushed to assist her.

'Elena!' He beamed at her, his admiration written large on his familiar freckled face.

Knowing that he loved her lifted her spirits. 'James! Looking more handsome than ever!'

They hugged fiercely then he jumped up into the carriage and retrieved her small suitcase from the overhead rack. She could have done it herself but he liked to look after her.

The porter passed them with his trolley and turned back. 'Is that you, Miss Fairfax?'

'It is. Good to see you again,' she told him, trying and failing to remember his name.

'Always a sight for sore eyes, miss.'

'Thank you.'

'I might not be here next time you come. Might be on the high seas. I'm planning to enlist if they need me. My father was in the navy. Very exciting it was, according to him.' He touched his cap and moved on with his trolley.

James wanted her all to himself and slipped an arm through hers. 'I brought the bikes, but now I wish I hadn't. We'll be home sooner.'

'We can push them, can't we? I've hardly any luggage.'

They collected the bicycles and, with her small suitcase precariously strapped on the seat of James's machine, they began the walk back to the farmhouse. Elena braced herself for his questions. Aunt Marion, she knew, would be very tactful and would wait until the time was right to enquire gently how she was feeling about the broken engagement. Uncle Ivor would look embarrassed but say nothing and Hermione would simply clasp her hands and whisper something sympathetic.

When her previous romance had ended in tears, Hermione had said gently, 'Better luck next time, Elena.' But it hadn't happened that way for Elena. This was next time and the results had been the same. James would come right out with his questions.

Proving her wrong, he said, 'I had a bet on Riggs to beat Cooke – Wimbledon finals. Won ten pounds!'

'Wonderful! How are you going to spend it?'

'I haven't thought about that yet . . . If there's a war and I go abroad, Elena, will you promise to write to me?'

'Try and stop me, James!'

She was surprised by the change in him. He was no longer a boy, not quite a man, but she could see how he would be in a few years' time. Bright, eager, confident and so good looking. The women would flock round him.

'How's the teaching going?' he asked.

'Good days and bad days. Mostly good, I suppose. How's Hermione?'

'Up and down but more up than down.' He stopped the bicycle and turned to study her face. Then he said, 'I didn't think you would ever become a teacher.'

He made it sound as if she had made a mistake. Perhaps she had disappointed him. The idea dismayed her. Defensively she said, 'What else do I know? I've practically spent my whole life at school, one way or another. It seemed the best option at the time.'

'It was my fault, wasn't it? They sent you away because I was born. '

'Not exactly. It certainly wasn't your fault, James. The family was in such a muddle. I think they needed to get the worst over without upsetting me. They meant well and I was happy at Leighton's. They wanted me to go back to Downsview after my training and find a local school and I was tempted but then I thought – why not go back to Leighton's and be independent? They wanted me.'

James allowed the subject to drop. Instead he asked, 'I notice you call Mother Hermione now.'

'She asked me to. She felt it made a clean break.' She shrugged. 'I call my real mother Nan because she thinks it sounds cosier and less formal than Mother and a little like Nanny. It was my choice!' She laughed at the memory.

James stopped to talk to Mr Jennings who was cutting roses in his front garden and the old man smiled at Elena. 'We should see you more often,' he told her.

'Thank you. I do love it here, tucked away in the countryside.'

'You noticed the butcher's shop has changed hands, I expect. Poor old boy died in his sleep a month ago. Tut!' He shook his head at the pity of it all. 'Still, his eldest boy's taken it over. Given it a lick of paint and started selling pies and pasties as well as fresh meat. Very good they are too.'

Somehow this interruption gave James the chance he was looking for. As they continued he said, 'I don't know why you thought Max was right for you, Elena.' He was anxious to talk to her properly before they reached home. 'I could have told you he didn't understand you. I'm glad for your sake that . . . that he . . . that you decided . . .'

'You did tell me at the time,' she reminded him with a half smile. 'I should have listened to you, shouldn't I?'

'Well, you found out in time.'

'No, James, Max found out in time that he'd made a mistake. He gave up on me. I'm not going to pretend it was the other way round.'

Concentrating on their conversation, their steering went awry and the bicycles' front wheels clashed and dislodged the suitcase, which had to be tied on again.

As they continued the walk he said, 'Well, you decided to end the first romance.'

'Only because he was married!' She gave him an enquiring look because that was the first anyone knew of the true reason for that particular fiasco.

James's eyes widened. 'Married? You've never said that before. You said—'

'I lied, James. I didn't want anyone to know what a fool I'd been. I could have ended up like my own real mother! Robert was a wonderful man, but he had a wife and two children and when I found out it broke my heart.'

'If he lied to you, Elena, then he wasn't a wonderful man.'

His eyes narrowed. 'He was a rat of the first order! A dyed-in-the-wool rat! As rats go, he was King Rat! Am I getting across to you?'

Elena sighed. 'Loud and clear.'

James nudged her with his elbow. 'To hell with all of them!'

She nodded. Why was it, she wondered, that it was taking her so long to find the right man? It wasn't as though she were suspicious of men. If anything she was too trusting.

After a long silence she said, 'Well, let's talk about you. I suppose by now you've found yourself a girlfriend.'

'Can't be bothered!' He shrugged. 'They're all too young and silly. They giggle and simper.'

They turned the last corner and the farmhouse came into sight.

He said, 'There's a big cook-up going on. All the usual. Did you bring your swimsuit?'

'No, but I left one here last time I came and I'm still the same size. It must be somewhere. How are your grandparents?'

'Fine at the moment but about six months ago they were worrying about Mother and that affected them. I was away at school, of course, but Mother didn't write and that's always a bad sign.'

Elena gave him a quick glance and found herself wondering how she would think of him if she had just met him for the first time . . . or if she were to meet him for the first time when he was twenty-one. He would be a grown man then. She wondered, frowning, if the war would be over by the time he celebrated his twenty-first birthday.

He said, 'Mother was upset for you, about Max. She said she knows what that's like! Being rejected. She felt for you.'

'Poor Hermione.'

As if he had been reading her mind, James said, 'In just over three years I'll be twenty-one!'

'Meaning?' She grinned.

'Meaning don't be in too big a hurry to let anyone else break your heart.'

'James, you have a very one-track mind.'

'I keep telling you – I like older women!'

They had reached the big gate and Elena held both bicycles while James unlatched the gate and swung it open. Marion spotted them from the window and came rushing out to greet them.

James winked at Elena and whispered, 'Think about it!'

By five o'clock the picnic was drawing to a close. The potted shrimps were no more, and all that remained of the tomato and cheese pasty were a few crumbs which Ivor inadvertently scattered over Elena and James as he shook the tablecloth and began to fold it. The two young people, still in their wet swimwear, were wrapped in towels, debating whether or not to have a last swim before going home.

Marion said, 'You two come home when you like. It's old fogies like us who have a longing to sit in a comfortable armchair and drink a civilized cup of tea!'

Hermione raised her eyebrows. 'So now I'm an old fogey! Thank you for that!'

James grinned. 'You could be a young fogey, Mother.'

'I'll pretend I didn't hear that!'

Hermione held out her hands to Ivor who obligingly helped her to her feet. She hadn't swum but she had caught the sun and her rosy face made her look much younger than she was. 'Actually an armchair does sound tempting,' she admitted, brushing grass from her skirt.

Marion asked, 'Shall I leave the rest of the apple cake?'

Elena said, 'I'm full up.'

'Ditto,' James agreed. 'I've eaten too much as usual. I shall probably sink if I go in the water again!'

Elena threw off the towel and helped with the packing of the picnic hamper and five minutes later she and James watched the older folk wind their way back towards the road.

Around them the afternoon was coming to an end with a slight breeze which ruffled the wild mint that grew along the water's edge. The River Otter was no deeper than five or six feet with a smooth pebbled river bed. There was very little weed and what there was grew in well-known places and could easily be avoided. Further downstream three young children splashed around while their mother kept a close eye on them.

James lay back and gazed lazily up at the sky. 'How many more times do you think we shall be here like this?' he asked.

Sitting beside him, she said, 'Plenty, I hope.'

'You'll meet someone and that will be it. All over.'

'He could come here too.'

'No. I wouldn't want that. It wouldn't be the same, would it?'

'James! Stop this. You mustn't be so possessive. I shan't be unreasonable about your girlfriends.'

He regarded her helplessly. 'You think you won't but how will you feel when you see me totally lovesick with my arm round a flighty young girl? I'm sure you'll hate it.'

'Of course I won't.' But would she? Suddenly she wasn't sure. She said quickly, 'I shall think I hope she makes him happy.'

'And if she doesn't?'

'I might have to push her in the river.' She looked down at him. 'Just because we're close friends it doesn't mean we can't share each other with other people.' It sounded rather trite, she thought uncertainly.

'Maybe I think it does mean that. Someone like that would come between us and nothing would ever be the same again.' He sat up and his freckled face was suddenly serious. 'Elena, would you marry me if I were older? And please don't say anything funny because I'm not in the mood.'

Elena's heart sank as she struggled to give him a fair and honest reply. She had known him as a friend for so long . . . He was staring at her intently, waiting for her answer.

'The honest answer is possibly,' she told him. 'Difficult to predict. Look at it another way. If, in say six years' time, we met up again and I am in my thirties by then, would you fall in love with me?'

'Probably. Very probably. Almost certainly! Maybe we'd better wait and see. We need a pact – one which ensures that I stay away from silly young women and you refrain from meeting any other men.'

'Right now that last bit sounds very appealing!' She hoped she didn't sound bitter. She didn't understand why her relationships with men were so unsuccessful. Was it her fault in some way? Was she expecting too much? Was she being influenced by her father's example so that she lacked trust? Was she always holding back, afraid of total commitment? It concerned her that possibly, deep down, she had no faith in the concept of true love.

'Is that a promise then?' James eyed her eagerly.

'I promise not to go actively searching for the perfect man!' She tried to speak lightly. 'How's that?'

He thought about it, his head down, not meeting her eyes. 'Better than nothing,' he mumbled. Looking up again, he said earnestly, 'Just bear this in mind, Elena – that if you get married before I'm old enough to ask you, I shall never forgive you! How's that?'

'Oh dear!'

'What is it?'

'You might one day discover that I have plenty of faults and am not your perfect woman.'

He moved forward and kissed her bare shoulder and she was shocked by her sudden longing for even greater closeness.

James smiled brilliantly. 'Let me worry about that!' he said and they stared at each other, unsure quite what, if anything, was happening.

Impulsively Elena leaned forward and kissed his cheek. 'Sealed with a loving kiss!'

She shivered and reached for her clothes and the moment passed.

It was fortunate for their peace of mind that neither could know that a few weeks later England would be at war with Germany or that the conflict would rumble on for six years bringing death and destruction throughout large areas of the world. Elena and James could not have begun to imagine what this would mean to millions of people – including them. Life would never be the same again – and neither would they.

# Thirteen

Snow fell for the fifth day, covering the grounds of the Leighton School for Girls with a crisp white blanket, decorating the trees and outlining the window sills and the tops of the doors. War had come just weeks after that carefree picnic, and James, headstrong as ever, had enlisted that autumn, eager to experience the thrills of warfare before it ended. Douglas had been conscripted in 1941, but mercifully both had returned unscathed physically, though James was, according to Marion, deeply affected by his experiences.

For Elena, the war years had dragged on interminably but although she feared desperately for both James and Douglas, she herself felt remote from it in many ways. Life at the school continued with few real changes. There were drills to be learned in case of air raids and there was a serious change in the quality of the school meals because of the food shortages. The pupils became a little shabbier as clothing coupons were issued, and prayers for the children's scattered families were part of every morning assembly.

The daily routine of teaching remained largely unchanged, however, and Elena felt comparatively safe, almost cocooned from danger, and fortunate not to be called up. She had flirted briefly with the idea of joining the Women's Auxiliary Air Force, but Marion had talked her out of the idea, suggesting that, as a skilled professional, she was of more value to the country caring for and educating the next generation.

The classes at the school had always been suitably small so that each girl could be given the attention she needed. Thus, on this day in 1946, only a few months after the war had ended, Elena had sixteen children seated before her. They sat with their geography textbooks open, their exercise books and pencils ready. Elena's main subject was geography, but she also gave piano lessons.

'Good morning, girls.'

'Good morning, Miss Fairfax.'

'I want you to turn to page thirty-two and study what you see – and without talking.'

Pages rustled and whispers were hidden behind hands as the children turned the pages and discovered a picture of two Dutch children – a boy and a girl, each in their national costume and wearing clogs.

Elena glanced round the room, checking on the pupils. This merited extra attention for whatever reason. Connie Silverton, who was slow and needed constant help to keep up with the rest of the class; Bethany Evans, in the front row because her eyesight was so poor that she could not read from the blackboard if she sat anywhere else; Madge Sturton, a surviving twin, so bright she could have been in the next class except for the fact that she was immature for her nine years and timid. And last but not least Amy Wendropp, brash, excitable and unpredictable. On the whole a decent class, but then most of them were well behaved because the school was known for its firm but kindly discipline and its tightly structured timetables. Elena knew from personal experience how valuable the school could prove to the many children who came from disrupted families as well as those who did not.

As expected, it was Amy whose hand went up. 'Please, Miss Fairfax, you said we could do the volcano. You said we could do Vesuvius.'

A chorus of voices joined her.

'You did, miss!'

'You said—'

'That will do, girls! I said we would learn about volcanoes when we studied Italy later in the term.' She ignored the mutters of disappointment and, smiling, continued. 'When we come back after half-term we'll be studying Italy, but in the meantime you can go into library after prep and look in the encyclopedias if you are desperate for information about volcanoes.'

Feeling cheated, the girls exchanged rueful looks.

Elena asked them, 'What is today's date?'

'Please, Miss Fairfax, it's January the—'

'No! Miss, it's February and it's Thursday.'

'Thursday, February the seventh,' she told them, 'and please remember how to spell February. Which letter comes after the b?'

'R, Miss Fairfax!'

'Good. Look up when you've written it.'

At last the class was settled, heads were bent and pencils moved across paper, and Elena breathed a sigh of relief. She sat back in her chair and began to think about James. As promised she had written to him once a month throughout the war but not all the letters had reached him. She had done her best to write cheerfully and to keep from him some of the worst aspects of a Britain in wartime – the daily radio reports of military disasters abroad, the newspapers full of loss of life, harrowing accounts of the bombing of major cities and the grief of widows and motherless children.

At the start of the war, James's letters to her had been something to look forward to but over the months and years she had detected a change in his writing. The letters came infrequently and told her less and less of his daily life. She detected a mournful undertone which later became a worrying reluctance to talk about the hell around him.

It had finally dawned on Elena that the young man she had known and loved was changing into a morose and nervous man and the fear took hold within her that he might end up like his mother – a prey to depression. To prevent this she had recently written with excitement about their upcoming reunion and the good times that awaited them. Now that meeting was looming and in less than three weeks she would be a guest in their home and they would be together again.

Although she longed to see him, she was troubled by how he would react to her after so many years apart. She felt the ties that bound them more strongly now, but would he remember that last day by the river when so many things were left unsaid?

The industrious silence in the room was interrupted by a knock on the door and Judith Lotts, the headmistress's monitor, came into the room.

'Miss Stanford says could you spare a minute. You have a telegram.'

As Elena left the room, Judith took up her position in the front of the class and prepared to hold the fort until the teacher returned.

Miss Stanford had replaced Miss Randall after she retired from her position as headmistress some years earlier. She was small and wiry with great energy, but without the previous head's dignity and, because of her comparative youth, she had less of Miss Randall's acquired wisdom. She was well liked however and was generally considered a good choice.

Now she handed the yellow envelope to Elena. 'I do hope it's not bad news,' she said.

Elena opened the envelope with trembling fingers and read the folded sheet inside.

HERMIONE DIED LAST NIGHT STOP FUNERAL SATURDAY AT THREE STOP PLEASE TRY TO BE THERE STOP DOUGLAS

Miss Stanford read Elena's expression. 'Oh dear!' she said.

Shocked, Elena tore her gaze from the dreadful words. 'It's my . . . It's Hermione – she's dead.' Even as she spoke the words they had, she thought, the ring of untruth. Not Hermione. She was too young. Elena had expected Ivor, maybe, but not Hermione. Poor James. Poor Douglas. Yes, she must be at the funeral.

Miss Stanford said, 'I'm so sorry, Miss Fairfax.'

Dazed by the suddenness of the tragedy, Elena realized that the headmistress was still speaking to her and tried to concentrate on what she was saying.

'I'm suggesting you might need time off from your duties to attend the funeral.'

'It's on Saturday.' Elena stared down at the offending telegram, trying to imagine how Hermione had died.

Not by her own hand, she hoped desperately. Suicide left all the survivors racked with guilt.

'Then perhaps you could take Friday afternoon off, Miss Fairfax. Would that help? I'll see whom I can find to cover for you. I'm so sorry. The death of a loved one is always such a blow.'

Elena stared at her blankly as she tried to find a way out of the darkness that surrounded her. She searched for words that somehow eluded her.

Seeing the extent of her shock, the headmistress rose briskly to her feet. 'Go to the staffroom for half an hour and make yourself a cup of sweet tea,' she instructed. 'I shall take over from you in class until you return.'

Brushing aside Elena's thanks, Miss Stanford held the door open and Elena made her way to the staffroom where the games mistress was relaxing prior to netball practice. Hearing what had happened, she sat Elena down with the biscuit tin.

'Sugar to ward off shock!' she told her. 'I'll make you a cup of tea.'

She chattered on to fill the unhappy silence, but Elena heard none of her conversation. Obediently she munched a couple of garibaldi biscuits as her thoughts skittered to and fro as she tried to plan her journey down to Devon. She wondered about James and the effect it would have on him. Since his return from the war she had heard nothing from him. How would he cope with his mother's death?

The same day a telegram was delivered to Downsview and Winifred received it. She read it and tucked it behind the clock, deciding to wait for the right moment to show it to her husband. He would not appreciate a phone call at the shop.

Millie set the table with a bad grace, resentful of the fact that neither she nor Cook had been allowed to know the contents of the telegram. Millie was now a married woman who only spent a few hours a day at Downsview because she had a husband and son to care for, but they needed the extra money. Her husband, who had been a sapper in the army, had met and married her on one of his home leaves and had later suffered a wounded leg from shell splinters, leaving him with a severe and permanent limp which prevented him from earning what Millie called 'a decent living'. Before the war he had been a sprightly young chimney sweep and his own boss – now he was a lowly storeman in a local builders' firm.

She made her way back to the kitchen, still smarting under the injustice of Winifred's decision.

Cook glanced up as she entered and said, 'Do cheer up, Millie. We'll know all in good time. No use fretting.' She opened the oven door and studied the corned beef hash. 'Blasted rationing!' she muttered. 'Blasted corned beef! The war's been over more than a year and we still need ration books. When the day comes to get rid of them, I shall throw mine on to the nearest fire!'

'Now who's fretting?' cried Millie, mocking her. 'It'll come right, all in good time!'

'Very funny!' She closed the oven door with more noise than was necessary and glanced at the clock. 'Nearly five! Let's hope His Nibs doesn't decide to come home early.'

Without waiting to be asked, Millie lent a hand to pull her upright. Cook had put on a lot of weight during the past few years and was becoming rather breathless and irritable.

The telephone rang and two sets of eyes swivelled in the direction of the sound and waited silently when Winifred answered it.

'Yes, we heard. It's terribly sad. No, Oscar doesn't know yet. It seemed best to tell him in person when he . . . Yes, of course you can. We'd be delighted to see you. How long before you . . .? Half an hour? Right. I'll ask Cook to put on a few more vegetables. It's one of your favourites – corned beef hash . . . Right then. See you soon.'

Millie beamed. 'It must be Elena. She loves corned beef hash. Shall I do some extra spuds?'

Cook nodded. 'I'll open a tin of peas. But it sounded rather serious. Mrs Fairfax's voice, I mean. Bound to be bad news because she said, "It's terribly sad". That's what the telegram's about.'

Millie's excitement faded. 'You mean someone's died? Oh Lord!'

Ten minutes later Oscar arrived home from the shop looking none too happy. As he hung up his hat he said, 'That idiot, Freddie – the new chap – has completely messed up Mydern's order. They rang me to ask if there was a mistake as I don't normally order in such quantities and Freddie had . . . What is it? Oh God! Now what?' He took the proffered telegram and read it. 'Hermione! God! How did it happen?'

Winifred shrugged. 'That's all I know. I haven't been in touch because I thought they would ask if we were going to be there and I wouldn't know the answer.'

He was stuffing his gloves into his pockets and began to pull off his heavy overcoat. 'Before you ask – I shan't go. Not really appropriate, is it?'

Winifred frowned anxiously. 'Why not? You did nothing wrong. I mean, Hermione left you for Douglas.' She took the coat, hung it up and followed him into the sitting room.

'I did nothing wrong?' He shook his head at her logic. 'You've haven't forgotten what happened earlier? Me and you.'

'Oh!'

He warmed himself at the fire and she hovered anxiously nearby. 'Surely that's all in the past,' she said. 'I do think—'

'You go by all means. Does Elena know?'

'Yes. She rang. She's having a quick meal with us then taking a late train to London. I think she hoped we'd be going as well and we'd all travel down from London together. There's a train around nine which reaches Exeter and connects with a bus.'

'She should have gone straight to London from the school.'

'But this way we get to see her. That's a bonus.' Winifred sat down. 'What shall we say if you don't go?'

'Say I'm not well enough to make that long journey. Say I can't just leave the shops. Say anything. What does it matter?' He rubbed his eyes wearily and raked his fingers through his still thick hair which was now mostly grey.

Winifred said, 'Poor Hermione. She didn't have a very

happy life and I was partly to blame. I wonder if she ever forgave me.'

He threw himself into the opposite armchair. 'We've been through this before, Win. You were very young and you were available and I took advantage of you because my wife turned away from me because Edward died.'

'That doesn't change—'

He held up his hand and continued. 'Hermione's depression seemed as though it was never going to end and . . . I took what you had to offer. It was my fault, not yours, but it was also circumstances.' He sighed. 'And then Elena came along, just to complicate matters.'

'I wanted us to leave and take her with us.'

'It's history, Win.'

'I still feel wretched when I think of it.' She regarded him unhappily.

He regarded her tiredly. 'Hermione wanted a child by me and your baby was the next best thing. She wanted Elena. She felt that in a way you'd stolen what should have been hers. I understood, but I should have been stronger. You were right – we should have left . . .'

Winifred was aware of a terrible tightness in her throat. Remorse, regret, whatever it was it was almost choking her as it always did when she tried to confront the past.

Oscar said, 'I think if we had walked out . . .'

'I know. You thought she would kill herself.'

He nodded.

'But we fell in love, Oscar! We let it happen because we were so in love!' She stared at him wide-eyed. 'Weren't we? I loved you. I thought you loved me. I thought . . .'

He sat back, closing his eyes. 'I wanted you. I didn't love you – not at first – but over the years.' He opened his eyes. 'I finally realized it when Hermione left. Without her constant presence to remind me of how badly I'd behaved. Now I love you very much, Win. If I don't show you affection often enough I'm sorry, but . . .' He held out his hand. 'Come here, darling.'

Winifred's expression changed. She jumped from the chair, ran to him and, kneeling, threw her arms round him.

She pressed her face against his chest, comforted as always by the sound of his heartbeat.

'As long as you love me, Oscar, I can bear anything.'

He stroked her hair gently. 'Can we finally put the past behind us, Win? I know you wanted another child once we were married, but –' he shrugged – 'it hasn't happened, and we have Elena and each other.'

The front doorbell rang and they heard Millie hurry to open it.

'You can go to the funeral with Elena if you wish,' Oscar said.

She shook her head. 'It is not really appropriate. I shan't go without you, Oscar. You're probably right.'

'Well, that's settled.' He heaved himself up from the chair and he slipped an arm round her waist. Together they went out to greet their daughter.

Despite the efforts of two pot-bellied stoves, the church in Ottery St Mary was very cold and the service unusually short. Outside the snow fell lightly as they huddled round the grave, watched by an unhappy gravedigger who muttered to himself and blew on his mittened hands to warm them. Elena had only just arrived in time to slip in at the back of the church and take up a position behind the other mourners. James and Douglas were in the front row and Ivor and Marion sat behind them. There were no choristers and the small congregation sang thinly to the organist's well-intentioned rendering of 'Abide with Me'.

Elena saw James turn and cast an anxious glance behind him, checking the congregation. She waved her hand until the movement caught his eye and he smiled briefly in return. So, she thought, reassured, he had wanted to make sure she was present.

'And now let us kneel and pray.' The vicar clasped his hands and Elena knelt, but she peeped through her fingers to look at Hermione's coffin which was topped by a wreath of flowers, presumably from the family. White roses and pink carnations. Very feminine, she thought, guessing that they had been Marion's choice.

At a point in the service, the vicar signalled to James and he walked slowly to the front of the church and turned to face the mourners.

Unfolding a sheet of paper he read aloud in a voice that trembled. 'My mother, Hermione, was a very loving mother and wife, and Father and I will miss her dreadfully. We've been a very happy family and my mother would want me to acknowledge the debt we owe to my grandparents, Marion and Ivor. They've helped us through the difficult times and shared the good times and Mother loved them both very much. She also loved Elena. We shall all remember Mother and nothing will ever be quite the same without her.' His voice broke suddenly and he crushed the paper and blindly returned to his seat.

Seeing his grief, Marion went forward and put an arm round his shoulders to guide him back to the family.

Elena was also weeping unashamedly and fumbled in her pocket for a handkerchief.

The vicar then spoke and they sang another hymn before the coffin was carried outside and they gathered round while it was lowered into the ground.

When they had finally laid Hermione to rest and filed slowly out of the churchyard, the silence was broken only by the sound of the gravedigger throwing in the first of many frozen scatterings of earth. Douglas walked with his arm round his son's shoulders and Elena walked with Marion and Ivor. The latter was bundled up in stout boots, a thick overcoat, gloves, scarf and trilby hat, but Elena could see by his red nose and cheeks just how cold he was.

'I know, dear,' Marion told her in a troubled whisper. 'We all wanted him to stay at home, but he refused. A drop of brandy in his tea, that's what he'll get when we reach home. In fact I think we'll all need that particular remedy.'

It was the first time Elena had seen the farm white with snow and in spite of the cold she acknowledged how beautiful and serene it looked. She barely had time to consider it before they all tumbled through the doorway and into the big kitchen where they took off their coats and hats. Shooed through from there into what Marion called her front room, they found a glowing fire and were soon settling gratefully into the cheery warmth. As people relaxed with Marion's 'remedy', the chatter started, muted at first but gathering in confidence. A woman from the village had come along to help Marion serve the meal in the dining room and while last-minute preparations went ahead for this, Elena went in search of James.

She found him in his bedroom, standing at the window, staring out across the white landscape.

Elena said, 'James, it's me, Elena.' For a moment neither spoke.

'Elena!' he murmured. Without turning, he said, 'Mother loved the snow. She was such a baby at times. We always made a snowman and . . .' His voice wavered. 'I was about nine, I suppose, and Grandmother said it was too cold to go outside but Mother just laughed and bundled us both up. We made an enormous snowman and we persuaded Grandfather to take a snap of us on his new Brownie camera – Mother on one side and me the other. It's in one of the albums.' He turned to face her.

He looked haggard and somehow diminished by sorrow. His black suit contrasted with his still-bright gingery hair, but his blue eyes were dulled and his expression bleak. Elena held out her arms and he stumbled into them with a strangled sob. They clung together for a long time while his body shook with grief. When at last they drew apart he sat on the edge of his bed and Elena sank into a nearby chair.

'What happened?' she asked. 'To Hermione, I mean. This is all so dreadfully sudden.'

He folded his arms across his chest as though to keep himself warm.

'Mother got chilled one day – she insisted on going for a walk across the fields when the snow first started and nobody wanted to go with her, and she got lost – don't ask me how, but I suppose the snow changed the look of the place – and she was out for hours. We were worried, and went out to try and find her. We still don't know where she was all that time. She came back of her own accord, Lord knows how! She was shivering and exhausted and went straight to bed. Grandmother took up a hot-water bottle and hot milk with honey, and I built up the fire.' He swallowed, faltering.

'You all did all that was possible, James.'

'I wonder. If only someone had gone out with her.' He gave a long shuddering sigh. 'Anyway, next morning she was feverish, but it was Sunday and she insisted it was just a cold and we shouldn't drag the doctor out on a wild goose chase. Monday morning she seemed better and got up, but soon went back to bed saying she ached all over and she began to cough . . .'

'Poor Hermione.' Elena could imagine it as clearly as if she'd been present.

'The long and short of it was that she developed pneumonia and the doctor said she was too ill to go to hospital and gave her some stuff to take and . . . and then she . . . that same night, she died in her sleep. Grandmother found her looking very peaceful so . . . Oh God, Elena! We should have saved her!' Tears filled his eyes.

Elena sat beside him and put her arm round his shoulders. 'James, it was nobody's fault. Just a succession of events that took a wrong turning. No one was to blame. You'll see that later when you've recovered from the shock.'

'I could have walked with her. She wouldn't have got lost with me beside her. I just felt lazy and couldn't be bothered. I keep thinking – I was away for all those years during the war and I don't think I realized how much she must have worried about me and Father. When I did get back I should have made it up to her. Bought her flowers or taken her out for the day. Something. Anything.'

He sounded so desperate that Elena began to wonder if he would be the next to fall ill. His wartime experiences had left him emotionally frail, she thought anxiously, and now his mother had died. She gave him her handkerchief and moved to the window to give him a chance to gather his wits and regain his equilibrium.

He said, 'Winifred and Oscar didn't come.'

'No. They thought your family would prefer it that way.'

He tried to smile. 'Can you stay? I wish you would.'

'Only until tomorrow. I'd love to stay longer but I have to be back at school first thing Monday.'

He shook his head. 'When I think back to that picnic – do you remember?'

She nodded.

'How I couldn't wait to be grown up and now I am and it's not so good, is it? Not good at all. Mother's been trying to cheer me up but . . . after what I've seen, Elena, I wonder what hope there is for us all. I can't begin to think about the future – and I can't bear to think about the past. The recent past, that is, and I don't remember much about my childhood . . . Mother was trying to convince me that I do have a future and it could be more than just bearable.'

'She was right. It can be better, James. It could be wonderful again.'

'Really? It seems to me that the war has ruined everything.' He looked at her with eyes full of despair. 'Everything is broken, smashed up. Whole countries and the people themselves. Life can't ever again be the way it was.'

Elena thought for a moment. 'I don't know, James, but I think it can be better if you have someone who loves you.' She fancied she heard his heart skip a beat.

Time seemed to stand still and then he stared at her, shocked by her implication. 'Someone you love? Oh God, Elena! Does that mean you've found someone to . . .? Oh!' His face crumpled. 'You've met some ghastly fellow! I knew it!' He held up his hands defensively. 'No! Don't tell me a word about him – I don't want to know.'

'I haven't met anyone, James,' she protested. 'Not exactly. Look, James, this isn't the time or place, but sometimes life . . . well, sometimes it needs a bit of a nudge. Like now, James.' She felt her words deserting her but struggled to go on. 'This "ghastly fellow", as you call him, has loved me for years and I've recently realized – I really am a bit slow on the uptake – that I love him too, but I've had to wait for him, thinking that he might one day propose. But I'm thirty-two now and so far no such luck.'

She saw the rush of emotions etched on his unhappy face. Shock, fear, disappointment – and then a sudden suspicion followed by hope. To put him out of his misery she said, 'You're the ghastly fellow I've been waiting for, James.' She smiled. 'It's been a long wait but here we are and it's up to us.'

He stared at her with disbelief. 'Are you serious? I mean, I'm not exactly who I was.' He ran agitated fingers through his hair. 'In fact I don't exactly know who I am any more. I've tried not to love you since I came home, knowing what a wreck I am. It didn't seem fair to ask you . . . for anything but friendship.' He laughed shakily.

'You're not a wreck, James. You're simply like many men who have been through hell. You're saddened and shocked, but you're still the James I know. I remember the real James. Inside you're still the delightful young man I've waited for all this time. So how foolish am I? Not to understand what was happening between us.'

'You mean that?'

'With all my heart. When you ask me to marry you – if you do – I shall jump at the chance. My answer will be yes, but I'll wait until you feel quite sure.'

His expression was changing to one of cautious hope. 'I haven't found anyone special either – not that I've looked. Not that I've ever wanted to find anyone else. I thought about the two of us all the time I was away – imagining we had a future together.' Restlessly he stood up, staring up at the ceiling. 'I wonder what Mother would say if she could see us. If she could look down on us.' He wandered to the mantelpiece and fidgeted with a small porcelain bowl. Then he turned to look at her, his eyes full of entreaty.

Elena said softly, 'I think your mother is watching us, James. She wouldn't abandon you. She's always adored you . . . The thing is, James, that I'll be thirty-three soon. If someone doesn't snap me up soon I'll be on the proverbial shelf! Elena Fairfax, a spinster of this parish!' She was rewarded with the faint smile which lit up James's woebegone face. The smile broadened into a pale shadow of his familiar grin.

'So you're asking me to ride in on a white horse and rescue you from spinsterhood?' he asked. 'I might be persuaded!'

'You might need time to mull things over?'

He closed his eyes and immediately opened them again. 'That's quite enough mulling!' He held out his arms and Elena stepped forward into the longest embrace and fiercest kiss she had ever experienced.

When at last he released her she held him at arm's length and they were both laughing. In James's face she saw a glimpse of the James she had feared might be gone for ever.

She said, 'I think Hermione would have approved.'

'Of course she would. She used to tease me about you. And Father will be pleased. It will give everyone something to be happy about.'

'But let's not say anything today, James,' Elena said. 'This is your mother's day.'

James hugged her again. 'I don't want to let you out of my sight, but I suppose we should go down and talk to people.'

'Yes, we must – your grandparents will need our help, but later, when they've all gone home, James, let's go outside and make a snowman especially for Hermione.'